DARKNESS RISING
Volume Four: Caresses of Nightmare

Books by L.H. Maynard & M.P.N. Sims

Shadows at Midnight
Echoes of Darkness
Incantations
The Hidden Language of Demons
Moths
The Secret Geography of Nightmare
Selling Dark Miracles

As editors

Darkness Rising
Enigmatic Tales volumes 1-10
Enigmatic Novellas volumes 1-6
Enigmatic Variations volumes 1-5
Enigmatic Electronic online
Best Of Enigmatic Tales
F20

DARKNESS RISING
Volume Four: Caresses of Nightmare

L.H. Maynard & M.P.N. Sims

PRIME O
Canton, Ohio

DARKNESS RISING 4
Volume Four: Caresses of Nightmare

Copyright © 2002 by L.H. Maynard and M.P.N. Sims
Cover art copyright © 2002 by Iain Maynard.
Cover design copyright © 2002 by Garry Nurrish.

All rights reserved. No part of this publication may be reproduced or transmitted in any form or by any means, electronic or mechanical, including photocopy, recording, or any information storage and retrieval system now known or invented, without permission in writing from the publisher, except by a reviewer who wishes to quote brief passages in connection with a review written for inclusion in a magazine, newspaper, broadcast, etc.

Published in the United States by **prime**
P.O. Box 36503, Canton, OH 44735
www.primebooks.net

ISBN: 1-894815-47-5

CONTENTS

Introduction to "In the Wheat"	Hugh Lamb	7
In The Wheat	Maurice Level	9
The Memory Of Trees	Phill Beynon	13
Going Back	Steve Redwood	26
Love Lies Underground	Scott Emerson Bull	35
Fields Of Mariah	Pam Chillemi-Yeager	48
They Never Come Back	William P Simmons	56
Essay on Geza Csath	Rhys Hughes	64
Matricide	Geza Csath	67
The Woman Who Collected Flies	Gerd Maximovic	74
The Daguerreotype	Richard Sheppard	85
The Cruelties Of Him	Brendan Connell	96
Lost In The Crowd	Simon Wood	107
The Drawstring	DF Lewis	113
The Penates	Donald Murphy	116
Last Bus Home	Andrew Roberts	132
The Catacombs Of Osimus	Alastair G Gunn	143
Charnel Wine	Richard Gavin	154
The Maestro and Monique	Martyn Prince	157
In Memories	Lucy Fryer	171
Essay on Pierre Louys	Rhys Hughes	190
An Ascent Of The Venusberg	Pierre Louys	193
The Elemental Child	Beth Lewis	199
Biographies		202

Introduction to "In The Wheat"
by HUGH LAMB

'Monsieur Level is himself a gay, light-hearted man, essentially Parisian in temperament. He is no morbid student . . . he is a daring sportsman, fond of all outdoors sports. When asked to explain the difference between his work and his apparent light-heartedness, he said that writers of sad things are usually gay in real life, while professional humorists are frequently melancholy'. So wrote H.B. Irving in 1920, introducing Level's book of short stories CRISES on its first English translation. Level's view of writers differing from their works holds true today, of course. Of the many horror writers I've encountered in the past 30 years, I cannot think of any who were not cheerful company. I've been more alarmed at some of the critics and researchers. Light-hearted or not, Maurice Level (1875-1926) was one of the finest writers of the *conte cruel*, that French speciality which delved into grim and wrenching horror. Level came from a military family, spending much of his early life in Algeria. He studied medicine and started writing to pass the long hours of the night shift in a Paris hospital. He very quickly was able to write full time, and became a regular contributor to the famous Grand Guignol theatre. 'In The Wheat', from CRISES, has not been reprinted in Britain for eighty years. It is harsh stuff. The *conte cruel* in the hands of a master.

Hugh Lamb,
Sutton, Surrey, England, 2001.

IN THE WHEAT
Maurice Level

With long strokes, slow and rhythmic, Jean Madek thrust his scythe into the wheat, and at the touch of the blade, the sheaths that quivered at the end of the stalks fell down with a soft frou-frou like silk.

He advanced, measuring his steps by the supple balance of his arms, and behind him the ground showed itself brown, spotted here and there by groups of stones, bristling with thick-set sprigs of reddish straw.

His old mother followed him, her back bent as she gathered up the scattered stalks, and seeing only her feet dragging their heavy sabots, her two wrinkled and knotted hands and her body covered with rags, one might have imagined she was some animal crouching on its four feet.

The sun mounted in the horizon. A heavy heat weighed on everything, wrapping the country in torpor, and the field looked like a large piece of ripe fruit, its sap rising in a penetrating perfume.

Gleaning steadily, the old woman grumbled: 'What's your wife doing as late as this? When's she coming?'

'She'll bring dinner at 12 o'clock.'

The old woman shrugged her shoulders: 'At least she's not overtiring herself! . . . '

'She's like everyone else. Whether she's here or at the farm, she's at work.'

'Oh! Work of that sort . . . '

Then, as if talking to herself as she continued to scrape the ground: 'Our master isn't here either this morning. Perhaps he stayed behind to give her a hand? . . . '

The man held back his scythe: 'What do you mean by that?'

'Me?... Nothing... Words... something to say...'

Jean went on with his work. The mother began again as if speaking to herself:

'My dead husband wouldn't have had it... When he went to the fields, I didn't stay behind to keep the master company.'

A second time the reaper raised his head. 'Why are you telling me that?'

'I was thinking, inside me, that your father was more suspicious than you are...'

The son straightened himself with a jerk:

'What is it? What do you mean? You must have some reason for talking like this...'

'If you must have it then,' blurted the old woman from her stooping position, 'people are gossiping about you and about Céline... Nasty gossip, too!'

'Who gossips?'

'No one... and everyone... What's more, you can't blame them; they can't help seeing what's under their noses.'

'Lies!...'

Without seeming to hear him, the old woman pushed aside a clod of earth with her foot and continued:

'I'm telling you for your own good. I'm your mother, and I oughtn't to hide anything from you... You can be angry if you like. But you've had your warning.'

'I tell you it's all lies. Céline is a good housewife, never tired of work; she has everything she wants... Why should she be unfaithful? Why?...'

The old woman made a vague gesture:

'Who can tell?'

Changing her tone she went on:

'Besides, I'm not saying she is... I'm only speaking for the good of both of you. She's young, she likes to amuse herself, to dress smartly to go to market on Saturdays. Temptation often takes people quickly. At the beginning they don't see any harm in it. They let someone give them a ribbon, a fichu, a comb for the hair, a watch-chain... And to be able to wear them they say they were bargains, got for next to nothing... that they picked them up on the road. Perhaps it's true...'

Every one of the slow words struck into the husband's brain. He thought of his wife's return one evening after she had accompanied the master to the town. He remembered that the following Sunday she had won a lace fichu and moiré ribbons. Above all, he saw the gold chain she said she had picked up on the road...

The monotonous voice of the old woman continued:

'It's not her that I'm meaning, of course! But a husband isn't always there: he's in the fields: he goes off to do his month's military service...' The man was no longer listening. His two hands crossed on his scythe, his eyes vague, he was absorbed in the recollections that crowded into his mind. All kinds of little incidents gave weight to the insinuations of the old woman: the master, a known libertine, very hard on all his workers, but always particularly amiable to him: the wife coquettish. And suddenly he remembered that in a week he would have to leave for a long month with his regiment.

A call rang out from under the big trees at the end of the field, and, looking up, Jean Madek saw the head and shoulders of his wife emerging from the gold of the plain, and a few steps behind her, swinging his short, thick stick among the corn, the master with his red face and big shady-brimmed hat.

And a laughing voice cried:

'Here's the pittance!'

One by one, the workers rose out of the corn, sat down under a tree, and began to eat their dinner.

Jean was silent, slowly cutting his black bread into pieces.

'Why are you so quiet, Madek?' asked the farmer.

'Are you ill?' added the wife.

'No, but the sun strikes hard. It must have been better in the house?'

The master broke into a laugh:

'You're about right there!'

The meal finished, everyone lay down for a nap. They would start work again when the sun lost a little of its ardour. Madek did not sleep. Lying on his stomach, his chin in his hands, he was lost in thought . . .

As two o'clock struck the men got up, went back to the field, and once more over the gold of the corn, unruffled by any breeze, there sang the rhythmic sound of the scythes.

When they were all at work, the master stretched himself slowly, and in a sleepy voice shouted to the wife of Madek:

'Come and give an eye here, Céline: have you by any chance a needle with you?'

'Yes, master.'

'Then come and put a stitch in my blouse. The cows are in the meadow. There's plenty of time before you need fetch them. The sun has turned. It's too hot here just now. I'm going over there under the apple-tree. Come to me when you've finished your sheaf. Come by the path so as not to beat down the corn.'

They smiled stealthily at each other. But Madek, who was watching, had seen. He made a movement as if to speak, then he lowered his head and went on with the reaping.

The old woman had gone. It was now his wife who followed him. When she had tied up her sheaf, he said, without turning:

'Didn't you hear what the master said to you?'

'Yes, I did . . . '

'Then what are you waiting for?'

'I'm just going . . . '

She fastened up her hair which had come undone while she stooped: and, her two hands flat on her hips, her waist swaying under her bright petticoat, she went along the path, a cornflower between her teeth.

He watched her being swallowed up in the verdure as one is swallowed up in the sea, and when she had quite disappeared in the shadow of the apple tree that stood out on the horizon, he set to work again.

His movements had lost their quiet ease of the morning. He went forward in jerks, stopping sharply, then on again, his head lowered, his jaw clenched, an ugly frown on his forehead.

All the old woman had said was fermenting in him like new wine, fitting in his temples, filling him with a sort of drunken rage. At first there had been doubt; then had followed certainty which had taken deeper root because of the incidents that had just happened.

He was advancing, and before him he seemed to see his wife and the master laughing and kissing each other in the shadow of the apple-tree.

He was advancing, throwing the weight of his whole body into his arms. Behind him the sheaves fell, and the field that his scythe devoured seemed to grow larger. Never in the earliest vigour of his manhood had he been able to work like that. From a distance, a fellow-worker called:

'Are you going to cut it all to-day?'

Without looking up, he replied:

'Perhaps.'

When he was only a few yards away from the apple-tree, he stopped, listening intently: murmurs reached him. A voice, the voice of his wife, said:

'No . . . He might be able to see us . . . '

And another rougher one replied:

'Keep still! He's at the other end of the field. It'll be half-an-hour before he gets here . . . Come closer . . . '

For some seconds he stood as if transfixed, livid under his sunburn, then with a sharp gesture of decision went on reaping. But he had slowed down. The sweep of the scythe was almost noiseless. The wheat fell to the earth without a sound. When he was almost under the tree he heard the sound of kisses. Pulling himself up to his fullest height, with a furious movement he lifted the scythe. Gleaming white in the sun, the blade leapt up, came down, and plunged . . . Two horrible shrieks rang out, and two frightful things, two heads, bounded up and fell again, bespattering the stalks that broke with a grating sound . . . The scythe flew up out of the corn waves, all red . . .

Madek threw it away, and waving his bloody hands in the air, roared:

'Help! An accident . . . They were there!'

THE MEMORY OF TREES
Phill Beynon

'They won't work anymore in this part of the forest, monsieur. They say that this is Saint Ferdinand's place. They will not risk disturbing it. I am sorry.' The French foreman shrugged his shoulders helplessly.

'What?' exclaimed James Allanson in outrage. Foreman Jean Dupris shrugged again. 'There is a legend about a local, holy man who cared for the trees. Some people even believed he could talk with them. They say he lived there.' Dupris pointed to an ancient, tangled glade of gloomy yew trees.

'Superstitious rubbish,' Allanson retorted. ' Go back and remind them who pays the wages.'

As the project's chief architect, Allanson hated the nitty gritty of site liaison. The chaos and mess of actual construction always seemed at odds with the purity of his original designs. Superstitious local workmen were just an added irritant. Angrily lighting a cigarette, he tried to imagine the gleaming, central plaza, with its bars, restaurants, swimming pool and other sporting facilities, set amidst a tasteful, naturalistic planting scheme of his own. But the tangled woodland in front of him seemed immune to such visions. All in all Renwick Holiday Development's latest project was not going well. The locals had opposed the holiday park from the start; the construction work was behind schedule.

Dupris returned. 'They say this part of the forest should be left alone Monsieur Allanson. They say it would be very bad luck to disturb the glade. They will not return to work.'

'Damn it! Whose side are you on anyway? ' Allanson retorted, "Renwick and the bloody consortium will probably fire us all on the spot!'

Dupris looked uncomfortable. 'They will not listen to me.'

Stubbing his cigarette out, Allanson strode over to the men, shouting at them in pidgin French. The men took no notice but merely stood frowning at him. 'Bloody hell! Do I have to do everything myself?' he roared. Turning, he climbed quickly into a stationary JCB. He stared for a moment at the vaguely familiar controls, hoping he could still remember, and then savagely twisted the ignition. The digger spluttered into life, shattering the heavy silence. Allanson grinned as the vehicle rumbled towards the glade. Some of the workmen ran forward trying to block it. Allanson shouted for them to get out of the way, wrestling with the machine to avoid them. He didn't see how close he was to the glade until a huge, gnarled and twisted branch crashed through the windscreen, filling the cab with broken glass and sharp, thorny twigs. Trying desperately to shield his face, Allanson slammed on the brakes but the vehicle's momentum carried it forward. With a tearing sound the branches ripped past him, lashing into his forehead and cutting his cheek and face. The JCB gave a final growl before crashing into a huge tree trunk.

Dazed and stunned, Allanson all but fell out of the broken cabin. Dupris rushed to help him. Allanson tried to wave him away but finally surrendered, leaning on the Frenchman as he staggered away from the wreck. Ignoring the enraged labourers and pointing to the tractor, he shouted at Dupris, 'Get them to sort that out and then give them the rest of the day off. I'll have to go back to the chateau and tell Renwick.' He limped over to the Land Rover, wiping his bleeding forehead with a handkerchief.

The chateau was a rambling, half-derelict edifice, set in the heart of the ancient forest, Brocilliande. The village of Trehorenteuc was some two miles away up a single, rough track. The endless trees pressed up hard against the house, smothering and choking it in a green embrace. It was difficult to tell where the grounds ended and the wild woodland began. Despite this, building work could be seen, for the chateau was eventually to be restored as a luxury hotel and restaurant. For now basic facilities for the work crew had been constructed in the west wing of the house, including bedrooms, a refectory style canteen and some basic exhibition and conference facilities.

Renwick was predictably incensed. 'Look, Allanson, it's your problem,' he insisted, angrily. 'You're site liaison. Get it sorted. I want to see progress not some bloody strike! We've both got too much to lose if things go wrong.'

'I'm not a personnel manager,' Allanson replied angrily, 'Most of them don't even speak English. If Dupris can't convince them, then how can I? Why not just draft some Brits in?'

'Too expensive and it'd take too long. Look, I can agree to the men being paid time and a half temporarily but you'll have to find a local solution. Good PR is vital to this project. Find out what this superstition's all about, and sort it out. I'm away tomorrow for a few days. Business at head office. I'll be bringing the consortium members back with me. So you'd better have something to show them.'

Later that evening in the refectory, Dupris joined a surly Allanson unexpectedly. He immediately felt awkward. 'Look. About earlier. I'm sorry. It's just that there's a lot at stake here and Renwick breathing down my neck doesn't help. Why don't you let me buy you a drink? It's what we English like to do if we behave like prats!'

Dupris looked blank at this last word, but readily agreed to the offer.

They drove to the tiny bar-tabac in the village. The few benches and tables scattered around the single room gave the impression of being in somebody's kitchen rather than a bar. Allanson spied a fading Playboy calendar in one corner, contrasting ironically with an effigy of the Virgin Mary in another. A small huddle of wizened villagers sat near the bar, smoking Gaulois and drinking local cidre, from large, bowl- like cups. Determined to prove himself in some way, Allanson insisted on getting the drinks in and he soon found himself chatting freely to Dupris, whose English turned out to be quite good.

'The thing is, Jean, things have to change. The park will bring jobs, tourists and money to the area. No one wants to cut down old trees, but we'll plant more. The forest will still be the forest. '

'Is the family still the same if the child becomes the father?' Dupris asked. Allan shook his head, bemused.

'The memory of trees is long, so they say, 'Dupris continued, 'maybe sometimes the best plan is to leave things alone.'

'Well, I don't have that option I'm afraid.'

'So what do you propose? '

'I haven't a clue. I thought maybe you'd help me.'

'What can I do?'

'You speak better French than me for a start and you've lived in the village for years!'

'True, but I wasn't born here. ' replied Dupris, somewhat taken aback. 'I am not even Bretton. These people are close. They respect the forest; even feel in awe of it. Soon you start to share that.'

'OK, but you must have some idea.'

'There is Father Chere. '

'The village priest?'

'Why not? Ferdinand is supposed to be a saint after all.'

'Good good!' Allanson replied, feeling his confidence return. ' Let me get you another drink old man.'

The next day a modicum of work returned to the site. The pay rise helped to smooth things over but some of the village men could still not be persuaded to stay and promptly quit the site, muttering darkly in thick Brettonese. Allanson let them go, grateful to be keeping the work going at all. Later he and Dupris drove into the village to meet with Father Chere.

At first the priest was friendly and helpful but once they described the glade and mentioned the long dead saint; he became very agitated, babbling wildly in French.

'What's he saying?' Allanson urged.

'He says, 'The Church knows nothing of this saint.''

'What do you mean?' Allanson shouted angrily at the priest, though Dupris tried to restrain him. Father Chere's eyes hardened, ' No saint. No saint!' then he descended into wild French again before slamming the door in the stunned faces of Dupris and Allanson.

'What did he say?' Allanson demanded.

'No saint but special, favoured,' Dupris translated

'Who favoured him?'

'The Guild of Foresters. He will not risk their displeasure or that of those they serve.'

'What guild? What's he talking about?'

Dupris looked momentarily troubled. 'I believe he is meaning a local trade guild, very old. Many such guilds in France in middle ages. You have them in England, too?'

Allanson nodded.

'I have heard stories,' Dupris continued, 'local superstitions about religious ceremonies held deep in the forest. Old religion, about the trees. The forest much bigger then.'

'You mean it was like some kind of cult, a secret society?'

Dupris nodded.

'Bloody marvelous. He's not even a real saint then. Just some local myth made up by a bunch of religious zealots. What the hell are we supposed to do now?'

'Maybe we should just leave things alone,' Dupris murmured.

The next morning Allanson was urgently summoned to the glade. A group of workmen stood huddled in a semi-circle, parting as Allanson pushed his way forward. Lying as if entangled in the thick hawthorn was the body of one of the work crew. Allanson stood in silent shock. 'They found him this morning, I am no expert but I would say he had been dead for some hours,' Dupris explained, pushing himself through the gathering. 'We've sent for the gendarme.'

Allanson nodded, his mouth dry.

'Oh shit! Does anyone know anything about this?' he demanded of the gathered group but they just looked away, muttering uneasily among themselves. 'Come on, one of you must know something, for God's sake!'

'Come, Monsieur Allanson, leave now, the gendarme will be here soon,' Dupris urged. Allanson allowed himself to be lead away. 'Bloody locals,' he continued uttering.

Allanson and Dupris had to go to Renne to give statements. Some hours later the investigating officer rejoined them. 'The deceased was one Maurice Relon,' he announced in halting English. 'Recently employed by your company as a construction worker but not from the village it would seem.' he added, turning to Allanson. 'Cause of death appears to be strangulation by an improvised garrote, namely a length of hawthorn.'

'Christ, you mean he was—'

'Murdered, oui! Time of death was approximately 3.00am this morning. He was killed where he was found.'

'You mean at the glade?' The officer nodded. Allanson could not take it in. 'Who? Why?'

'Do you live in Trehorentuec?' the officer suddenly asked Dupris, seeming to ignore Allanson's questions.

'Oui, for seven years.'

'But you are not from the village?' Dupris nodded.

'I thought not, you do not have their manner,' he finished, turning back to Allanson. 'The village is a close community, oui? They do not take kindly to outsiders. I understand there was some opposition to your development?'

'Of course, but there often is. It's nothing serious.'

'Perhaps. Trehorontuec is very protective of its forests. There are many stories about the place, bad stories,' the officer added.

'Superstition, that is all,' Dupris replied. 'They respect the forest, as I have come to do.'

'Maybe, but these are not superstitions.' The officer pulled out a handful of files from a nearby cabinet. 'Disappearances, accidents, other killings. Go back many years. All in same area. All unsolved, many implicated. Previous owner of chateau, Monsieur Letrec, he implicated in last killing, 1973. But no proof.'

'So?' Allanson asked.

'You ask who or why such a thing would be done? The man found where he killed, oui?' Allanson nodded, the officer continued, 'Little attempt to hide body, oui?'

'OK, so they did a bad job of covering up?'

'Or they meant for you to find it,' the policeman finished.

Dusk was falling as Allanson drove back to the chateau, having dropped Dupris off in the village. The evening light transformed the trees into dark shadows, their branches reaching out like spider webs capturing the last of the faint sun. The solitude sent his mind thinking about the murder, and its implications. A sudden jolt shook him out of his reverie. He had slid off the main track. He wrestled frantically to bring the Land Rover under control. Trees loomed out of the twilight causing him to swerve. Screeching to an abrupt halt, Allanson found himself by the glade. The police had already cordoned it off. Without knowing quite why, he got out and walked to its edge, struck by the watchful silence of the place. The thin red tape ran around an almost circular wall of thick, impenetrable hawthorn, interspersed with young birches, enclosing six huge and ancient yew trees.

Allanson shuddered with unease and turned to leave but suddenly noticed something protruding from the disturbed ground near where Relon had been found. Furtively stepping over the cordon, he stretched out to pick the object up. It was a small, clay amulet, very old, with a design embossed on it. Inspecting it, he realized with a start that it was a primitive image of a tree. Slipping it into his pocket he hurriedly withdrew and drove swiftly back up the track, acutely aware of the endless, towering trees, pressing in on him with their ancient immensity.

That night he dreamed of the glade, silver in the moonlight. The thick hawthorn seemed to curl back, forming a living gateway. He stumbled onto his knees before the mighty yews, staring past the temple pillars of their trunks to the distant, ribbed and vaulted roof of the canopy. In that moment Allanson understood the annoyance with which the trees regarded the tiny irritant that was man. Beneath their slow strength and great age, humanity was but a low, crawling thing; brief and dizzy, easily crushed by angry roots and savage branches.

He tried to cry out a denial but the trees mocked him with febrile whisperings, which slowly took on the anguished cries of people. Turning in sudden fear Allanson saw the dead man, Maurice Relon, entangled in thick hawthorn. Hands reached out to him, begging for release. Behind Relon, fading deep into the tangled hawthorn, Allanson saw other men, women and children, all clawing helplessly to escape; their bodies cut, lacerated and punctured by cruel thorns and barbs. In terror Allanson ran, sharp branches snagging at his clothes as the trees tried to pull him back into the forest's pitiless heart.

He awoke shouting and flailing at invisible assailants. Heart pounding, he scrabbled to reach the bedside lamp. The moon shone through the branches of the trees outside, casting a shadow of prison bars across the floor. At last his flailing fingers found the switch, bathing the room in blessed light. He shivered, suddenly realising that the window was open. He slammed it determinedly shut. Heading back to bed, he glanced down at the floor and noticed a light dusting of fresh forest earth between the bed and the window. He was sure the floor had been clean earlier. Angrily he swept it away then lay awake for a long time, haunted by the dream's vividness. Eventually the constant tapping of the branches on the window sent him into uneasy sleep.

The dream's vivid horror was not diminished by morning. The forest seemed oppressive. The endless procession of trees, made him feel watched and claustrophobic. The police continued with their enquiries, making it impossible for most of the building work to continue. It made little difference anyway as the rest of the village workmen had quit soon after the body had been found. Allanson retreated to the half finished room that pretended to be his office and decided to check over the chateau plans and deeds again, as a way of keeping himself occupied. There were several different ones, made at different times and as he worked, a small discrepancy caught his practiced eye. There was no doubt about it. A tiny room was marked on the 1956 version, which was not shown on the most recent one. He rechecked the deeds but there was no mention of it there.

The excitement of his find momentarily distracted him from the dream, but that night he found himself inside the glade again. This time he was dressed in long robes and holding something in his hands. Trembling he looked down and saw a kind of ceremonial knife, smooth and darkly stained. The hilt was gnarled and carved from a single stake of wood. He awoke in fear and was unable to sleep again that night.

The next day, despite feeling tired, Allanson went in search of the mysterious room. Dupris tried to pin him down to talk about the police disruptions but Allanson managed to avoid him. The house was huge and rambling with many twisting corridors and odd rooms. His route took him towards the centre of the house. It was a relief to get away from the ever-present trees. The plans brought him to a small stretch of corridor close to the centre of the house. Checking the wall carefully he finally found a half boarded-up door, hidden behind crumbling plaster. Eagerly Allanson began tearing the rest of the board aside. The door beneath was plain and unadorned except for a single faded symbol. Gasping in surprise, Allanson took out the clay amulet. The symbols were identical.

Forcing the door, he stumbled into a most extraordinary room. It was perfectly square with no other doors or exits, but his eyes were drawn towards a giant stained-glass window that filled one entire wall, stretching from floor to ceiling and bathing the room in rich greens and browns. Beyond the glass Allanson could make out an enclosed courtyard funneling sunlight down through the window to create a sense that he was not inside at all but outside, in the deep forest under the green canopy of the trees. Excitedly he approached the stained glass window and suddenly began to tremble for it depicted a scene of nightmare. Diminutive human figures were dancing around an enormous yew tree, faces upturned in rapture. The image seemed to echo his dream and the room's strange lighting reminded him of Saint Ferdinand's glade.

Despite his initial unease, Allanson began to feel strangely fascinated by the room. Few shared his enthusiasm, however, when he finally declared his discovery.

'I do not like this place, Monsieur Allanson,' confided Dupris. 'It makes me feel like a trespasser.'

'I think that's the general idea. It's like a church. A holy place.'

'Or unholy, monsieur.' Allanson shuddered momentarily. The room did have a tense, expectant atmosphere, as if great powers dwelt here but were sleeping. He wandered what would happen if they were to wake up.

That night he dreamed that the glade was full of rapturous worshippers and he found himself joining their dance. The image faded, becoming the picture on the stained glass window in the glade room. A shadowy figure knelt over a hole in the floor, beckoning to him. Then Allanson woke up gasping, his nightshirt damp with sweat. Dupris found him later that morning, frantically poking and prodding the flagstone floor of the glade room.

'Monsieur Allanson, what are you doing? We have all been looking for you.'

'I'm looking for something. It must be here.'

'What are you talking about? You should come away!'

'No! I have to find it.'

'Find what?'

'Answers.'

'Find them later. We have more important things to worry us. What about the murder? The gendarmes are still here. Monsieur Renwick will be back tomorrow. Still no progress, oui?'

'The answers are here, Dupris. I know it! If I can just find them, I'll know what to do!' he replied, continuing with his search. He gave a sudden shout, 'Here! This one's loose. Help me.' In exasperation, Dupris handed him the crow bar. Slowly Allanson levered up the flagstone, reaching into the darkness. 'I can feel something.' Grunting with the effort Allanson heaved up an ancient wooden chest. Eagerly he forced the lock and threw open the lid.

The chest was full of bundles of papers, letters, ledgers and legal documents, many, clearly very old. 'What is this?' Dupris asked in astonishment.

'Answers.'

'Answers to what, Monsieur Allanson?'

'The glade, Saint Ferdinand, the Guild. Everything.'

'This is foolishness. We have more important things to do. If the papers are valuable then maybe we should let the experts look at them.'

'No!' Allanson cried, stunning Dupris with his vehemence. 'They're for me, only for me. I was meant to find them, don't you see?'

Dupris shook his head. 'You have been under much strain, Monsieur. At least let us go through them together in the office. Leave this room,' Dupris finished, trying to sound reasonable.

'No. I must read them here. Get out, all of you!' Allanson snarled. Dupris backed off, motioning for the others to follow. Reluctantly he left, a very worried man indeed.

Allanson would not leave the room after that and would tolerate no interruption to his 'work', the rest of the project forgotten in his obsession. Even Dupris could not reach him. When Renwick returned the next day, Dupris did his best to explain about the murdered workman and the continuing police inquiries. Lead by Dupris, Renwick stormed over to the glade room. 'What the hell is going on James? The consortium will be arriving in the next few hours and we've got a murder and police crawling all over the place!'

Allanson looked up from the papers strewn all around. He smiled, 'Renwick, Dupris. Come for a progress report? Don't worry. Everything will be fine so long as we all do the right thing.' Renwick fumed incoherently.

'It's all here,' Allanson continued, eagerly clutching a sheaf of papers. 'The Guild is real,' he said, turning to Dupris, ' and it survived into the modern day. Monsieur Letrec, the chateau's previous owner, was the last guild master! All of this, the house and grounds, they've belonged to The Guild of Foresters for centuries. It still belongs to them.'

'What the hell are you talking about, James?' Renwick roared. 'This land was bought fair and square. Our solicitors can deal with any outstanding legal matters. Right now we've more immediate concerns. I want you ready to address the consortium tonight and I don't want any mention of dead bodies. Do you understand?'

Allanson nodded vaguely, watching Renwick turn and storm out. Dupris followed, glancing helplessly back. Smiling to himself, Allanson reached into his jacket and brought out a strange, ornate knife, with a gnarled, wooden handle. He cradled it in his hands for a while before placing it reverently back in the bottom of the wooden chest next to the clay amulet. Yes. Everything would be fine, so long as Renwick and the consortium obeyed their wishes he thought, looking reverently up at the stained glass window.

Renwick looked around the converted refectory with satisfaction. The business dinner had gone down well. Dupris had done an excellent job of wining and dining the consortium members, and if all went according to plan, ten of the wealthiest financiers in Europe were about to sign and seal the contract for the forest park. Only Allanson's absence at dinner left Renwick anxious.

'I understand there has been some local opposition,' one of them spoke up.

'An accident of some sort so I'd heard,' replied another.

'You must forgive us if we seem a little anxious but there is a lot of money at stake,' finished a third.

'Of course I understand. I assure you there will be no more delays,' replied Renwick. 'Our chief architect has everything in hand. In fact why don't I hand you over to him right now?' he finished, catching sight of Allanson edging into the room.

There was an uncomfortably long pause before he spoke. 'Welcome to Brocilande, the oldest forest in Europe. Most people don't realise what that really means. The forest is old, much older than you or I could possibly imagine. After a while that fact begins to work on you, just ask any of the locals. The villagers don't want us here and neither do the trees. During my time here I have had a unique opportunity to reflect on this and I strongly feel that we should heed their wishes and abandon the project. They will not tolerate our interference. To continue will be to invite disaster for us all. There has already been one death. Let's not be the cause of any more. I implore you to end this folly right here tonight. They will not wait any longer.' And with that he abruptly left the room. Dupris looked worried, but Renwick was shaking in anger as he stood up to quell the tide of outrage from the floor.

'What kind of a joke is this?' shouted one, joined by a chorus of agreement.

'One death already?' shouted another. The room exploded into uproar.

It was late when Renwick confronted Allanson outside the glade room. 'What the hell do you think you were doing back there?' he demanded.

'Trying to do you all a favour,' Allanson retorted.

'You nearly made a laughing stock of this whole enterprise.'

'Have they agreed to call it off?'

'What? Of course they haven't you bloody idiot! Fortunately I managed to bring them round. We're drafting in some Brits. The first thing they'll be doing is bulldozing that damn glade! With any luck, our losses will be minimal!' Renwick retorted.

'No!' Allanson gasped. 'You mustn't. You've got to tell them, Renwick. Tell them!' he shouted, grabbing the older man's jacket.

'I will do no such thing, James. For God's sake man, get off me!'

'You don't understand but I do. It's all in Letrec's papers. They won't allow it. Not now, not ever!'

'Who won't allow it?'

'The trees, Renwick, the trees!' So saying he backed into the glade room, slamming the door in Renwick's face.

Renwick's frantic hammering soon ceased and Allanson heard his footsteps recede. Now, as he stood before the image of the giant yew, he felt calm. Deferentially he removed his clothes and knelt in abeyance before the stained glass window. Words, rustling like wind through leaves, echoed in his head. 'Who will make the sacrifice?'

'I, as guild master and as the masters before me, claim the right. I will make the sacrifice.' Allanson replied, swiftly drawing the wooden handled knife across both wrists in turn. His blood began to pour out, flowing slowly towards the stained glass window. Allanson felt the first change immediately. His feet and toes seemed to twist and contort, pushing outward into the cracks of the stone floor and down, deep into the soil beneath. He went rigid, bleeding arms jerking upwards as his whole body stretched towards the distant sky.

Renwick returned to the refectory looking for Dupris. The dinner party was just beginning to break up, when every window in the room shattered, scattering glass in all directions. People shouted in alarm as thick leaves and branches poured through the broken panes, reaching and groping. Renwick hurled open the French doors but was met by thick impenetrable undergrowth, as if the entire forest was pushing right up and into the chateau.

Fleeing into the depths of the house, he was plunged into sudden darkness as the power went down. All around, Renwick could hear the cracking of stone and timber and the occasional human cry, swiftly muffled. A section of wall and ceiling crashed downward. Instantly Renwick was smothered in a mass of thick clawing branches. Struggling for breath he suddenly felt them recoil as hands pulled him free. It was Dupris, clutching a burning torch. 'They do not like the fire.'

'What the hell is going on?' Renwick gasped.

'It is the trees, they are angry.'

'That's absurd, man!'

'Look around you. You cannot deny what you see. We must find Monsieur Allanson.'

They ran through the house, dodging collapsing ceilings and walls as the trees continued their relentless attack. Dupris savagely forced open the glade room door and stumbled inside, skidding on the blood soaked floor. 'Mon Dieu!' he gasped. The stained glass window was smashed. A huge, towering yew tree filled the courtyard, choking the small room. He shouted Allanson's name frantically before finally catching sight of the remains of Allanson's blood-soaked clothes, entangled in the roots of the tree. Dupris stared upward in horrific comprehension.

Behind him, Renwick screamed. The blood and the impossibility of what he now saw, finally ripped away the remnants of his sanity and he hurled himself bodily at the tree, tearing and smashing at it with his bare hands. Dupris tried to shout a warning but thick branches snapped downward, grabbed him and hauled him off his feet. The torch dropped from his hand. He screamed as the he felt the pressure tighten and his ribs begin to crack. 'M. Allanson, if you can still understand me, stop, for pity's sake!'

Abruptly the tree loosened its grip. Dupris gratefully breathed in lungfulls of air. Whispered words rustled through his subconscious.

'You are Jean Dupris?'

'Yes yes!' he choked. ' You remember me, Monsieur Allanson?' he gasped in relief.

'Yes. You knew James Allanson. He wishes you to be spared so that you may bear witness to what befalls this night.'

'Stop this please. Spare them, I beg you! '

'No! They are already lost. James Allanson says you must go now!'

'But Renwick?' Dupris replied weakly.

'None shall be spared. Go, while you are permitted.'

'How? I cannot get out, no one can!' Dupris cried helplessly. But the voice was silent. Far above him, the night sky was clear.

With bitter resolve he began to climb up the huge yew as fast as he could weeping Allanson's name. The trunk soared straight up the centre of the house, sending its leaves and branches deep into every nook and cranny of the doomed chateau. Dupris climbed on, desperately waiting for the tree to crush him or else hurl him down to his death. But no such moment came. At last he reached a section of roof where the trees could not reach him. He sank back trying to block out the screams and interminable breaking of stone as the forest slowly crushed and broke the chateau.

The authorities arrived early the next morning. The chateau was a deserted ruin. A single set of footprints led away towards Saint Ferdinand's glade. Throughout the morning search parties found the crushed and broken bodies of the chateau's former occupants. They were all tangled deep in the undergrowth of the forest. No one could explain how they had got there or what had happened to the house. When the police entered the ruin they found that it was filled with twigs, broken branches and leaves, which, in their passing, left only the memory of trees.

GOING BACK
Steve Redwood

'You see, Jenny, I never did forget you, I remembered you longer than you can ever imagine. And you are fine now. Ah, but the price I am paying, the price!' I hear the voice, but I can't see the face in the dreams, or I see it as one might see an image from beneath waves in the sea, bobbing, flickering, distorted. But I know, I sense, who it is. And I sometimes wake with tears on my cheeks, and it seems as if they are not my own.

* * *

When they woke him the first time, Simon Brent went to visit her grave. It was in one of the few cemeteries left in the country, preserved for tourists. It was still just possible to make out the name: Jenny Smith. Such a common name then. Jenny Smith: 1989-2008. Not even twenty years old. A living, suffering creature mashed down into two trite words. Smith. Jenny.

Two words that could still accuse him after a century. And would probably accuse him for many more.

The tombstone itself was crumbling and decayed. And inside the grave, would even bones now remain?

And would it serve any real purpose to disturb the memory of bones?

But it was something beyond logic, something he had to do, though they had told him it was still impossible, that it always would be impossible. He should enjoy the miracle he had been offered. Many of the Returnees, they told him, died soon after they were taken out: 'cured' of the disease which had killed them, but instantly attacked by others that had been patiently waiting their turn, like polite persistent worms in a queue. Or was it Time itself that was killing them? That was why they had revived him, before the stipulated moment. If they put him back...

But at least his greatest fear had proved unfounded—he still had a 'soul', whatever that was, his emotions had not been frozen out of him.

He knew because of the tears that blurred that common name

He returned to the Centre annexe and turned down the brave new life they offered him. He would wait. Wait for the impossible.

* * *

Jenny Smith is preparing for the disco. The fashion this year is the nano-skirt, and she's pleased, because she knows her legs are her best feature. She isn't exactly plain, and with her black hair cascading down as it does, she doesn't go unnoticed. But she's never been able to compete with the really pretty girls.

She wonders whether Simon will be there tonight. She senses that he's a bit different, though he tries to hide it, to act like the louts he hangs around with. She can tell he's interested, too, but so far she's put him off. He's a bit young, and she's slept with enough boys to know that it doesn't gain you any respect—or even a decent orgasm, most of the time.

And anyway, she always hopes that one day she will meet someone really special, someone to take her away from the drabness of life in a small seaside town.

Perhaps tonight will be the night. She says this each time she goes out.

Everyday dreams of an everyday girl.

* * *

The second time they woke him, the impossible had become possible. In a way.

'You don't *look* two hundred years old!' was how Alex Feynman, the Director, greeted the man whose drive and money had founded the Centre. The man who had set one condition: that he be cryogenically stored, and revived to see the end result of what he had set in motion.

Feynman tried to explain the science to him, but how do you explain a guided missile to a man used to a club? A word processor to a person scratching on rock? After the brightest brains had battled with the ideas current in Simon's time—time travel through distortion caused by spinning black holes, tachyons, time slippages, exotic matter, chronons—two hundred years later, as is the way with science, it was none of these. All Simon Brent understood—or really cared to understand—was that the time traveller if you could call him such—could now double back on himself, as it were, like a knitted jumper unwinding back into its original ball. It would be a journey of the mind only, the body remaining as an anchor on reality. The traveller would be an onlooker, only able to see what he had already seen before, do what he had done before. It was a very limited form of time travel, a literal trip down memory lane. The past could not be altered, because of the Paradoxes involved.

Simon Brent almost gave up then. But he sensed that Feynman was holding something back. He probed and pressed until finally he learnt what it was.

* * *

Am I going mad? Bloody schizo? I keep seeming to catch echoes of voices, well, *one* voice, in my head, or rather, not even a voice, because there are no words, more like a presence, like a fine mist slithering into the cracks of my mind. For no reason I suddenly feel disgusted and angry, somehow terrified of myself.

I saw Jenny Smith in the street today, and that's when the presence seemed strongest. I felt a sort of panic, for chrissakes, an urge to cry. But it was gone in a few seconds. Thank God it's Saturday, and club night for the gang. They scare me a bit, but at least we always have *fun*, we always end up doing *something*.

* * *

Feynman stared through the viewing panel at the body of Simon Brent, almost lost behind the array of equipment. That crazy old bastard! He should have expected something like this. You don't put yourself in cold storage for two centuries just to *see* a time machine! Yet how could they have barred access to the man who had made all this possible? Who could have suspected he would lock himself in like that?

The early tests had seemed to show that it was, as expected, impossible to create a Paradox, to break the causal loop. The 'travellers' claimed that they were aware of everything they were doing (had done) but were powerless to change anything at all, however much they tried. It was like being observers in a dream, like watching a film of yourself. Indeed, it was not even certain at first that they *had* returned to the past. They might simply have been remembering everything they had already done. Unless they changed something, there was no absolute proof that it wasn't a case of total recall induced by the Transmitter.

Until the Zavinsky case scared the shit out of everybody.

DARKNESS RISING 4: CARESSES OF NIGHTMARE

* * *

At first it was all blackness, nothingness. The centuries in the cryogenic vaults were a journey through emptiness, with just a sudden flash of awareness—the first time he was woken?—before more darkness, and then the images skimmed by like clouds chased by a storm. The theatre where they would soon exchange all his bodily fluids, the day the Prime Minister visited the Centre, the opening of the first lab, the day he heard he'd made his first million, cold sex with cold women, the headlines of the local paper stabbing at him . . . and suddenly he is there again, the day of the disco, and reverse time is slowing down like a video tape at the end of the spool, and he sees her walking on the other side of the street . . .

* * *

Jenny Smith is well and truly pissed off. There are only the usual holiday yobs at the disco, with a small bunch of locals, most of them with no intention of dancing: the pubs have shut, and the only place to get a drink is in the nightclubs. They lounge around, getting more drunk, more self-confident, more obnoxious. 'God's fucking gift to the toilet bowl,' her friend Mandy, declares loudly.

The Sinclair brothers hear that, turn their heads, and think Jenny has said it. Their piggy eyes glower. Their friend Simon looks uncomfortable.

Not long after, they coincide at the bar. Josh does his chat-up line. 'Want your twat filled with something to remember?' he asks.

She rounds on him scornfully. 'What, *that* thing there? That wouldn't fill a Barbie doll!'

'Fucking bitch!' is Josh' witty reply.

'You mean 'butch'!' adds his brother. He looks round for admiration.

So when Simon asks her, a few minutes later, for a dance, she tells him to go screw himself. She actually quite likes him, but anyone who hangs around with first-class arseholes like those Sinclairs . . .

'Fucking snotty tart!' growls Josh, and Simon, pretty drunk himself by now, nods in agreement.

Hostility simmers until chucking-out time comes, and they all stagger, quite drunk, into the street. The brothers, as they head towards their motorbikes, deliberately jostle the two girls. Simon is already on his bike, and revving up when he sees Jenny.

'Going to the club next week?' he calls out hopefully.

Mandy answers. 'You joking? We can find better pricks than you lot in a bloody gorse bush!' She laughs uproariously.

'And bigger cocks in a farmyard!' adds Jenny, her speech slurred.

Simon revs up angrily, and roars off down the street, skidding dangerously as he takes the corner too fast. The brothers give the girls V-signs, and follow him.

Jenny and Mandy hold on to each other for support as they cackle over their triumph for a few minutes, then Jenny totters off towards home, which is just ten minutes' walk along the almost deserted seafront. She stops to pee in the ornamental gardens, and is just stepping out, still yanking at her tiny skirt, when she hears the roar of motorbikes. Somehow, she knows who it is, but she isn't particularly scared because it's all only been for a giggle and, besides, she knows that Simon fancies her.

* * *

If it had been a nobody, a loner, someone whose life hadn't greatly impinged on the life of others, it might have been all right, any small changes cancelled out by the levelling-out effect of entropy.

But Simon Brent . . .

* * *

To change the past was *almost* impossible, but not quite, as Zavinsky had shown. In a routine trial, they put Zavinsky, who had scored extremely high in parapsychic tests, in a locked room for ten minutes, sitting at a table with a pencil precariously balanced on its edge. Zavinsky had to remain absolutely still, in order not to dislodge the pencil. Everything was filmed, and the film put away in a lead safe.

Then they sent him back an hour, a period that included the time spent in the locked room, and told him to try to make his past self dislodge the pencil.

There was the usual flickering, lasting no more than a second, as if a silver sheet had rippled in blue light. They undid the straps.

'I did it!' Zavinsky shouted, 'I made the pencil drop!'

'What are you talking about?' Feynman asked irritably. 'So what?'

'I made the pencil drop!'

'We know, we already filmed it.'

Zavinsky stared at them. 'But on the film, the pencil didn't drop!'

'Of course it did, I remember quite clearly.'

In the end, to show Zavinsky how wrong he was, Feyman took the film from the safe.

The pencil had remained on the table all the time.

Zavinsky's slight movement had distorted *everybody's* past.

Had, in effect, replaced it with a new one, in which the pencil had fallen.

But he, Zavinsky, still remembered the original past.

The implications were so shocking that that night Feynman had even told his wife about it, though this was strictly against the rules.

Now he stood helplessly outside the chamber, waiting for Security to break down the door, wondering why Brent had gone back, trying to console himself with the thought that he couldn't possibly have Zavinsky's extraordinary mental power. And even Zavinsky, after all, had done no more than nudge Schrödinger's Cat.

There was a flickering, as if a silver sheet had rippled . . .

* * *

They only intended to frighten her, but the drink was in them, and they remembered her mockery, and Josh took out his penis meaning to frighten her even more but it worked too well and she began to scream so they grabbed her and covered her mouth and the feel of her body helplessly twisting in their arms changed the nature of the sport and they hurled her to the ground and yanked down her underwear and pushed rough fingers inside her. But in the end it wasn't the brothers who did it, they were too drunk to get erections, so they dared Simon to stuff it in, prove he was a man, and he found he was harder than he had ever been and he thought he might just rub it against her not go right in of course but the moment he felt her heat it was impossible to stop. He came after a few clumsy thrusts, and suddenly what had been thrilling was sordid and disgusting, and the Sinclair brothers were staring at him almost fearfully. He felt drained and frightened and confused, and pulled her knickers back up again, lifted her to a sitting position, and stroked her hair back from her twisted face, almost tenderly: a boy may know the meaning of shame even though he does not, cannot, know the sickness of violation. The brothers threatened her with terrible reprisals if she talked, though it was all bluff, and they stumbled to their bikes, frantic to get away from the scene, with a blind hope that sheer distance might save them. Only fear, very little guilt, not then.

Jenny Smith, after all, was always flashing it around. Everyone knew that. She was a tall, gangly girl, who worked as a veterinary assistant, and smelled vaguely of animals, and had rough hands, and had asked for it by taking the piss out of them. And in the darkness Simon Brent couldn't see her eyes . . .

***

She is staggering along the side of the road, aware only of the pain and the bruised flesh and the need to vomit, and doesn't move away when she sees car lights approaching, and the lights of another car, coming from behind her, are blinding the driver on her side of the road . . .

The everyday dreams of an everyday girl shatter and splash over the windscreen.

***

There was always a suspicion that she'd been raped, of course—they found the semen in her, and no boyfriend came forward—but that suspicion was at first directed towards a middle-aged man who'd been seen on the sea-front just a little time before. By the time he was cleared, no one remembered the three youths, not even Mandy, who had anyway seen them roar away long before Jenny had left her. It was a holiday town, and the holiday season, and few of the people in the nightclub had ever seen each other before.

Simon Brent was twenty before he had the first glimmering of what might really have happened that night. He met a girl with flashing eyes and nervous gestures on a train in Belgium, and a month later went to visit her in Verviers, near the German border. He tried to kiss her after her mother had gone to bed, and couldn't understand the trembling, the sweat on her lips, the panic in her eyes. Only when she told him how someone had once molested her in a lift, when she was a teenager, did he begin to understand.

He returned from Belgium with memories of rain and greenness, and fear and longing mixed in a young woman's eyes, and the repressed memories started to claw their way out.

He began to wonder whether it had been an accident, after all.

Guilt was a maggot in his mind that grew fatter day by day.

It was then that he began to plan the impossible.

***

He tried to stop his younger self going to the nightclub at all. The easiest solution. But that other self was refusing to even admit his existence.

He was near despair. He was only here because a crime had been committed. That crime had led to a timeline of two hundred years. Both Simon Brents—the owner of this strong brutal young body, and the would-be intruder in his mind—*had* to converge to become the Simon Brent of the future who entered the Transmitter.

And he now saw something else with horrifying clarity: when he returned to the future, either that future would be very different from the one he knew—in effect, a parallel time line—which meant that in the original time line *the crime had still been committed;* or it would be the future he had just left, and again *the crime would have been committed*, otherwise he would never have had himself frozen in order to reach that future.

There was just one hope: if he didn't return to the future, it was just possible that the future he remembered would never exist, and the Paradox would have wiped itself out.

But he was powerless to influence his younger self. He knew this, even though he repeated to himself like a mantra, 'Zavinsky made a change, so I can do it.'

The young Simon was getting drunk. Would this weaken his mental hold? Possibly. He skimmed along the timeline between now and the attack on the girl, like a spider racing backwards and forwards across its web searching for its prey.

And found the moment.

He saw himself, just after leaving the disco with the girls' mocking laughter ringing in his head, skidding on something—probably something like fish and chips thrown into the road. He had almost lost control of the bike.

The skid. There was the answer. It had been so close. Only luck and instinctive reactions had enabled him to keep the bike upright. There was a moment—one, maybe two, seconds—when with the drink and the anger and the unexpected danger the young Simon's mind would be vulnerable. *That* would be the moment to strike.

If he had an accident, his friends wouldn't just leave him there. They would stop and help him. They wouldn't pass the gardens at the exact moment Jenny Smith wandered into view still adjusting her panties.

Perhaps the Paradox of the causal loop would still be there. Perhaps any change he made now—if he did make any—would simply be erased. There was no way of knowing. But he had to try.

He saw the bend coming up, gathered himself. He reminded himself of how he had felt when he had seen those headlines the following day, and as the wheel began to slide hurled himself around the young man's brain to disorientate him...

As the bike hurtled across the road into the building on the corner, he had time for a final thought:

Does Time have a moral dimension? Can it make ethical choices?

***

'Yes, I know time travel isn't possible,' Feynman declared.

The others looked at him with suspicion; they guessed there was more to come.

'But a hundred years ago I'd also have known you couldn't have a thousand people living on Triton, or photograph dreams, or transplant brains.' Tired old arguments, valid enough as they went, but hardly worthy of a top physicist. Because, despite some specious theoretical reasoning, Time itself simply would not allow time travel. He knew this better than anyone, had wasted his whole life on fruitless experimentation. And yet he still had this crazy inner certainty that it really was possible to travel into the past—or the future. An obsession that made him a laughing stock in the scientific world.

No, it was more than an obsession. It was a multitude of shadows that came to him when he was half asleep, that whispered forlornly and talked about the undiscovered and untapped power of the neutrino, and said, 'Remember, all time is eternally present', and it all made sense until he woke up in his lonely bed, and dawn chased away the spectres.

***

I dread Peter noticing, because how can I explain to him why I wake up crying when I can't even explain it to myself? I'm now even surer of my love for him than when we got married. So why am I dreaming of Simon? I hardly knew him, just vaguely fancied him a long time ago, that's all.

If you're there, Simon—and I know it's you—then yes, I know you wouldn't have had that awful accident if I hadn't been so rude to you outside the disco. We were just having a bit of fun. Saturday night banter. I did want to get to know you, I really did. But not while you were with those loutish friends of yours.

My friends tell me it wasn't really my fault you skidded like that. But the fact still remains that if I'd been friendlier, you wouldn't have ridden off in such a temper.

And yet, I don't sense anger coming from you at all. Something quite different.

Ah, if only there were some way to go back and do it all over again.

You might stop haunting me then.

LOVE LIES UNDERGROUND
Scott Emerson Bull

Amekayla was on love's mission. On its wings she flew through Castle Woods, her feet barely touching the ground as she followed the path lit for her by the scarlet moon. He is there was all Magda's message had said, but those few words conjured a vision of the clearing where she had first made love to Elias. If Magda was to be believed, that same hallowed ground held her lover, buried alive.

She stopped to catch her breath. The trees around her seemed familiar, but it was hard to tell. During the day, Castle Woods was bright with nature and the remembrance of love, but at night it became a place of shadows and things unseen. A sharp wind rustled through the leaves whispering cautionary words—'Go back, my child'—but Amekayla could do no such thing. Her love would not allow it.

Rain fell as she began to move again, making the ground slick and treacherous. She moved slowly, knowing that she was approaching the clearing. She pulled her coat tighter and felt for the dagger she had placed in its pocket. The touch of the cold steel brought her some strength, but would it be enough?

Then she felt it. Something was up ahead.

'Elias?' she called.

There was no answer. The wind died, silencing the trees. Rain still fell, but it did so soundlessly. All around her time had stopped. A chill rose from her belly, leaving the bitter taste of fear in her mouth.

'Magda?'

Again no reply, only dead silence. She felt the trees watching her, their branches twisted in morbid welcome. 'Friend or foe?' she wanted to ask, but knew the answer. They were merely observers, glad for some excitement to relieve their immemorial boredom. She passed beneath them and saw the clearing up ahead, carved in silver by the moon. Craggy with rock, except for patches of moss and lichen, there was little vegetation. On the day they had come here, Elias had spread a blanket out on the one flat piece of ground. Tonight that spot was covered with a roiling violet haze.

Amekayla approached slowly, her heart pounding. She watched as the haze billowed up in tiny clouds, then came back to lick the earth. It seemed designed to tease her and as she got closer, she saw why.

Beneath it she saw a freshly covered grave.

'Goddess be with me,' she said, and entered the clearing. The silence around her now was maddening. She knelt down before the grave and with a wave of her hand parted some of the mist. It recoiled from her warmth, then slipped back into place. Was this some spell, she thought? She placed her hand through the haze and touched the grave. The earth was warm, as if the midday sun were beating upon it. With both hands she separated the haze and slipped inside it so she could lie atop the grave. It was the right size for her, just as it was the right size for Elias.

The mist engulfed her and she heard a voice from the ground.

'Amekayla.'

Goddess above, she thought, had she found him? She slipped open her coat to reveal the nightgown she wore underneath and let the ground's dampness seep into the silk. It felt like heaven.

'Please be you, Elias,' she whispered.

As if in response to her words, the ground beneath her moved. It felt like it was trying to embrace her and Amekayla did not resist. It seemed so natural and its touch so familiar. She cooed Elias's name as arms appeared from out of the ground, strong arms and hands that knew just how to hold her and just where to touch her. She sighed as an entire body covered in dirt rose from the grave. She was offered lips and she kissed them, tasting the fertile richness of the soil. The worries of the last hours slipped from her mind. She had Elias now. Her love had awakened him.

Then it all went wrong. What she thought was her lover suddenly tightened its grip, as the sounds of the forest returned with a fury. Wind howled in her ears, as the violet mist that had clouded her mind pulled back to reveal the ugly mud creature that held her. She screamed at the thing to let go of her, but it just stared at her, its dirt face twisted with lust.

The thing freed itself from the ground and threw Amekayla onto her back. She kicked at the creature, but it was on her quickly, forcing her legs apart. Its cold, slimy hands ripped through her nightgown.

Goddess, help me, she thought, and focused her mind. She relaxed her body and looked up at the thing towering over her. Mud dripped from the creature onto her stomach and breasts. Still focusing, she locked her gaze onto the thing's hollow eyes. You want me don't you, she thought. The creature looked at her, startled. 'Then take me,' she whispered, and watched as a smile passed across the thing's face. Then, just as quickly, the smile turned into a look of utter horror. Amekayla had pulled the dagger from her coat, and with a twist of her hand, had relieved the creature of its manhood.

The thing leapt to its feet and stumbled away into the forest. Amekayla threw the thing's penis away in disgust, as laughter came from the edge of the clearing.

'You certainly ruined his day,' a woman's voice said. From out of the woods, the violet mist parted to reveal a beautiful woman of fifty years, though Amekayla knew Magda was much older than that. Bright green eyes shown out from between long twists of black hair streaked in silver. The mist played over her body, slipping in and out of her heavy black robe, feeding on her powerful aura.

'Where is Elias?' Amekayla asked, as she pulled her coat around herself.

'He is well buried, child. And buried he shall stay until you have learned your lesson.'

'What lesson?'

'You know very well what lesson. I only hope you come to your senses before it is too late.'

Amekayla stood up, her stance defiant. 'Your words are lies. I need no lesson. I know my love for Elias is stronger than any magic you can throw at me.'

'Your love?' Magda laughed. 'You have much to learn, child.' And with that she disappeared into the mist.

* * *

Amekayla stayed in the shower until she had used up nearly all the hot water. Even after the last traces of the creature disappeared down the drain a thin layer of filth seemed to cling to her body. She felt soiled by the magic that had fooled her into thinking that thing had been Elias.

Coffee was brewing downstairs. Amekayla's grandmother was making breakfast. She had lived with her grandmother for the last eight years, ever since her parents had been killed in a sudden fire. Amekayla had been twelve and just awakening to the powers within her; an awakening that happened to coincide with her first tentative changes into womanhood. Grandmother had been a strong part of that awakening, guiding and teaching her. Amekayla could put it off no longer.

She would have to tell her grandmother about Elias.

In the kitchen, she found Grandmother feeding their three cats. She wore a green terrycloth robe and her long cinnamon hair was twisted into a loose braid. She was sixty-one, but looked at least a decade younger. Amekayla always felt slightly jealous of her grandmother's beauty.

'Oh, Kaylie. What is it?' her grandmother asked, as soon as she saw her. Amekayla couldn't find the words to speak. Almost at once the tears came.

'Oh, sweetheart. Sit down. Let me make you some tea.'

Amekayla sat down and wiped her eyes, as Grandmother made the tea, taking it from an old tin canister from the top of one of the cabinets. Soon, a mug of it was sitting in front of her. It smelled of fresh dew and cloves, like a welcoming morning. Amekayla felt its relaxing powers as she drank. She kept her gaze on the rich brown liquid. She couldn't bear to look up. Her Grandmother began to stroke her lightly on the cheek. She had touched her in this same manner for as long Amekayla could remember. It was only when she was older that she realized that there was magic behind it.

'I sense love and jealousy and fear,' Grandmother said. 'Who is he?'

'His name is Elias,' Amekayla said finally. Her voice sounded distant and small.

Grandmother nodded. 'A young man?' she asked.

'Older.'

Grandmother took her hand away. She was suddenly up and moving about the kitchen. Clearing dishes. Watering herbs. Amekayla knew she had been purposely left to her thoughts, so that they might escape and fill the room. After a time, Grandmother poured herself coffee and sat back down.

'My first lover was older,' she said. 'As was your Mother's. I suppose I should not be surprised. And your love has placed this man in peril, am I correct?'

'Yes.'

Grandmother closed her eyes. Amekayla felt a flurry of emotions. Love, hate, fear, desire. She thought of the dreams she sometimes had of her mother lying in her casket, a bouquet of flowers clutched in her lifeless hands. She thought of how her mother's eyes would open, the same ice blue eyes that was the trait of all the women in their direct bloodline. It had always seemed like her mother was trying to warn her, but of what?

'You fear him dead?' Grandmother asked finally.

'I don't know,' she said, and then everything about Elias began to tumble out, as if she had lost control of her emotions. She told of how she had met Elias in the library when both had been reaching for the same moldy novel by Trollope. How they were soon having coffee, Elias reading passages from the book, as Amekayla sat there like some quivering schoolgirl. She told of watching his lips and how artfully they formed the ornate sentences.

'You fell in love first?'

Amekayla paused, as she considered this answer.

'Yes,' she said.

Grandmother stared hard into her eyes and Amekayla wondered how far into her mind she could see. There were dark thoughts she kept hidden in the shadows, but she wondered now if they were hidden really all that well. After a time, her grandmother frowned, then took another sip of coffee.

'Where is he now?'

'Buried somewhere in Castle Woods.'

'Dead?'

'I pray not.'

'Then someone put him there. Who?'

Amekayla got up and walked towards the window that looked out on the backyard.

'She calls herself Magda. She merely taunted me at first, telling me I was too young and frivolous to hold the interest of a man like Elias. I thought she was jealous, but she claims to have no interest in him. She says she wants to teach me a lesson.'

'Go on.'

'After a while, she began shooting spells at me, little nuisance things like giving me my period on the night that I had hoped to . . .' Her voice trailed off.

'Magda is a witch?'

Amekayla nodded. 'Yes, she says she represents an old coven.'

'And you believe she has cast some strong spell on him and hidden him under the ground away from you?'

'Yes.'

'And you believe this? You believe such strong witches exist?'

'Don't you?'

Grandmother got up and joined Amekayla at the window.

'No, I don't,' she said.

Amekayla looked at her, puzzled. 'But you? Me? I mean . . .'

'We're practitioners, Amekayla. We have sensitivities that allow us to control powers that existed long before man or woman. But strong evil witches? No, Kaylie, I don't believe they exist.'

'But Magda?'

' . . . has fooled you, child. She's weaving spells around your mind. She is nothing but a trickster.'

'But I was in Castle Woods last night,' Amekayla said, and she went on to recount her evening's experience. Grandmother listened in silence as she described the mood of the forest and the violet mist. She winced as Amekayla described the attack of the mud creature. When Amekayla finished, Grandmother put her arm around Amekayla's shoulders.

'Take me to this place, this clearing in the woods.'

* * *

They drove along Westlake Boulevard to the outskirts of town, passing the stone gates of Grandview Cemetery. A small collection of cars gave evidence of a funeral. The thought of all those bodies underground made Amekayla think of Elias, not that she had ever really stopped thinking about him. She wondered if he was in a coffin or if he was lying with his skin naked against the dirt. She shivered at the thought and banished it from her mind.

They entered Castle Woods through Reservoir Road. Amekayla directed her grandmother to where she had parked last night, a small dirt patch along the road that was used by hunters in the fall. It all seemed so different during the day, completely alive with the sounds of nature.

A narrow path took them into the woods. The sounds of nature were muted here, as if in deference to this cathedral of lush green. They walked for sometime in silence, both of them listening to the woods. It was Grandmother that finally broke the stillness.

'The trees don't feel much like talking today,' she whispered.

Amekayla nodded. 'They weren't much help last night either.'

Very little sunlight was able to break through the trees, and it gave the woods an eerie feeling. They walked until Amekayla recognized the trees that had seemed so taunting last night. Their branches seemed to have softened now. They neither urged nor discouraged their presence.

'We're close, aren't we?' Grandmother asked.

'It's just ahead.'

'Are you frightened?'

Amekayla hung her head. Her palms were greased with sweat.

'Relax, Kaylie. Such magic doesn't work well during the day. Listen carefully. See how normal everything sounds, how normal it all feels?'

Amekayla listened and tried to focus. They walked the last few yards and entered the clearing. The sun was bright on the rocks and dirt. It clearly showed no evidence of a grave.

Her heart sank. 'But last night?'

'... was a trick, Kaylie.'

'But....'

Grandmother placed her fingers to her lips. Listen, she motioned, and Amekayla heard the same deafening silence that she had heard last night.

'Some of the charm remains,' Grandmother, said. She looked around with her face filled with what Amekayla thought was awe. 'I've never felt anything this strong.' She closed her eyes and began mouthing words in a tongue Amekayla did not recognize. The temperature around them dropped a degree or two, then, as if someone were gently turning up the volume on a stereo, the sounds of the woods returned.

'There,' Grandmother smiled. 'Perhaps not so strong after all.'

'So it was all a trick?'

'So it would appear.'

'Then none of it happened? It was all in my mind?'

'Yes.'

'Then Elias isn't buried in the woods?'

'That I don't know, child. Though I can feel a strong spell here somewhere. The sunlight has disguised it some, but it is here nonetheless.'

'Then we must look for him!'

'No. The night will be the best time to capture the spell. Besides, we must prepare you. Come. We should leave this place.'

'Wait,' Amekayla said. Something on the ground had caught her eye. When she saw what it was, she pointed it out to her grandmother.

There, just on the edge of the clearing, was a perfect example of male genitalia fashioned out of mud.

* * *

They were in the attic stooping beneath elaborate spider webs. 'Help me with this,' Grandmother said, and they put their weight against an antique wardrobe that barely fit beneath the cramped ceiling. It creaked as they shifted it a few feet to the right, revealing floorboards made of a darker wood. Characters were carved on each corner of the boards, lettering that Amekayla recognized from her set of runes. Grandmother knelt and traced the outline of each character with her index finger, then laid her palm flat on the boards. Then she raised her hand and the eight wood screws that held the boards in place rotated and rose in unison. They hovered in mid-air until Grandmother plucked them one by one and placed them in her pocket. She lifted the boards to reveal a square object wrapped in lamb's wool.

'You must be the first to touch it,' Grandmother said.

Amekayla reached out slowly. The object gave off energy like heat from the sun. She lifted the object and felt its weight in her hands. It was heavy, but the lamb's wool felt soft and warm. Inside the wool, she found a book.

'That is a Grimoire, Kaylie. A book of magic and spells.'

'Why have you never shown me this before?'

Grandmother lowered her head. 'I thought the days of such magic and covens had passed. What I felt in the woods today proved me wrong.'

Amekayla ran her fingertips over the cover. It was hewn from black slate and decorated with what looked like carved bone. As she touched the carvings, they shifted on her, arranging and rearranging into different patterns. When she went to open the book, her Grandmother stopped her.

'There is no need, Kaylie. Spread out the lamb's wool and place the book on top of it.'

Amekayla did as she was instructed.

'Now concentrate on what you have lost.'

She closed her eyes and focused on Elias, recreating his body, his soul, everything she knew about him, until he'd become a breathing living creature in her imagination. When she reopened her eyes, she saw the same image in the detailed carvings of the bone.

'Good,' Grandmother said. 'Now breathe across the pages.'

Amekayla knelt down and drew her breath across the book. As she did, a gush of wind came from the corners of the room sending the book open and its pages fluttering like an antique kinescope. The moving pages created images, and in them Amekayla saw all of her experiences with Elias, from the first time she had seen him in the library to the last time she had made love to him. The book also pulled Amekayla's emotions to the surface as if it needed to analyze them, and perhaps it did. She felt herself on the edge of tears, when suddenly the pages stopped.

She looked down to see that the book was open to a page of ornate hand-lettered script. She bent over slowly and read the open page.

'Dowsing?' she asked, not a little disappointed. 'But isn't that what people do to find water?'

Grandmother nodded. 'But it can also be used to find bodies.'

'Bodies,' Amekayla repeated. It made it sound like she was looking for someone who was already dead. 'Will it help me find Elias?'

'If you let it.'

She turned back to the book, but already it had closed and the lamb's wool was weaving itself around the outside.

'But I didn't get a chance to read it.'

'You already know it, Kaylie.'

Amekayla closed her eyes and indeed there it was, already burned into memory.

'Now go to your room and sleep,' Grandmother said. 'You must rest for tonight.'

'But Elias . . . '

' . . . must wait. This magic will serve you well, but only once the sun has gone down. Until then you must rest. You will need your strength.'

Amekayla nodded. When she reached the door leading downstairs, she stopped and looked back at her grandmother.

'Will you go with me tonight?' she asked.

'I am always with you, Kaylie.'

Amekayla nodded and left the attic.

* * *

She slept until sundown. When she awakened, she found her mind had already prepared her for the evening. Her body was ready, too, as adrenaline mixed with her blood and energized her heart. She focused, draining her mind of emotion as much as she could, though fear pushed hard at the edges.

She dressed quickly in jeans and a sweatshirt. The Grimoire had told her she would need a personal item of Elias's, and without thinking, she took out the bookmark she kept under her pillow. Elias had left it behind on the first day they had met.

No, a voice in her head told her, he did not leave it behind. You took it, didn't you?

Amekayla shook the voice from her head. Was the magic of the Grimoire here to help her or hinder her? She tried not to think about it. Instead, she fingered the bookmark. It was made of green satin and anchored by a pixie cast in pewter. She had wound several of Elias's dark hairs around it to help strengthen their love. She wondered about that charm now. Had it worked too well? Never you mind, she told the voice, and placed the bookmark inside her bra, so that it would be close to her heart.

It was time to go. When she went downstairs, her grandmother was nowhere to be found. Amekayla had expected this. This was her fight alone. She put on her coat, with the dagger still in the pocket, and beneath an angry moon drove the ten miles to Castle Woods.

By the time she got there, the moon had abandoned her behind the clouds. The chill of dread snaked through her blood, but she shook it off by focusing on what had to be done.

She searched the ground for a fallen limb. Finding one, she broke off branches until she had fashioned it into a 'Y,' then balanced it in her hands. It felt right, though to be honest she felt ridiculous. She took out the bookmark, removed one of the strands of hair, and wound it around the branch. She knew she should use them all, but she couldn't bear to do that. It would mean admitting to herself and to the gods about what she had done and she couldn't do that. To do so would show a loss of faith in what she believed her love had become, and purity of heart was the last thing the Grimoire had told her she would need if she wanted to find Elias. She only hoped that this was what the book had meant.

Time to begin. She stepped into the woods and began dowsing by holding the limb loosely and keeping the point an inch or two from the ground. She felt stupid and the trees chattered at her as if they agreed. Had her mind not been so intent on feeding her images of Elias buried underground choking on dirt, she might have laughed. Instead she felt frustrated. After several more minutes of dowsing, she threw the limb away in disgust and fell to her knees.

'Damn it,' she cried. 'This will never work. Elias is lost and it's all because of me.' Anger choked her voice. 'I had to have my way, didn't I? Damn you, Goddess. Why have you given me such powers?'

The wind broke suddenly in the trees, crashing like a wave against the breakers, silencing Amekayla. She huddled to the ground, suddenly aware of having been impetuous. The trees, energized by the wind, began to whip at Amekayla with their branches. She got up to run away, but a large limb knocked her back to ground. She fell on her dowsing rod, breaking it.

'Damn it,' she cried, and the wind died down. As she went to pick herself up, she found another stick close by on the ground, this one readymade for the task, as if it were a gift. She wound Elias's hair around it and began dowsing again. Almost immediately, the stick twisted and fought in her hands, as if it was trying to turn itself into a snake. It was gift indeed.

Amekayla followed where it led. It took her away from the direction of the clearing and towards a part of the woods where she had never been. Here the trees were denser, like an over anxious crowd straining to watch the action. She focused as hard as she could, to keep her emotions at bay, knowing that deep inside she was scared beyond belief, not least by the powerful magic she held within her hands.

Now the rod was pulling her and she had to run to keep up with it. She leapt over roots, dodged branches. Eventually the rod slowed down, but only so that it could abruptly bend hard towards the ground. She pushed her hair back from her face and what she saw made her breath catch in her throat.

The rod was vibrating wildly and she had to let it go, but already it had done its job. She knelt down to the ground and ran her hands over the freshly dug grave the rod had led her to. This time there was no violet mist, only the fresh sweet earth. The dirt moved easily, but it seemed he was buried deep. She cursed herself for not having brought a shovel, but if he was buried in the flesh, and not some form of casket, the shovel might injure him anyway. She began to dig with her hands, but stopped when she became aware of another presence.

'Very impressive,' Magda said.

'Leave me alone.'

Magda walked towards her. The violet mist enveloped her, making her look transparent. The black robes were gone, replaced by a diaphanous gown that made her look almost angelic. What a blasphemy that was!

'So you have a strong witch's blood in you,' she said. She looked at Amekayla as if she were some sort of museum piece. 'Surely that could not have been from your mother. Such powers skip generations.'

Amekayla looked at Magda with disgust. 'What do you know of my bloodline?' she hissed.

'More than you do, child. And more than your Grandmother will admit to you.'

Amekayla felt in her pocket for the dagger. It was still there.

'Leave me alone,' she said again.

Magda walked to the head of the grave. 'I cannot do that, child. I am here to see that you are taught the lesson you have coming to you. Do you remember what else the Grimoire said you would need? The one thing that still troubles you? Tell me, how can one so dishonest have purity of heart?'

'My love is true,' Amekayla said.

'Is it?' she asked, and as she did, a mud creature appeared from behind a tree. Then another one appeared, and then another, until at least a dozen stood staring at Amekayla with their dead eyes. 'Do you want to prove your love, child? I can provide you as many lovers as you can handle.'

'I don't want them.'

'Don't you?' Magda took a step towards one of the creatures and began caressing its chest with her hands. 'Look at how strong they are. Such arms could make a woman melt, don't you think?'

'They're disgusting.'

Magda laughed. 'A bit dirty perhaps,' she said. 'But at least you won't have to breathe a charm into them to make them want you.'

Amekayla's face went red.

'Oh yes,' Magda said. 'I know all about your feeble little spell on Elias. Not that it takes much magic to bewitch a man. You really aren't that ugly, you know. A bit plain perhaps, but not anything a man wouldn't want.'

'I wanted him to love me,' Amekayla said, her eyes focused on the grave beneath her.

'And you still can,' Magda whispered, then gestured towards the creatures. 'But only after you have loved all of them.'

'No,' Amekayla cried, as the creatures grabbed her, pulling her off the grave. She tried to fight them off, but they were too strong. They tore at her coat, and she watched in horror as the dagger fell to the ground. One of the creatures grabbed it and tried to slash her face, narrowly missing.

'Easy boys,' Magda said. 'You don't want to hurt your new girlfriend.'

The creatures wailed in a confusion of lust. They shoved and pushed each other, each wanting to be the first to have her. Amekayla was able to free one of her arms and she punched one of the creatures in the mouth. Its head disintegrated from its shoulders, then its whole body collapsed back into the ground. One down, she thought, but more of them kept coming. They appeared one after another from behind the trees, until they were everywhere. Amekayla closed her eyes and prayed. She couldn't win this battle. Elias was lost. Her whole world was crashing in and all for the vanity of a schoolgirl crush.

Enough, the voice in her head cried out, and this time she recognized it as her grandmother. They are real only as long as you believe them, it said. Magda is strong but not that strong. Refuse to believe the lie!

Amekayla closed her eyes and focused as she felt her coat and sweatshirt being torn. She focused as she felt dirt hands pawing at her breasts. She stayed focused as she fell to the ground amid the mounds of dirt that seconds ago had been creatures. Amekayla brushed herself off and looked at Magda, who looked shocked. Then anger soured her face.

'You,' she said.

Amekayla turned to see her grandmother standing behind her.

'I thought your kind was dead,' Grandmother said.

'You thought wrong.'

Magda wrapped her arms around herself, twisting her gown in such away that it appeared to lick her body with flames.

'I've no quarrel with you,' she said.

'You do now. Now go away. Go back to that coven of ancient fools you live with.'

Magda burned into a pall of smoke before Amekayla's eyes. 'This isn't finished,' she hissed, and suddenly the air was filled with violet mist. Then she was gone.

Grandmother motioned to the grave. 'Finish what you have begun, Kaylie.'

Amekayla fell to the grave and began digging as fast as she could. She worried that by having angered Magda, she might have removed the spell, and Elias might be dying at that very moment. Rocks and stones cut her hands, but still she dug faster. She cried out with relief when she found an arm. Not a dirt arm, but a real human arm. She grabbed it and pulled, and out of the dirt came Elias.

'Oh Sweet Goddess. Let him be alive!'

But Elias was not breathing. His body lay limp in her arms, his eyes rolled back into his head. Amekayla tried to breathe into his lungs, but nothing happened. She felt for a pulse and listened for a heartbeat, but nothing was there.

'No. Don't be dead. You can't be dead.'

Grandmother placed her hand on Amekayla's shoulder.

'You know what must be done, Kaylie.'

Amekayla looked at Elias. Even without life, he was beautiful. She traced the outline of his lips with her fingertips. 'But I love him,' she said, but she knew Grandmother was right. She laid him back on the ground, and reached inside her bra, taking out the bookmark. Her hand shaking, she slowly unwound the last of Elias's hairs from the satin. The pewter pixie seemed to smile at her, as if it understood her guilt. She placed the bookmark flat on her hand and slowly drew her breath across it.

Slowly Elias moved. Like a baby wrenched from the womb, he groped at the world uncertainly. He coughed violently, his lungs forcing out chunks of dirt and dust. Amekayla watched him, tears streaming down her cheeks. She wanted to touch him, to hold him, but she knew it was wrong to do so. When finally Elias composed himself, she saw the horror in his eyes and her heart tore itself to shreds.

'I'm sorry,' she said, but she could see her words had not registered. Elias backed away from her slowly, his frightened eyes darting between her and her grandmother. Then he was gone, running through the forest as fast as his feet could carry him.

THE FIELDS OF MARIAH
Pamela Chillemi-Yeager

Daylight brought nightmares to Mariah. It was only in the darkness that she felt safe. Darkness calmed and soothed her. It eased the screaming of the day, the searing brightness so strong and high she thought she might go mad.

'Dark now,' she said as she stumbled out of bed. 'Night.' Then, as she did each night, Mariah drew a cool bath. She eased into the water and carefully washed her pale, tender skin. Gently, slowly, as if by cleansing her body she could also wash away her pain and fear.

'Safe,' she crooned as she ran a sponge over her belly and thighs, 'safe.'

And as she dried off with a fluffy towel she almost believed that she was indeed safe. That the nightmares of a sun-drenched field and tall, whispering grass would slide away from her just as her bath water swirled down the drain.

When she was dry she rubbed lotion and oils into her skin and scrutinized herself in the mirror. A tall, lean body was reflected. A wavering reed, all angles and planes. Mariah smiled at her spareness, at her small breasts and flat belly, so different from the women in the village. So blessedly tall and lithe and lean.

She slipped on silk underwear and a soft cotton dress. Then she walked to the window, smiling as she opened the tidy mini-blinds that hung there. Her smile was instantly swallowed in a low, guttural moan. For night had yet to fully come. Brilliant ribbons of light slashed the sky. Vivid streaks of orange and purple that made Mariah cry out in pain and fear.

Too soon, she thought, scrambling away in terror. Too fast. She closed her eyes and lay on the floor, panting and moaning.

When at last full darkness came, Mariah stood on wobbly legs. She pressed her palms to the windowpane and felt the helix of fear which had been coiled in her stomach loosen. This time she really was safe. And when she reached the library and breathed in the good smells of lemon polish and old books, she would almost be happy.

It was strange to feel this way, her mother had told her. Strange to loathe the light and prefer books to people. 'Come to the fields, Mariah,' her mother had urged, 'come to the fields, you silly girl.'

But Mariah had resisted and made excuses. She had read her books, biding her time until she was old enough to move away to the city, with its beautiful concrete. To the city, teeming with people who did not bother her or make demands. Where she could sleep during the day. Where she could read when she pleased and work at night in silent, antiseptic nursing homes with only the cries of the dying to disturb her.

Mariah really did not mind the old people, often, when they cried out in their dying, she paused from her work and smiled, happy for their release, blessing their passing.

As she listened and mopped, she thought of her village, her hometown, of its thick, suffocating woods that bordered the fields. She thought of the mists hanging over them like sane ghastly shroud.

She remembered the vast, moody sky and the glaring sunlight filtering through it onto the tidy cottages and endless fields of green.

She thought of the women in their brightly colored kerchiefs and muslin house dresses, their bodies thick and heavy from birthing. The stocky men with their toothless grins and dirty fingernails.

It was not for her, those people. It was not for her the land that carried secrets in its mouth like a hound gripping its bloody prey.

She had fled from the people and the land on the day when she had finally gone to the fields. The fields where they chanted and danced about until Mariah ran screaming through the rustling grass and the soft clouds of Queen Anne's lace that brushed her ankles as she ran.

Yes, the memories came during her long nights in the nursing home. But they were just that—memories, and Mariah was wise enough to let them drift though her mind like clouds floating in a summer sky. For memories could not touch her or chant into her ear, they could not take away her tidy high-rise apartment and the blessed concrete and her beautiful books.

Mariah slipped on shoes, gave thanks for the darkness and went out into the night. A soft summer rain fell from the sky. It lay on her skin like a prayer, cosseting and soothing her.

She walked through the city, past restaurants and shops with brightly colored awnings. She walked through crowds of people, black and white and brown. Round and thin and all wonderfully oblivious to her.

Mariah smiled at the flower shops with their bouquets and baskets of blooms, She paused to look at one window featuring a little stuffed bear clutching a spray of assorted flowers in his paw. Too loud, she thought, turning away from the bright reds and vivid purples. Her eyes came to rest on a crystal vase filled with pale pink rosebuds and baby's breath. Lovely, she thought, resting her palms on the cool glass. So pale and sweet.

She imagined taking the flowers home with her, of carefully removing the petals so as not to harm them. She thought of scattering them on her white eyelet bedspread. Of taking off her clothes and lying on the petals, rolling in their fragrant softness. They would ease her into the sleep of daytime, the sleep that kept her sane. She looked at them wistfully and decided to treat herself to a bouquet at one of the street vendors after she was done at the library.

She continued walking until she reached her destination. Grand it was, the library. So different from the small one-room building back home. She opened the door and took in its high ceilings and endless rows of books. She loved the place, and during her months in the city, had become familiar with its every arch and curve, loving its every lintel and beam.

She quickly walked to the classics, pulling Socrates and Tacitus off of the shelves. Then she moved to the poetry section, delighting in the assortment of offerings by Shelley and Byron and her favorite, Emily Dickenson.

She held the books to her chest, a small flush of pleasure warming her. How she loved her books. Loved their neat, orderly pages and the tidy rows of lines laying out the words that sang to her. She went to a corner table, sat down and picked up the volume of poems by Lord Byron. She held it up to her face and smelled it, breathing in the fine smell of old paper and leather. Yes, she thought, running her hands over the paper. Oh, yes. The night and the concrete and the books. Oh, yes...

After an hour of reading, Mariah heard the friendly tones of the night librarian announcing the library's closing. So soon, she thought, running her fingers over the scarred wooden table where her treasures sat. She gathered them up and headed downstairs, fussing as she paused to look over the various titles, trying to decide which one she would take home with her. She settled on the Byron. And as the librarian handed her the book and her card, Mariah noticed a sticker in the lower right-hand corner of the book. A small oval with an eye painted on it, a small eye with an even smaller tear below it. How odd, she thought, She shook her head and walked towards the door, her heels clicking across the floor as she went.

A blast of heat greeted Mariah as she stepped out into the summer night. She walked immediately to a flower vendor and treated herself to a lovely bouquet of lilies and babies' breath, just as she had promised herself. She held them to her face and tried to decide which was more delicious, the soft, pretty flowers or the old, musty books.

Then she continued to walk through the heart of the city, taking it all in: screaming sirens, the clinging of trash can lids, the shattering glass and the intermittent snatches of music blaring out at her from cars and windows and boom boxes. Above it all came the mingled tongues of men women, a potpourri of Spanish and English and Vietnamese. Some fast, some slow, understandable only for their visceral heat.

Mariah walked, smiling, confident in the darkness. She passed clusters of women in neon spandex and stiletto heels, their faces bright with color; young, bare-chested men with muscles rippling beneath tamed flesh; teenagers in bright t-shirts and ripped denim, chains around their necks, the insignia of their gangs on baseball caps pulled snugly on their heads.

A beggar staggered toward her, a brown paper bag in his hand. He lurched past Mariah, his body reeking of sweat and desperation. As he moved beneath a street lamp, she saw the drooping of his right eye, the large tear spilling dawn from it, leaking, oozing onto his hollowed cheeks. Her stomach tightened. For a moment she could not breath.

The man stumbled and dropped the paper bag. Mariah watched it blow over a steam vent like tumbleweed in a desert. The sounds of Latin music drifted by.

Mariah stood, shaking, staring at the crumpled paper. She bent down, reached for it and gave a sharp cry as a shard of amber-colored glass sliced her hand. Blood dripped down on the crumpled paper, over a crudely drawn eye with a single tear.

In the distance came a soft rustling noise and the sound of laughter.

* * *

Mariah sat on a bench pouring ice water onto a wad of paper napkins. Blood lay on her hand like a dark veil covering the face of a grieving widow. She winced as she cleansed the wound as gently as she could, grateful to the kind waiter at an outdoor cafe who had given it to her.

A faint rustling sound pricked her ears. Mariah froze and discarded the bloodied napkins.

'Lovely lady, may I join you?'

'What?' Mariah peered up into the face of a bald-headed man in black leather. He leered down at her, a gold stud in his nose. 'No,' Mariah stammered, 'I was just leaving.'

The man bowed and flashed a toothless smile. As he walked away, she saw the tattoo on the back of his head. A large winking eye with a single tear. She sat, gape-jawed, as the man turned once and saluted her before he was swallowed up in the crowd.

Stay calm, she told herself. Take your flowers and your book and go home. She dropped her gaze to the book of poetry in her lap. The sticker was gone, and Mariah gave a shaky laugh. She would go home and slip into her silk chemise and read the lovely words of Lord Byron. She would arrange her flowers in her best vase and put them on her bureau where she could enjoy them. A nice book of poetry and some flowers to ease her into sleep and rid her of the strangeness of the evening.

As she went to gather her flowers, she saw that the book was not a collection of poems at all. That it was not even a hard cover book. That it was in fact one of those cheap dime store paperbacks she abhorred.

Lying in her lap was a trashy romance novel replete with a swashbuckling pirate embracing a buxom woman in a crinolines gown. 'What?' she murmured. The figures began to whirl and dance about, winking at her as tears streamed down their faces.

Mariah hurled the book away with a small cry. In horror she watched the pages fly out, the words swirling out of it like emblems in the night, chanting and circling her like buzzards.

The flowers in her lap began to open. Tiny pale buds blooming into giant orange and purple flowers. Opening, blossoming like the time lapse commercials she had watched on her small black and white television set. Pistols thrust up from the centers of the strange bouquet. Pistols oozing white liquid like the seeping glands of a readied lover. Pearly white fluid like the spurting milk from a suckled breast.

Mariah gave a sharp cry and jumped up. Images assaulted her, a dizzying film reel of sunlight and tall whispering grass. The rustling began again, echoes of chanting wrapped around it like a shroud.

She held her hands to her head as the images continued, faster and faster, a dizzying carousel of pendulous breasts, turgid cocks and bloodied mouths. The bright sunshine and the endless fields of green.

Vertigo howled around Mariah like mad dogs as the memories continued in rushing waves of skin and sweat and the angry purple heads of thick penises.

Angry and purple, driving into a young girl barely a woman. A girl who lay twisting and screaming beneath them.

Thick purple, her mind screamed. Purple like the dusk that terrified her.

She began to run through the streets, knocking into people, rushing past them. Her hand began to throb as blood spurted from her wound anew. *Come to the fields, Mariah, Come to the fields, silly girl.*

Past the library with the books that could not save her. Past the striped awnings and flower shops with cuddly stuffed bears that exploded as she ran, eyes flying out of their plush round bellies. Eyes winking and seeping tears.

(little lamb)

She staggered into an alley, the rustling and chanting calling her as surely as it sickened her, laughter and chanting. Gibbering tongues in the filthy mix of macadam and chipped concrete.

(little lamb)

Mariah looked up and saw the old beggar with his stench. She saw the biker in his shiny black leather, spinning about, the tattooed eye on the back of his skull winking madly.

A wave of nausea gripped her. She bent down and retched. Pain lashed her to the ground. A tearing, A sundering deep within.

(come to the fields, little lamb)

The smell of death in her nose and something else, something ripe and fertile as well. No blessed release for her as for the old people in the nursing home. Only a sudden, glaring light and dozens of eyes upon her.

She wept as they came, the people of her town with their fat, naked bodies. Their toothless mouths chanting and the impossible rustling of a thousand blades of grass.

They came with their hands reaching up to some dark lord whom Mariah didn't want to know. Some force, some abomination that demanded this. That shaped them and held them and drove them. Drawing her back to them with totems of paper and skin and flowers and the eyes that wept as they finished what they had begun, what she had fled from. What she had feared without true recollection.

Their voices chanted as they had in Mariah's nightmares. Syllables and words found in m written pages. Kept only for this which they did.

She screamed as tendrils of grass erupted through the concrete, snaking around her, tying her and holding her fast. The flesh of her vulva ripped open. Blood poured down her thighs onto the serpentine alley, the bright red color she had been so afraid without knowing why. Waves pain of came with the last memory,, the memory of the day she had been drug to the fields. A sunlit day. Her mother leading her, pulling her while the others waited in the foot-high grass as they waited now in the filthy alley.

Blood roared in her ears as she remembered the birthing, her birthing. The woman born of the child in the fields. Long and lean, an unfinished colt, fleeing before the process was complete.

(little lamb, little lamb)

(little lamb, little lamb)

The chanting grew higher in pitch, splitting Mariah's breastbone. Her heart lay exposed, a quivering mass that beat faster and faster as they forced her head down. They chanted louder. Higher. Faster still. Her skull split inside her body, shards of bone shooting through her organs. The intricate webbing of her brain pulsed as they danced. And as they cavorted, she ate of her own muscle and tissue, ate the inner parts of the unformed Mariah. Endless screaming and shouts of joy filled the alley as she birthed, chewing organs and muscle and sinew until at last she crawled screaming out of the dark tunnel of her own mutilated sex.

Agony flared through her as the long limbs, which had pushed through her as she consumed herself contracted and plumped with flesh. What was left of her face sloughed away like the bath water that had swirled down the drain of her sparkling white bathtub. Bones knit and covered her redeveloping brain.

Mariah lay, weak, dazed as her body continued to form new organs, new cells covered by fatty flesh and shortened bones. A single tear fell from her right eye as they fell upon the birth sac, the shuddering mass of organs and tissues left behind.

The men came forward then. All hot insistence and howling rage. Pummeling and driving. Severing what was left of her with vicious asperity.

Mariah moaned, too weak to struggle as they held apart her new, meaty thighs and entered her. Thrusting and grunting their vicious heat while a screaming tore through her.

Above the roar of her own agony came a flicker of power. A dark joy as they entered her and filled her with their pearly white sperm. The life-force nourishing now as pain and terror receded and gave way to her becoming. A becoming as inexorable as flame to tinder. The colt dying to fleshy heaviness and singular purpose. Part of the hive. Part of the whole.

She felt herself growing stronger as they rode her. Fleshy legs gripped them, strong, doughy arms held them until at last they finished, leaving her filled with a pleasure she had never known. Completing her, making her whole . . .

She woke in the fields, knowing by the smell of moist earth and grass that she was home. She gingerly felt her fat body, caked with blood, still weak from the birth. The little lamb. Killed and birthed as they were all killed and birthed, suckled and entered until she was complete.

She sat up, no longer afraid of the daylight or the strange and exotic blooms of orange and red and purple that she now realized she had never seen in all of the months she had been away.

A kind-faced, kerchieffed woman smiled down at her and held a ladle of cool water to her lips. She washed Mariah and dressed the nipples of her pendulous breasts and her woman's parts with salve.

Mariah gave way to the woman's ministrations, vaguely remembering her own efforts to cleanse herself when she had been in her tiny apartment, when she had been an unformed colt. A terrified colt whose turn as the lamb she had feared and fled, wandering through the dirty city. Losing herself in rows of words in an effort to escape. How silly that time in the city all seemed. So foolish to want words when the only words needed were those chanted in the rustling fields of green.

She slipped a muslin dress over her stout body already knowing she was with child from last night's pleasuring. A daughter, she thought as she took the kerchief the woman held out and slipped it on her head. Her own little lamb whom she could feed and raise while she worked at her stove and swept her hearths.

They walked together into the village, Mariah smiling as the woman pointed out a young girl of thirteen, red-faced, arguing with her mother. She imagined the taste of the girl's milk when she attended her birthing, her first official birthing as chanter and reveler now that she was a woman. Her belly rumbled as she thought of the birth sac and how delicious it would taste. The younger men feeding on those sacks and coming out of themselves in their own way when their time to be birthed came. Of the pleasuring that would follow as the men and women coupled in the endless fields of green. Her fields now. The fields of Mariah.

She looked at the nearby woods, at the mists hanging aver them, all white and gray and beautiful, Home again. Healed now. Born.

THEY NEVER COME BACK
William P. Simmons

Beth listened to her parents fighting and wished she could roll the air up like a blanket and hide.

That afternoon, the girls had cornered her by the swings.

It had been unusually cold and Beth hugged herself when she walked by the jungle gym. A few yards away, Susan and the other girls played on the swings. Beth envied their closeness.

Susan stared at her when she walked by. Susan Myers lived in the richest part of Harper's Mill, and she didn't let anyone forget it, especially Beth. Hardly a day went by when Susan didn't make it a point to insult her in front of the boys.

'Hey, Bum-Rag!'

Beth ignored the peal of Susan's harsh laughter.

I won't give them an excuse, she thought.

She'd promised her father that she'd try harder to make him proud. She would do anything to make him love her again, like before Billy had gone away. Before he looked at her like he had a secret.

'Do your parents shop at the thrift store?' someone shouted.

'No, she's wearing her brother's old clothes,' Susan said.

Beth stopped. She didn't want to, but her feet refused to move.

No one had a right to talk about Billy.

'You shut up about my brother!'

Susan stopped swinging. Her lips reminded Beth of pale worms when they grimaced.

'Why?' Susan asked. 'Everyone knows he was a retard.'

The other children stopped playing their kick-ball game.

'The principle caught him in the bathroom with Mary's sister.'

Beth felt swallowed by shadows, cornered by the low rustle of jackets.

'They were doing something *filthy!*' Susan added.

The boys across the field watched with growing interest. Beth wanted to scream at them to mind their own business, but Susan held her attention like a snake charmer.

'Do you know what happened to your brother?' someone asked

'Sure she does! Everyone knows where *he* went.'

'Billy didn't go anywhere!' Beth stammered. 'He got sick. He died!'

'Oh, he's dead alright,' Susan said, standing so close that Beth saw herself reflected in her eyes.

—Like her father when she spilled milk at the table or said a word she heard in school—

'The Away-Men took him,' Susan said.

Beth blinked.

Why did she have to go to school? Why couldn't she stay at home?

'The Away-Men take the people no one wants,' Susan said for everyone to hear. 'No one wanted your brother. When they found him with his hand in Mary's sister's dirty place, your parents *had* to send him away.'

'You take that back!' Beth clenched her fists until her palms smarted.

'They never come back,' Susan said.

Anger coated Beth like hot oil. That's when she noticed how pretty Susan's dress was. And the mud. 'You don't know anything!' she said, but her words sounded far away, muffled.

'I know that your brother wasn't the only one who went away.' Susan insisted. 'Mr. Crisler's family gave him away when he forgot who he was. And Kelly Mason gave her husband to them when he came back from the war.' Susan leaned close enough for Beth to smell the chili from lunch. 'And if *you* get in any more trouble, they'll send you away.'

But Beth wasn't listening. She bent and grabbed a handful of cold, wet mud. A moment later, it made a satisfying smack against Susan's dress.

'Why'd you do that!?' Susan backed away, wiping at her dress. She only succeeded in smearing the stain deeper. 'I don't want to be sent away! *I don't!*' she cried.

A moment later, the lunch aid was pulling Beth across the playground. The rest of the afternoon had been a blur of angry faces and harsh words until her father picked her up. On the way home, she tried to explain that it wasn't her fault, but he wouldn't look at her.

'No more,' he said between pinched lips.

Her mother was waiting in the living room. She kneaded her hands and looked from Beth to her husband.

'Your room!' her father shouted.

Beth mounted the stairs. After she opened and closed the door loud enough for them to hear, she tiptoed back to the stairwell. As she listened to the growing anger in their voices, she thought about her brother. She recalled hazy smudges of his face and the warm, soft curl of his fingers. In the half-light of memory, she recalled the pudgy slope of his chin and his soft blue eyes.

She tried to remember his voice, but the din from downstairs distracted her.

She'd been reading a magazine the morning her mother came to tell her Billy was gone.

'But where is he?'

'He passed on, honey.'

'When will I see him again?'

'When they leave, they can never come back.'

'But that's not fair, Mommy.'

'No. No, it isn't. So promise me something, all right?'

'I guess.'

'Promise you'll be good when Daddy's home. Can you do that, Baby? Can you be a big girl and do that just for me?'

Beth didn't like the way daddy looked at her when they were alone.

His eyes followed her when she did her homework and ate dinner. Sometimes, when she looked up, she imagined his eyes would bulge out and smother her. And now he was angry at her again.

'Give her another chance, Paul.'

'It's too late. We're going.'

* * *

Beth couldn't sleep.

She snuggled in a warm ball and wondered what the *Away People* would look like as shadows cast by stray waves of lamplight stretched across the wall.

No one had come up to yell or spank her. When her mother tucked her in, Beth asked if she was in trouble. 'No,' her mother said, avoiding her eyes. 'It's okay.'

But she'd been crying. She still was, Beth heard her low sobs through the wall. A familiar lullaby, it rocked her to sleep.

* * *

The next afternoon, when Beth came home from school, her mother waited by the door. 'Here, put this on,' she said.

'But I'm already dressed.'

'Don't argue, damn it!'

Beth blinked. Her mother never said words like *that*.

'Just bundle up.'

'Why?'

'We're going on a trip.'

'All of us?'

'Your father's warming up the car.'

* * *

'Where we going?' Beth asked her father.

'To see your brother. Wouldn't you like that?'

'But Billy's gone,' she said.

'We're going to visit his grave,' his voice shook. 'Hey, you trust your father, don't you?'

She nodded, glad when he looked away.

The world blurred past in a parade of road signs, snow-caked yards, and dusty windows in leaning houses. They followed the road leading outside Harper's Mill for about ten minutes. Finally, the town bled into dark, wild hills.

Beth had mixed feelings about seeing Billy. She hadn't been allowed to the funeral because Mom didn't want her having nightmares. She wondered what would be horrible enough to give her bad dreams. After all, Billy had been her brother. *Was he still? She didn't know if people stayed related to you after dying or not.*

Beth waited for her mother to joke or point out something funny along the road like she usually did, but she sat with her face against the window. Getting in the car, her face had looked pinched and pale, and Beth wondered if she was sick.

They turned onto Davidson Road, past the field where Beth sometimes played when the air was warm and sticky like carnival taffy. It wasn't warm today. Even with the heater blasting, she shivered in the back seat.

She wished her father would stop looking at her.

* * *

She looked out the window at Hampten Hill Cemetery as they pulled to a stop. Beyond rusted gates, marble stones dotted a wide stretch of ground like faceless grey heads. Flowers decorated the newer graves. Funeral wreaths waved in the shrill wind like crippled limbs. She looked for an end to the cemetery, but it seemed to stretch on forever. The ground was hard beneath her feet when she stepped out. Cold air slammed her face, and her breath made ghost trails that circled her head.

Her father got out of the driver's side and came around quickly. His eyes darted back and forth like liquid pinballs.

'Come on, mom!' Beth called.

Her mother covered her face. 'Go on, honey,' she said. 'Mommy's got a headache.'

'Don't you want to see Billy?'

'Your mother isn't coming,' her father snapped, pulling her hand. When he did, her mother didn't look up. They took a frozen gravel path through the middle of the cemetery. Beth struggled to match her father's pace as they sank deeper among rows of somber tombs and staring marble heads.

They walked until the noises from town, already faint, bled away completely. Silence pooled thick around them, and her father didn't look in a talkative mood. His eyes were bloodshot and his face wrinkled in concentration.

Beth thought his lips mumbled, but she couldn't understand what he whispered.

Several of the stone slabs were large and impressive glittering in the late afternoon sun. When Beth followed her father past a line of trees down a little hill, the memorial stones became less elegant. Several looked like haggard slabs of clay that hadn't been allowed to harden properly. Most were chipped. A few were so old that she couldn't make out their names or dates, chipped from too many Northern winters.

She had to pick her legs up to make it through thick snowdrifts.

When a flock of birds cried in the sky, Beth turned to watch them.

The gravestones blocked her view of the road.

She tried to make a note of where her father led her after that, but as they twisted between shrubs and trees and stones, she became disorientated. Finally, after what felt like hours, they stopped in a section of land where the trees looked sick.

'Do we see Billy now?'

The forest leaned around them like several linked, gnarled arms. Cold light splashed across the snow. Swaying trees cast moving shadows across the graves as her father squeezed her shoulder.

'Billy's in there,' he said softly. His eyes were wet. When something snapped behind them, he turned to look.

Beth didn't like seeing him nervous. She liked even less the darkening air and the sensation of being watched.

When he turned, his face was pale. He smiled to show that everything was okay.

'What's wrong?'

His smile was uneasy. 'Nothing. Nothing at all, sweetheart.'

He pointed behind her.

'Billy's in there.'

The building was low, wide, and built of wood beginning to rot. Ice-cycles hung from splintered eaves like dripping fangs. A wooden door poked from its middle. She'd seen buildings like this on television. It was where they put dead bodies in the winter. She felt that the building watched her closely with two dirty windows like dusty eyes.

'In there?' Beth asked.

Her father nodded.

'Why'd you put him in there?'

'That's where the children go,' he said. 'It's okay, go look.'

She heard his impatience as he nudged her forward.

She took one step. Another. The air felt thick around her, and her legs moved slowly, as if wading through a pool of water. She felt her father behind her like a great, looming shadow. As she approached the shack, a sliver of sunlight slashed the windows.

Something moved inside.

Something scampering behind the window.

Beth stopped.

'I don't want to,' she said. 'I don't want to go in.'

What if Billy wasn't the same brother she remembered? What if he didn't like her anymore?

The wind brushed her hair like cold, thin fingers.

'Come with me,' she said.

She didn't care if he called her a baby or not. She wasn't going in there alone.

'Daddy?'

She turned, expecting him to be angry.

She *didn't* expect to be alone.

She blinked and looked behind her.

'Daddy?'

She stared across the vast, silent field of graves. First confusion, then panic rose

61

like bile in her throat. Howling winds swept specters of snow across her feet.

'Where are you?' she screamed.

'Daddy?' The question echoed between memorials and grey slabs.

She was alone.

* * *

An hour later, she hadn't found her father or the road.

Although the land stretched flat and clear for miles, there was no glimpse of the road, no trace of the path, which had followed in. She no longer hoped to see her father walking in the distance, arms outspread, smiling. Slowly, like a dreaded whisper, the terror of her abandonment had hit her. Her father wasn't coming back.

And she couldn't find the road.

And night was coming.

They never come back, Susan had said.

Beth tried four times to find her way out.

Four times, she found herself deeper among the stones. Tears of frustration welled in her eyes and froze to her cheeks. A horrible thrill of fear slid down her back. Something else had been bothering her, something that she hadn't allowed herself to think about. As she stopped to gauge where she was, she couldn't keep from admitting it any longer.

The forest was also gone.

She should have seen its branches waving behind the stones. She saw only miles of darkening air and cold marble eyes . . .

* * *

Night, when it came, fell like a horrible, stark sheet of black, obscuring the narrow wedges of space between the stones. She soon had to feel her way along cold, sharp edges to keep from tripping. She couldn't help but think that they moved closer in the dark.

Beth squinted in case the gravel path or road should by miracle appear, but the shadows thickened with the finality of dirt filling a burial hole, obscuring all but the thinnest rays falling from the late-night moon.

She stopped to catch her breath and looked at it.

It was high and full in the sky.

A horrible idea formed. She resisted looking up again until she ran another half mile. When she stopped, she slowly looked up. The moon was still there.

It hadn't moved.

The moon was supposed to move...

The scurrying, a low, rusting whisper, was barely loud enough to hear.

I'll keep walking and everything will be okay, because bad things don't happen to kids.

And then the air peeled.

She realized that the screams filling the night were her own.

Thin, willowy arms stretched the darkness before her. Lanky, bent bodies crawled through folds of rippling air. The men looked like wet meat scarecrows. Gnarled faces like dried black fruit twisted in dumb anger. Hateful eyes smoldered like dying embers, and the air reeked of rotten pumpkins and old soil.

—*They never come back, come back, you can never come back*—

It took her a few moments to process what was happening. When she did, she turned to run but stones blocked her way. Marble slabs larger than they could have been surrounded her.

'It isn't fair!' she cried, beating her fists against the unyielding marble.

The men gibbered in the night, scurrying closer.

For the first time, sheer, uncompromising panic washed over her. Regrettably, she stayed conscious. 'I'll be good!' she whimpered. 'I promise I will!'

The men crinkled wedges of night between their bleeding fingers.

'Daddy!'

They loomed above her.

'Please?'

Panicking, she freed an arm and slapped the closest one. Its face spilt like a dust ball, spilling smoke and ashes.

Wet, hard hands yanked her up and carried her to the shed.

The *Away People* looked exactly as she'd thought they would.

GÉZA CSÁTH (1887-1919)
An Essay of Introduction by Rhys Hughes

For those who speak not a word of Hungarian, which is the majority of the talking world, it may be helpful to point out that the author Géza Csáth is actually pronounced something like: GAYSO CHATTER! It may be helpful, or it may be pompous. He was a genius. He died a narrow physical wreck in the wake of a grand psychological mess. Quite mad, but the war was even less sane. The Hungarian nation has produced a number of supremely talented writers, in all genres, who remain virtually unknown outside that ancient furious land. Many were born when Hungary was much bigger than it is now. As a consequence, the contracting borders have left their hometowns stranded in other countries. Mór Jókai, one of the truly great historical novelists of the region, grew up in Komárno, which is now just over the Danube in Slovakia. Géza Csáth entered the world in the south, in Szabadka, in present day Serbia. It was a cultured age, but Hungary was due to crumble, together with its cooler sister, Austria, and very lean times were written on the potshots of Sarajevo, 1914. It was not quite a case of ploughshares into swords. It was worse than that: iron bedsteads and railings into bayonets and bombs. However, before the mustard gas was brewed, Central Europe was swathed in coffee steam and sweetened with waltz tunes. Only its depths were properly agitated.

There were a few ominous ripples in Csáth's youth. Disagreements with his conservative father, the early loss of his mother, the silencing of his hopes for a career in music. But he was more practical than his later history might suggest. He enrolled in the Budapest Medical School and took a degree in general medicine. He went on to specialise in neurology and became something of an expert in mental disorders, first from the outside, and then with the addition of a growing opium addiction, from within. His years as a researcher with the renowned Professor Moravcsik also contained the bulk of his literary efforts. In his spare time, he wrote music reviews, a play and almost a hundred strange stories. It was the twilight of Mitteleuropa's Silver Era, an age whose absurdities, reflected in the fictions of Musil and Kafka, seem almost modern in their sense of frustration and boredom, and more closely matched with our own than those of the period of reconstruction which exists between. It is one of the reasons why Kafka is rarely assumed to have lived so long ago as he did. Csáth is another writer, more incisive and terse than Kafka, whose concerns seem to reflect our own fear of bureaucracy, a fear that is as vague as it is ineffectual, doubtless locked away in a filing-cabinet lost somewhere in the guilty labyrinths of our own inefficiencies.

But for Csáth, the bureaucracy in question was never alien to the community. It was not a pointless system imposed on ordinary life. Rather, its cruelties were developed from the bottom up. They included the awkwardness of sympathy and superstition. In 'Father, Son' there are no true oppressors. There are not even any mistakes to blame for the situation, which is barely a tragedy, but horrible all the same. Many of his other stories do not consciously seek menace, or else caress it softly when they find it. The adjuncts of the art-nouveau movement frequently intrude, directly in the ophidian shape given to his work by the artist Attila Sassy, whose etchings inspired new tales as well as decorated those already written, or indirectly in the languorous loomings of his romantic passages, with their wise and cryptic heroines. Conversely, many pieces have the detachment and brutal precision of a medical report. A few, such as 'Matricide', adopt both approaches at the same time, the two styles having decayed and fallen into each other. The dreamlike qualities in this and others are not used to provide escape from the horror, but to merely embroider it, draw it out in swirls, like the smoky curlicues and gossamer tendrils of any fashionable interior. For Csáth, evil is the basic furniture of life. The style of its design is less important, a minor quibble of aesthetics rather than ethics.

As his taste for opium grew stronger, and his distaste for his own weakness deepened to a perilous level, Csáth sought a certain redemption in the massive war that had just commenced. But his madness was amplified by his exterior conditions and duties. He survived the giant hell but returned to a more condensed nightmare. Unlike Jaroslav Hašek, that other sentimental cynic of the perfect page, Csáth did not embrace politics, satire and practical jokes. He shot his wife instead. His imprisonment in an insane asylum was terminated by a daring escape. On the way back to Budapest, he discovered that the Hungarian borders had already shrunk beneath his feet. He was now in Serbia and had to cross a demarcation line guarded by soldiers. They refused to let him pass and warned him off at gunpoint. He backed away and then abruptly swallowed poison. The Hungarians are experts at suicide. Before they can graduate in this most serious of disciplines, there are levels to be achieved, stations on the route to nothingness, little termini, practice runs. For Csáth the most significant of these were opium and morphine. He reached the first promptly at the age of twenty-one and arrived beyond the last exactly a decade later. So in essence he will always remain a young man, the tales that survive him glowing abominably with the static energy of waste, frustration and ultimate doubt.

MATRICIDE
Geza Csath

When fathers of fine, healthy children die young, there's trouble. Witman's two boys were four and five when he said goodbye one sunny, windy November afternoon. He just died and, all things considered, didn't leave much sorrow. His relict was a beautiful woman, gentle and rather selfish. She had loved him just so much; but then, she'd not given him any cause to worry either. A tepid love's more excusable in a man than in women whose lives are protected, given meaning and value by this powerful if often irrational feeling. We can, however, pardon Mrs.Witman, since she has after all brought a couple of good-looking, strong boys into this world. They lived in a two-storey house that had a shaky wooden stair, and the other tenants appreciated blonde Madame Witman when she appeared in the street in mourning. Though her waist had been quite narrow and her eyes childlike when she was young. She was, as a human being, neither good nor bad—she kissed her two boys as seldom as she spanked them. In fact, there wasn't much they had in common, as it turned out.

The boys played the long afternoons away from home here and there in the quarter, showing up late in the evening. They talked little, and that between themselves. Their father's spirit gleamed in their tiny black eyes. They got up into attics, sniffed about old crates and boxes, and chased cats up to the roofs through vents, creeping over the walls high up in back and around the old, smoke- stained chimneys. While summer lasted, they swam in the river and trapped birds in the woods. Mrs.Witman fed them and gave them fresh underwear on Saturday night. She even walked them to school on enrolment day. Otherwise her life was tranquil and she grew plump. Six months after her husband's death she made acquaintance with a bank clerk, handsome, young, wide-shouldered, and clean-shaven, with a rosy, high complexion. Mrs. Witman found him attractive, and although it seemed hard and tiresome, she flirted with him. The clerk began escorting her, keeping her company, and took tea and kisses from her. Out of mere lazy boredom the fellow didn't drop her.

Witman's sons hardly paid attention to their mother or her lover; they were busy with their own little schemes. They entered high school; they grew tall; their small muscles stretched taut as steel wires along their strong, thin bones. They managed their studies easily in fifteen minutes every morning. School was unimportant in their lives. For them life was an aristocratic job, so from an early time they'd quite naturally arranged their time to suit their own needs.

In one obscure corner of the attic, they had set up a small infernal studio. Here they concealed an assorted collection of arrows, guns, knives, pliers, screws, strings. On gusty autumn evenings they would finish supper and slip quietly, quickly down the street, leaving their mother absorbed in her cheap novels. They would run off exploring over half the town. They would ambush stray dogs with a noose and drag them home, tying up their muzzles and lashing them to a board. Their little lamp flickered in the damp brume of the attic like a distant candle in a haunted house deep in the woods. With careful, thrilling slowness they would begin work. The dog's chest would be slit open, its bleeding blotted as they operated and listened to the animal's terrible, helpless moans. They would stare at its beating heart, take the warm, throbbing little mechanism in their fingers and destroy first the sac, then the chambers with tiny stabs. Their curiosity over the mystery of pain was insatiable. Often they would torture one another, agreeing together on pinching and hitting. Animal torture grew into a serious, ordinary passion in them. Their methods elaborated steadily, and they exterminated whole regiments of cats, ducks and chickens. And no one knew what they did. They concealed their activity with a mature carefulness.

Actually people in the building paid little heed to them. On the first floor there was an elderly law clerk seldom home, and a seamstress employing four girls. On the second floor there were only the Witmans and their landlord. He was the previous owner's son, a very young man who cared little for the house and its tenants. There was a glassware shop and a dry goods store on the ground floor. Nobody ever saw any customers in them. The Witman lads could use the whole place for their purposes. No one was ever to be seen in the small, little courtyard. Only the lone sumac in the center of it, which had ventured its last leaves and flowers years ago, could have sensed that not everything was right here. Yet, as everywhere, life went on, even in this small, two-storeyed building. Perhaps only the two boys found it enjoyable, since they planned tomorrow and the day following.

One September night they returned panting, red-cheeked, dragging a trussed owl behind them. They had gotten up into the belfry of the old church for it. It had taken them a whole week of searching and observation and discussion as to how to snare and kill it. And they'd succeeded. Their eyes shone; they felt the hunter's strength in their shoulders as they came galloping back through the dark streets, exultant. Long ago they had grown interested in that owl. Its head was like two huge eyes. Old marvels lay hid in its mind. It lived a hundred years, more . . . That owl they wanted desperately.

Now they had him. They plucked its fine feathers from its breast one by one, watching the flames of its pain flaring up in the bright eyes of the mysterious bird. Then they wound wire about the wing stumps, the feet, and beak, and stared a long while silently at the nailed bird. They remarked that the bird was in fact no more than a house, into which Torture has moved, residing there until the owl is killed. But where actually does it live! In the head, probably. They decided to leave it like that over night: going to bed would thus be more beautiful and exciting. And while undressing they were thrilled, listening for a sound from the attic. Their limbs were suffused by a rigid elasticity, as though the hapless power of the tied, twitching creature might yet come swooping over them. And so they slept.

In their dream they roamed vast prairies, galloping madly on great white stallions. They flew to earth from dizzying peaks, swam through bloody, warm seas. All the suffering and pain of the world twisted, screaming and shrieking beneath their horses' hooves.

The sunny morning smiled at them, and they jumped lightly out of bed. They took breakfast from the maid, Mrs. Witman usually sleeping till ten. Then they hurried up to their owl, and finished him off in an hour. First they removed its eyes, then sawed the chest open, freeing its beak so as to hear its voice. That voice, that horrifying voice piercing their very bones, surpassed everything conceivable. But because of it they had to execute it quickly and bury it, fearing someone below might have heard it too. It had all been worthwhile though: they were quite content.

That afternoon the elder brother left by himself. He had seen something in a house. Through the window there'd been a girl scantily clad in a pink slip, combing her hair. He'd stopped at the corner and gone back to peek into the room again. Now she stood at the far end of the room, her back towards him, her white shoulders glancing in the light. The boy went through the gate. An old woman approached, but the girl combing her hair appeared at the same time at the end of the corridor. The boy walked towards her and said that he would like to see her up close—she was very pretty. The girl stroked the smooth cheek of the slender boy in his short pants: with a jump he embraced her, his lips fastened to her face. Meanwhile a few doors opened in the hallway. Girls put their heads out, and then withdrew them quietly. There was a blue night light at the end, and the girl led the Witman boy down. They dropped the curtains and the afternoon sun filtered yellow into the perfumed room. The girl stretched out on the carpet and let herself be caressed and kissed without moving. Witman's elder son thought of the owl: through his mind it flashed—why is everything in life that is beautiful, exciting and wonderful so inexplicably horrible and bloody too. The necking soon grew boring. He rose disenchanted, waiting and staring at the female. He mumbled goodbye, promising to return. What was her name? he asked, and learned she was called Irene, which he thought beautiful. At last he said, Goodbye, Ma'am.

That day the Witman boys strolled the meadows until very late. Nothing about that afternoon was mentioned. The elder remarked that beings like humans lived in the air, you could feel them floating past when there was a breeze. They stopped, shut their eyes, spread their arms. The elder asserted that giant, ethereal women with soft bodies swayed about him, touching his face with their breasts and backs. In a while, his brother said that he too felt these women. In their beds at home they talked about the women of the wind, and opened their window to them to let them enter. And they came, slipping soundlessly in, barely touching the sill with their velvety backs, floating, swimming on the air to the boys, reclining on their pillows and blankets. They stretched their necks towards the boys' lips, and drew away in languorous, airy movements. All night they remained in the room, linked in an undulating ring, hovering, smiling towards the window and gliding back to the boys, lying above them, snuggling down on them. They left when the first rays of the warm sun glowed into the room, departing, as they'd come, with slow, dreamlike gestures, evaporating into the morning's freshness.

That day the Witman boys went to her together. Coming home in the warm May afternoon from school, they took the street to the house and slipped past the gate. She came smiling to greet them; dishevelled and laughing loudly, she led the two Witmans to her room. They dropped their books, knelt on her carpet, and pulled her down, kissing, biting, caressing her. She laughed through her shut lips, and closed her eyes, too. The boys glanced at one another, and began to strike her. Now she laughed with her mouth wide open as though she were being tickled. The Witmans took hold of her. They shoved her down, tumbled her about, pinching and hurting her. Panting, she allowed the boys whatever they liked. After a while, the boys stopped their play, their faces flaming, and snuggled against the pink silk of her gown. Then they collected their books, saying she was the prettiest woman they had ever seen. She said she liked them too, but if they came back they'd have to bring her something, flowers or candy. The elder Witman answered that she would be very pleased by what they'd bring her. She walked them to the gate and kissed their hands.

After supper they shut themselves in their room and talked about her, agreeing that their experience had surpassed all the former adventures incomparably, including torturing the owl.

—That's the only thing worth living for, the younger said.

—It's what we've taken all that trouble to find, the other said.

The afternoon was warm and bright, and they headed off for school without their books. They walked straight to the girl's window. No one there. They turned away. The curtain lifted and she looked out. They stopped. She opened the window.

—Coming tomorrow at noon! She said with a grin. Come along, and remember to bring me something. She waved, and shut the window.

They blushed. Just having seen her set their hearts racing.

—We'll bring her jewelry, rings, a gold bracelet, the elder Witman said after a while.

—Right. But where'll you get them?

—Mother's got some. We'll ask her for them.

—She won't.

—We'll get the key to the glass cabinet.

—She never lets that key out of her hands.

—She's got four gold bracelets and seven rings.

—She wears three more on her fingers.

In the evening they hung about the vitrine, looking over their mother's treasures. There were among them two lovely bracelets studded with pearls and rubies.

They asked Mrs. Witman to show them her things. Stubborn, the blonde woman chased them out. She felt quite distant from her sons, and was even a bit afraid of them.

The boys discussed matters out in the street.

—You can't ask her for anything.

—Never.

—She won't give up a thing.

—No, not her.

—We should break that cabinet open.

—She'd wake up and raise hell. Then we won't be able to take her anything.

—She won't wake up.

They were full of hatred for their blonde, blue-eyed, fat and lazy mother. They'd have liked to torture her, too.

—I break one of the little glass sides with my knife handle. That's all the noise there'll be. You hold the light, I reach in and get the rings and bracelets.

—Let's not take them all!

—Oh yes, we take all of them. She doesn't need them. We'll leave nothing for her. Let her yell her head off.

They dashed to the attic and studied their tools. They picked a chisel, a pair of pliers, checked their torch, and stuffed it all in their pockets. Then they scurried down and went off to bed. But first they peeked at the crack under her door and determined that their mother's room was dark. Undressing, they decided not to leave before midnight. They left their socks on to make sure their steps would be silent, and went to bed both peaceful and alert. Leaning on their elbows in bed, they planned in a whisper that they'd drop in on the girl at noon, when school was out. They'd hide the treasure in the attic, taking out a piece at a time. In the morning they'd deny everything. If their mother tried to beat them, they'd just scram. The picture of her anger and helpless blubbering when she couldn't find her jewels simply delighted them. The possibility she might wake up simply didn't occur to them again. They got out of bed as it grew late, opened the window, and leaned out into the pleasant May darkness. The barking dogs and the rattling cars of the trains that divided the hours with their passing didn't shorten the time of waiting.

When at last the tower bell struck midnight, they made ready. They lit their torch. The younger Witman took pliers, the file, and the light; the other took the jack-knife with its long blade opened. He went first. Calmly, confidently, he crept across the dining room in the middle of the apartment. The elder boy opened the door to Mrs. Witman's bedroom. The hinges didn't even squeak. They breathed easier. Mrs. Witman was fast asleep, peacefully turned to the wall. Her wide, fat back in its knitted nightgown was presented to them. They stopped at the cabinet.

The boy lifted his knife to bash in the small glass side. He hesitated, then struck at the glass. The rattling was fearfully loud, as loud as though somebody had thrown a carton full of glassware from the roof of the building. Mrs. Witman stirred and turned over; getting up on her elbows, she opened her eyes. Annoyance was expressed on her face, and a stubborn anger; but she never made a sound, because the elder Witman boy leaped towards her bed and plunged his knife into her breast. The woman dropped back again, throwing her right arm wildly up. The younger one was already holding her legs down. The older boy jerked the bloody knife from his mother and plunged it back again. There wasn't any need for that because she was dead. Her blood trickled under the blanket.

—Well, everything's under control, the older one said. Let's collect it all.

They removed the jewelry from the cabinet: the bracelets, brooches, rings, and the gold watch. They laid it all out on the table, sorting the newly seized booty and dividing it in turn.

—Let's get moving. We have to wash and change.

They went back to their room and washed their hands. But there wasn't any need to change because not a drop of blood had touched their clothes. Then they returned to the scene. The younger Witman lad opened the dining room window while he waited for his brother who locked Mrs.Witman's door from the inside, climbed out the window, and came back in through the opened window of the adjoining room.

The street was black; a deathly stillness covered it, but they hurried because the church bell struck one and they wanted to get their sleep. They undressed and fell into their beds exhausted by the excitement. In a few minutes both were fast asleep.

In the morning they were wakened by the cleaning woman who came at six-thirty on the dot. She knew Mrs. Witman never woke before ten, so she didn't go to her room. After cleaning up in the dining room, she woke the boys as usual. They quickly washed, ate their breakfast, and disappeared. This time the treasure was in their pockets.

—Let's do it before school!

—Okay.

—We've got to make class on time!

—Especially today.

—We'll be called home by eleven anyhow.

—Let's make it fast.

The gate was open. They met no one on their way to the girl's door. They went in. The woman was sleeping, her face hot. They uncovered her and kissed her, taking the precious things from their pockets then. They dropped them on her belly, on her breasts, on her thighs.

—Look what we brought you.

—It's all yours.

The woman came to very slowly. But she smiled, and hugged the hard little skulls of the two rascals to her. She thanked them for coming to see her, and turned back to the wall.

—We'll be back today or tomorrow.

Then the boys said goodbye, and ran off towards school.

THE WOMAN WHO COLLECTED FLIES
Gerd Maximovic
(Translation Isabel Cole)

The room was dark, the curtains half-drawn, the light of the moon which sailed between the clouds mixed with the reflection of the erect, floodlit spires of the cathedral and fell through the window into a room on the fifth floor of the house, where Angelina lay in the dusk on her wide bed, behind the screening curtain swam television, bar, the pictures on the walls.

She half-lay and half-sat, in the blue shadows which marked the drapery of the setting sun which spread for a few minutes over the dark red, the black roofs of the old centre of the city. A little studio lamp shone at the foot of the bed and cast a shimmer on Angelina's features, making her white face glow almost golden. The left arm lay slack over the plump cushions covered in heavy green silk; the right hand was raised to her lips, in her fingers a slender white cigarette, the fingernails red claws; her hands trembled slightly.

Her narrow face gazed steadily into an indeterminate distance, her green eyes gazed sharp and full of unveiled tension. Thin grey wisps rose from her full, unpainted lips, after she had sucked the smoke deep into her lungs. When she smoked her lungs expanded, her bosom expanded, the red silk robe drew tight, parting at stomach-level and disguising very little there, least of all the long slender legs, also bathed in rust-red light, lending her something of an Indian goddess, a high priestess with whose help human sacrifices are celebrated.

Not until the second glance did one notice the telephone that rested on a footstool next to the wide bed, her blue-black hair nearly reaching down to it. The telephone was as silent and mute as the entire evening; outside, behind the double panes, the street hummed quietly and anonymously. Outside the window the winter had unfolded after a sudden outbreak of cold, covering the double panes with frost flowers amidst which eyes, too, grew, gazing greedily at the creature in the red robe.

Crushing out the half-smoked cigarette in the ashtray, she thought once more that it was time to finish with Rodney. This one last evening. Then she would give him marching orders, would send him to the Devil. He was really starting to get on her nerves, and that was a rare occurrence. She still had control over the situation; she did not want to lose it.

She tried to picture the inside of her head, the fine gray mass, the many convoluted twists in which she had stored so much experience over the years since she had begun to play with men. She leaned her head a little to the side and thought how delightful it was when one felt how the sober calculation functioned. She sank into the shadows, purring like a cat, licked her lips, looked into the distance; like a picture book she opened up her eventful life, she detected the barbs, heard the men's songs of triumph—and heard them whimper. Lit a new cigarette.

It was important to do everything as soon as there was a strong feeling together. This spiritual closeness was not always present. She thought of the studio, the hot lights, the studied smile, the melting mask under which she sweated. Her thoughts jumped, hardly to be held on to in her head, as if an alien will were thinking with her. At last she saw herself in the glass bathtub, in the frothing green water, saw herself sink beneath the golden faucets.

She had covered her eyes with large sunglasses which gave her somewhat the appearance of a bloodthirsty insect which—now that she had nestled into the seat of her Lancia—crouches in the red, open calyx of an enormous flower to suck in the nectar from deep tanks, with proboscis and feelers which reach into the depths. She rolled out of the parking lot with opened sun-roof, drove at full throttle for several blocks, and then shot the ramp to the nearby overpass, cutting in front of a large silver-gray Alfa Romeo, which, somewhat slower than her Lancia, had been about to head straight down the right lane.

An ordinary manoeuvre. She snapped up the sun-shades to ward off the breeze, and for a short distance let her Lancia roar along the highway until her hair flew like whip-cords in the wind and the wind pressed her blouse tightly against her body, with little air bubbles here and there, as if she had just gotten out of a fresh bath. Then, as she switched from the fifth to the fourth gear and further, and as she skidded to the traffic light, her cars exhaust spat black clouds as if it were puffing hectically on a cigar.

The car that she had cut off a few minutes before loomed threateningly large in her rear-view mirror, had changed lanes, rolled on the left beside hers. She took in the driver with a fleeting glance, saw a firm, browned face, half-turned to her, saw a slight smile, looked into brown eyes, saw black hair full of pomade, as was the fashion now. The triple eye of the Cyclops high above the street, swaying beneath the blue of the sky, had opened a green eye to rust-red facades. Angelina flew across the grey concrete road and over the sticky patches of tar, faster really than she had intended, as if driven by a demon, into the city, the silver Alfa magically drawn on, dancing in the rear-view mirror.

At the next traffic light, as the cyclopean eye worked itself up to yellow, she pulled her car into a tight curve in the direction of the train station, onto the cobblestones, to settle the question once and for all. The silver-grey car skidded across the intersection with squealing tires in a bold manoeuvre, just like her, without blinking, and then settled in behind the red car with a cosy roar. She snorted black smoke onto his windshield, thundered down the express street past the train station. The Alfa followed without hesitation. She had gotten wedged in behind a truck, let up on the gas, the Alfa now abreast of her.

The man with the pomade-gleaming hair gave her challenging glances, as if he had no need to pay attention to the road. A grim smile played about his lips. Then he yielded to a Mercedes which edged up behind him with flashing eyes, drove past the truck, down the street, hesitated there a little, as if unintentionally, to see if Angelina would follow. She followed. Then they flew down the street like two thunderbirds.

She thought of that evening when tigress and tiger had met. They had spoken with that growl in their voices which showed that both were balancing on the crucial point, that they were circling each other like two satellites on extreme paths, that they were two comets which hissed across the sky and that they had set out on the long journey through the endlessness of space, at last to meet another fixed star. And, voila, there came this magician from the theatre, who had been engaged for a guest season, the magician with the black hair and the broad hands.

She tried to picture him without closing her eyes. She never shut her eyes to the truth. Except for his hair, a completely ordinary boy, but who must possess, hidden somewhere inside him, a magnetic anchor which did the job with women. Only with those who, like he, could balance their consciousness on their fingertips, Tigress and tiger. The two elements. Primeval forces. Lightning and thunder.

Her face had remained unmoved while she thought. The telephone stood beside her, hardly visible, and silent. Night had fallen over the city; the cathedral towers shone still brighter, the frost flowers stared more lasciviously. She dreamed of penises, which hung like garlic braids from the ceiling. She dreamed of sweet mouths that had to be closed. She dreamed of a last night in Rodney's arms. Something like a romantic shadow glided through the room as she realized that, for a second, emotion and intellect had fused in her mind.

She looked at the electric alarm clock, which turned its silent rounds behind the console, hidden under pale red illumination. Soon it would be eight o'clock, and Rodney would come. She lit another cigarette. She shouldn't smoke so much. It was unusual, it was not her way. She would drink a little sherry to calm her nerves. She swung her legs over the edge of the bed, drew the red robe closed, slipped into the terrycloth shoes and went into the kitchen with her own natural grace.

It seemed to her as if she saw a dozen men rolled into one, standing in the door, leaning against the frame, his hands folded over his chest, his eyes bloodshot, rolling. He seemed drunk. Spoke much too quickly, in an agitated, toneless voice. She laid her head to the side and listened into the past, to hear what he had to say to her. But he, who had made such a good impression before that one could almost have fallen in love with him, said nothing differently than other men in his position. What was the good of all the pleading, what was the good of the tears? She would never go down with a sinking ship.

She opened the door of the refrigerator, and the light shone in his eyes, made his face disappear; all that remained were his shed tears, as if drops of blood had fallen in the freezer. There, somewhere, she must have laid the bottle. She could not find it. But then in her mind's eye she saw traces in the ice cubes, saw the frozen blanket of snow on the slopes of the embankments, saw the mirroring ice of the frozen ponds, saw the ice-skating children, saw Rodney balancing on the ice with the camera.

Again the near-paralysing memory of that summer returned. An implacable flywheel drove the unsorted thoughts into her consciousness. In the darkness that lay over the farmhouse, owl eyes stared, gleaming gazes in which the alcohol spilled over, near the fire, in the petroleum lamps. Rodney and Angelina were forged together in their thoughts, rolled through the garden chained in thoughts, rose straight into the sky like coupled comets. They dove into the crowds, bathed in the gazes of the others, gathered points, found scattered points of contact, smelled envious eyes, squinted at the twisting back staircases in the minds, where new constellations, connections and constructions emerged. One more marble in the box, a gleaming, glass bead, the cards newly shuffled, the cards newly added.

The night rushed over them, filled them with the caustic smell of lox and tobacco, drove dry drinks behind their brows, in the mirroring eyes, went the shortest distances, knew shortcuts which must inevitably lead to the goal and shoot out somewhere into the darkness, where the crickets chirped in the grass, in the bushes, at the edge of the forest, where the central European insects made a pandemonium as if they sat in an amplifier to make themselves audible.

The stars jingled above their heads, bent their long necks stiffly, the stars jingled in the refined necklines of the women, rose and sank and described their seismographic curves in the pre-programmed heads, dammed the quicksilver there with hot dikes, let it flow again, stopped up the paths which it usually took: Short circuits crackled through the night with bright sparks, with blue flames they sprayed into the sky, rolled behind the mirroring eyes as ghostly images, executing a spectral dance which was supposed to show which phantoms back there, black and squat, had gained form and life and bent in love, with knotted hands, over the silver silhouettes.

The people recognized themselves in each other on different levels, in different stations of their development, in different degrees of maturity and development, grasped, sensed, insisted that it was not only a matter of grasping the self in the other, but of confirming oneself in him and thus waking oneself to life, now for oneself alone, and also in a certain sense for later smoke-impregnated evenings and nights. Nowhere near all of the ropes, which swung through the air, had been grasped, too numerous were the ends cut off and smeared with tar, but even there the heat of the open fire melted what had sealed their ends.

There was an attic into which one could vanish by way of a back staircase. The crowd was not as large as it might have appeared at a fleeting glance. Angelina and Rodney, seized by a sudden hot rage and desire toward one another, stumbled upstairs, groped through the darkness which was illuminated only by the meagre reflection of the flames through a glass window. It almost seemed as if they were dragging their booty up the stairs, as if it were time to overthrow the conditions of nature once and for all. Angelina's hair blew in Rodney's face like the ghostly fingers of a spider, but there were no alarm- or trip-wires that could have warned him; moreover, he was objectively playing a different role, and she was the beetle scented with flowers, who had given him signals with her perfume. Anyway, both were a little drunk, in spite of all their calculation, but that only meant an equality of weapons.

With that hot rage in which covetousness and hate are so closely woven, ready to topple over at any moment, to change course, to wage war in one way or another, or to resume it with other means, they fell upon one another, literally fell upon one another from the first moment they left the last rung of the ladder. Tugged, dragged, bit each other over to the bales of straw that towered up invitingly in the wan light of the moon, which illuminated the only window, in the form of steps, suitable for every convenience and position.

In these minutes, where each expanded monstrously from a length of only a few centimetres, they were like wild animals struggling with one another, taking possession of each other, each devouring the other, sipping from one another, like primitive savages driving their spears into one another, attempting to elicit whatever nature presented them in the other, who registered every gesture, every expression, every snort, every groan, every moan and sigh in the uncertain wavering light, who wrote down all this DNA with implacable precision and sharp consciousness, engraved in the slates of their brains, fixed forever, information and knowledge. Weapons. Now, now was the moment when the other unveiled himself, now, now one got to know him, now, now was the irrecoverable opportunity, these drunken minutes in which their dammed-up feelings exploded, where they did not pretend, where each was at the mercy of the other and each pumped the other full of that which he had and extracted what the other had to give.

The battle raged for a long time, the concept of time, dependent on motion, was lost, or rather changed its character. Gradually their feelings slowed down, slackened their rhythm, gradually they glided out of the zone in which they cramped their jaws, in which their tongues were knots, their lips tight lines, and their eyeballs rolled. Gradually they glided back into the zone of the ticking feelings, the calculated gestures, their status was normalized, compared to what they otherwise considered usual, the battle began to dissipate, retreated from the hot sphere where the tanks had rammed into each other with glowing motors. In time one saw only the silhouettes of the battle figures, frozen in their last movement, almost monuments already, with weary, slackening gestures, phantoms, which melted into the background.

She found the bottle of sherry on the kitchen table, drank a glass and blossomed. She felt the summer stir in her veins, stepped, grazing the glass case clumsily, nearly losing her footing on the slippery floor, into the parlour in front of the large mirror to regard her slender body, carefully observed the bronze goddess, swung her hips, regarded the black triangle, shuddered at the thought that this evening she would once again suck Rodney dry, then to discard his empty hull.

She felt glowing streams of molten iron course across her body, beginning at her nape, then flowing down rapidly, freezing in the cavities, laying hold of her entire body in an extravagant gesture. Before the furnace of the sun she saw the spiders struggling, threw back her head so that the black-blue hair flew, and watched as the male was devoured to pay tribute to his offspring.

In the bright mirror she saw the face of her mother, saw her lips trembling with rage, saw that she was about to strike her Angelina, heard this, tonight you'll stay at home, which would not last long. The first boy in the upper-school, that had been like the beat of a drum. Once her body was aroused, once the tigress had the smell of blood in her nostrils from the welts she had drawn across the boy's back the way one scrapes off wallpaper. He had been the best in his year, and, when the butterfly did not let itself be blinded, wandered long in confusion through the building in which he had once celebrated his greatest triumph.

She had raced along the wide street, the street lined with men who danced in the air like swarms of flies and left their marks, red and yellow, on the windshield of her Thunderbird. Like flies she had collected them, laid them under glass, had studied them under glaring white light.

The telephone exploded in a shrill tone. An arrow lodged in her heart with trembling shaft. Something made a move in her, her pulse rose, at the same time she was flooded by a fearful feeling of release, people of action are bound most terribly by uncertainty. She reached for the receiver as if into the midst of life.

Hello . . . .

A voice which climbed the precipice, Angelina, it's me. Rainer's breathless voice. Can we see each other again? Angelina, please?

For a moment she had the feeling that the climbing iron was tearing out of the cliff wall, a heavy barrier shifted in her head; then her face relaxed, her voice grew calm.

Really, Rainer, she said, it's pointless for you to call me here.

She smoked a cigarette again, her movements were unbalanced, her cheeks, when she took deep breaths of the smoke, were as if marked by a grave illness. She had sunk deep into the cushions which embraced her body like a substitute lover who, with all his warmth, was still unable to soothe the terrible unease in her mind, the excitement of her nerves, the shaking of her voice, the flighty thoughts and hands. She lay as if buried, and if the light had not been so thin one could have thought that her cheeks were tinged with an unhealthy grey.

She thought as if pursued by dogs. The images pressed in upon her. They welled up as if riding on the bloody lava of a volcano. When the cigarette was unable to calm her childish impulse, she bit into a pearl necklace, which she gathered up from the bedside-table. Poison pearls. She tasted blood sweet on her lips.

There are evenings that pass as if one were riding on silver arrows. There are bars that lose their gloomy charm when they are filled with the right words and turns of phrase. There are people who blossom, who come to life when they are drenched with the warm rain of other present times. This is the secret story of the inner life of human beings. If you shut someone long enough in a dark room, every paintbrush can mimic the sun. Angelina, the girl with the great qualities, had been shut up among all the men, and there at last one had come who had flung open her windows.

Somehow they had staggered, walked, flown through all these bars, which he, of course, did not know, winged, soused, drunk. For certain it was not the alcohol that took away the inhibitions of the two, who were well versed in the art of the dosage of hard liquor. It was the secret magnetic pole that drew their floating crusts together and urged the spark-spraying friction and union.

With a groan Angelina stirred in her cushions, crushed the cigarette in the ashtray, dropped her hands as if she were being opened like a book, felt herself grow heavier, felt the hot, heavy body, drew herself up on his arms, sank her fingernails into this back, and felt at last how he would fill her once and for all, and with all senses. The hours were wrapped in pale cloths, which would make them cool and congeal, hours that one had to capture, which one had to hold onto as long as this dull, dusky darkness lasted.

Nine thirty. The divine bastard had not come. Had not called. Had simply left her lying there. Spat upon Angelina's mind and body. Lay in a cesspool in the arms of another woman. It was as if fireworks drove Angelina out of the cushions, rage flooded her eyes with red, she bent back on her bed, her body jerked, she felt her breasts, felt here and there, and realized with terrible wrath, with incomparable rage, that the ignorant prick had simply left her lying there.

She bit into the cushions, for if she was to suffocate, she did not want to suffocate within. She clawed at the furs with her red fingernails, imagined that a great male tiger was lying there, whose heart could so easily be torn from his body. She saw his phallus, this ridiculous, sensitive spot, saw how the sausages hung from the hooks in the butcher shop while the pigs sank into the gutter, bled to death, back in the slaughterhouse. She saw all this.

She sat up straight, lit another cigarette deliberately, wanted to keep thinking. She pressed her free hand around her body as if she were afraid it would fall apart otherwise. It was good that way. She was calm now. She wrinkled her forehead, drew her eyebrows together. Her consciousness, that splendid mechanism, told her that she would lose her mind if she were not careful. Told her at the same time that Rodney had started something with her. Told her that she had Rodney to thank for everything.

She gasped for breath. Crumpled up the cigarette. Lit a new one, quite unconsciously. That was it. That was the thought. That was the black spider, which had slumbered in her consciousness, nourishing itself from her best juices. The psychological master, Rodney, the master spider. Yes, what she herself had done with so many men for whom she had conjured up her radiant appearance, cool, precise and calculating, whose wishes she had raised as if in an express elevator to the top of the house and multiplied them and enhanced them, whom she had first taught what they could be, what they were with Angelina. The scoundrel had started with her exactly that way.

From their first meeting he had sensed the fascination that he exerted upon her. The lofty banter, the idle talk which, if it had been written down, would have at most given cause for wrinkled brows the next day, he had succeeded because she had given him an advantage, a kind of trust, and he, skilful and brutal, had bound her and enveloped her and involved her in a ridiculous, tragicomic affair. The deeper she fell into his trap, the more she had betrayed of herself, thus making it possible for him to set traps, cautiously, in more distant rooms which were still closed to her reason, traps in which his precious prey was to be caught again and again.

Ten o'clock. The alarm clock glowed red. She staggered away from the bed as if drunk, the mummified men of her past reached their arms toward her, their desiccated faces grinned with yellow teeth. She had to destroy this scoundrel, had to lay his psyche in ruins. She raged. She had to free herself from this man. Ten o'clock. The swine had not come. Ten o'clock. Red-glowing alarm clock. Sterile wisdom of glass and plastic, electric wands that fed it.

In front of the transparent glass doors, behind which the brown-hued contours of the park, in its midst the broadcasting centre, were limned, she remained standing, in this summer, scrutinized her appearance coolly and as if to banish all doubt that she was desirable. Saw the blue-black hair flowing down upon her shoulders. Saw the narrow, pale face, the high forehead, the direct challenge, which every man was forced to answer. Saw the green eyes, which knew their dominion over the world of men. A scrutinizing look at her body. The silk blouse buttoned high on this summer day, neither semi- nor fully transparent, since it was neither a display nor a general merchandise store. The skirt, slit up the side, was also somewhat longer than usual, with silk-embroidered hems, a self-confident, cool charm that neither squandered nor threw away what was to be given only with care.

Indeed, her figure was almost painfully stirring. The curves on which nature had experimented so long, for so many millions of years, and which could only have come into existence in harmony with the minds of men, followed certain curves pre-programmed in the brain, called up patterns and signals, associations, made the mouth water, as if a bell were being rung which shrilled inaudible but loud in the cerebral zones. Since the men chased perfection in their way, in the attempt to approach that which nature and society permitted them to hold as their ideal, the hot terror which overcame them at the sight of Angelina was shadowed by the foreboding: should one take one's ideal image, should one pluck this rose, and what would happen if?

Toward twelve o'clock she was calm at last. The dishevelled, rumpled hair hung over her shoulders, the tracks of tears had dug themselves into her make-up, her fingernails were broken. The things in the world and in her head were sorted out again, to a certain degree, orderly. She decided that she would go to bed soon. She pulled herself together enough to clear away the dishes, empty the brimful ashtrays and clean up the apartment a little. She sensed her mind grow clearer as she performed these simple chores. These were simple things, which went quickly, which worked. They also proved to her that she was once again fully and completely and rightly focussed on reality that her senses were beginning to normalize themselves, which the things, which had shifted to the wrong places in her soul, had returned to their old positions. Now she suddenly remembered things that had escaped her behind the blockade of her rage, her sorrow and desperation. As if of its own will that day's drama returned to her, she needed only to glance at the newspaper, which lay untouched in the corner.

She also sensed memory press into her skull, her thoughts stirred in her mind like independent beings; they came creeping into her consciousness with tiptoeing steps. Once again she felt hot, excited pangs in her heart, but now she bore the realization. A hard, grim smile played about her lips as she headed for the kitchen to fetch scouring cloth, rags and caustic substances. On her way she cleared away the long knife, which was meant for cutting bread. She laid it in the sink in a caustic solution, in the vague hope that the blood would dissolve by itself over night so that she would not have to dirty her hands. Then she returned to the bedroom, secured the curtain and turned on all the lights. Red, dark red, congealed, it shone out at her. Fleetingly she remembered again. They had wanted to go to a pig sticking. Nothing had come of that. Strange, that in life all wishes are fulfilled after all. She made a feeble, playful attempt to remove the blood. It was hopeless; blood is best removed when still damp, with cold water, but of course only when it is not present in large quantities. Really she had meant this cleaning action only as a demonstration.

Now that she was calm, it was time to clear away the cleaning utensils. Tomorrow she would think of some way to get rid of the bloodstains. She turned out the lights in the kitchen and the hall. In front of the glass case, which was closed by a glass door, she stopped. She looked at Rodney. He was a rather unfortunately crucified hrist, for the clothes hangers had not held. Even in death one could see his ignorance. With his open eyes he stared past her unceasingly, as if he wanted to punish her with scorn. is mouth was twisted. emotely the pose of the victor, in which she had seen him last, could be glimpsed. She thought one could win a pri e at an e hibit of modern art with him. She kissed the pane, but odney did not return the tender greeting.

She lay in bed and turned out the lights. She saw the moon sailing behind the closed curtains. She saw the red dial of the alarm clock. The telephone lay in the dark. There was a smell of blood and sherry.

THE DAGUERROTYPE
A MODERN GHOST STORY
Richard Sheppard

I

'A man, sir, should keep his friendship in constant repair.' Or so said that most eminently quotable chap, Samuel Johnson, and it was with that in mind that I felt a sharp blade of guilt cut me as I saw Major Carroll burst through the doors of my club. I had not made any effort to contact my friend in the past few months, nor he me. Judging by his haste and disheveled appearance, he required a good friend, urgently. You see, Major Carroll and I had been close companions throughout most of our adult lives, indeed ever since we had graduated from Magdalen a good twenty years ago. Back then we were so full of and hope for our glorious futures, and to a greater or lesser extent we were not disappointed. Carroll (in that most noble tradition of his family) joined the army, and had distinguished himself during his service in India. It was said that he was the first Englishman to re-enter Delhi after the '57-'58 mutiny, after which all Indian affairs were taken from the hands of the East India Company and served (with far greater efficiency) by the Crown. I, had been less driven by any family tradition to uphold (being an orphan) and had no real ambition to travel or help my fellow man. Instead I took to illustration, with which I had marginal success in the field of children's books, with the occasional diversion into sketching the scenes of various grisly crimes for the recently created police force. It was something of a queer double life, to be detailing the gossamer wing of a pixie one moment, and the next to be turning my skills to a common drab, stabbed by some drunkard in an East End den. However these two pursuits kept me in sherry and cigars (and the occasional luxury) well enough. Unlike Carroll I had never married, and had firmly resolved to stay a bachelor. Coupled with this I owned a pied-a-terre in Berkeley Square, inherited from my late Uncle Tiberius. With neither wife nor landlord to empty one's purse, you might be surprised at how pleasurable life can be.

The night that Major Carroll violently pushed through the doors of my club, I was enjoying yet another of my pleasures; a few drinks and lively conversation with a good friend. Professor Callum Metzer (whose name you may recall from various small minded condemnations of his infamous 'selected breeding' experiments) and I had just finished a fine repast of baked trout in the Club restaurant and had retired to one of the low, cramped nooks of the library. There, surrounded by a gently smoldering fire and two imposing cases full of dreadfully important tomes with a good meal inside of me and a fine cognac about to join it, I felt completely at ease. Contrary to me, Metzer was quite agitated, his bald head darting about on top of his tall, lanky frame like a jack-in-the-box on a spring. I had been relating to him the story of a certain police inspector of my acquaintance who had asked me to sketch the bisected eyes from murder victims. The reason for this was that (according to the good inspector) the trauma of a violent death would be so great that the last image the victim would see would be indelibly recorded on to some part of the eye. Trusting nobody else but me with this theory, the inspector had commissioned to sketch every single part of the eye in the finest detail possible. I explained to Metzer once we were ensconced in a library nook that whilst this had resulted in a tidy profit for me, it had yielded no fruits for the police.

'At a guinea a sketch, the only crime they might detect is me robbing them blind. Do you realize how many different parts make up the human eye? At a guinea a piece?' I said, wallowing in my own good fortune.

'Certainly. According to my Gray's Anatomy, one has the retina, ciliary muscle, choroid, hyaloid membrane—I say, isn't that Clive Carroll?' Metzer said, staring past the bar to the visitor's entrance. I looked, and indeed it was Carroll, and in a highly agitated condition. His robust frame was heaving in exertion under his rumpled evening clothes, and his short, black hair was in a bird's nest tangle. He was looking around wildly, and once he had sighted me, approached our nook with great haste.

'Clive! Good to see you, as always. Are you quite all right, old chap?' I said, signaling to the alarmed barman to bring another brandy for my friend.

Clive collapsed into a chair. 'Thank God you're here, Roderick. If ever I have needed a good eye and a sympathetic ear, it is now. Hello, Metzer,' he said. He had never had any time for science or the scientist.

'Good evening, Major. What on earth is the matter?'

'Yes, Clive, tell us. You're beginning to scare the natives,' I said. The rest of the club had noticed his arrival and was staring in disapproval and concern at our table.

'Oh. I am sorry, Roderick, but I did not know where else to go, I've sent Pandora away to her father's estate. Anyway, this may be perfectly suited to you. Both of you.'

'If we can help we will, but what the devil's wrong? And why have you sent your wife away to Scotland?' I asked.

'It is no longer safe. I tried to explain that to her, but I dared not show her the image. It's just not right, Roderick.' With that Carroll collapsed into an over-stuffed armchair, sipping brandy and staring with wide, frightened eyes into the fire. This was most unnerving. I had heard tell, both from the Times and his regiment, of the bravery he had shown at Delhi, and anything that could cause him to run to earth like a frightened animal was a grave matter indeed.

'Right, how about we all go to your house and see to this?' I said, more agitated than I wanted to let on. Clive looked away from the fire and to me with a grateful smile.

'Oh thank God! Please, I'm sure that if I'm not the only one, it won't dare move. Things will stay the same. Please, Metzer, I would also like your opinion on this.'

'As you have said, but I must confess I have no idea what 'this' could be.' Metzer said, swirling his snifter around between long, bony fingers. Clive was already getting up to leave, and practically dragging me along behind him. With a raised eyebrow, Metzer took a final sip and followed us out into the night.

II

The three of us hastily pulled on scarves and gloves as we stumbled through the high winter winds and through the warren of narrow, stone streets that led to Carroll's house in Lambeth. We saw nobody else on the streets at this hour, and no lights lit in any window. Occasionally I would try to talk to my friends, but the cold wind would take the words away and throw them into the dark night above our heads. When we finally reached our destination I received cold comfort; I had visited the place many times by day, and had barely noticed the building itself, thinking it to be simply a house. Now in the dead of a winter night, with the first flurries of snow settling and melting on my coat, I almost cried out with fear. The building seemed to loom its full three stories over those around it, the gable windows hanging over the windows like the heavy forehead of an ape or common ruffian. The windows on the ground floor were so dark that they appeared to never end, and be portals to some oblivion. Cautiously Carroll led the way up the steps, and as we passed the black iron railings that ringed the front, I could quite easily imagine some malicious wind plucking me from the ground and hurling me down on their wicked spikes. Finally, after what seemed like an eternity of fumbling and fear, the door was opened and we pushed inside with undue haste.

'Bad show not having a fire lit for us, Clive. Where has your man got to?' I said.

'I have sent all the servants away, I could not risk them becoming drawn into this thing. They're safe, now. Please, come through to the drawing room, have a whisky.' Carroll said, and herded us into the front room. Once inside Metzer began to start up the fire and I poured drinks for all three of us. Soon enough we were warming up again, and with some of Carroll's fine whisky inside of me, I knew that we could take on whatever was troubling my friend.

'Now, Clive, if you please, what on earth is the matter?' I asked.

'Have either of you heard of Louis Dageurro?' Carroll replied.

'Certainly.' said Metzer from his seat. We had dragged the three best chairs around the fire in a horseshoe, as if we were about to fight off the Indian hordes.

'Roderick?' Carroll asked.

'No,' I replied, 'but I presume he's has something to do with the daguerreotype.'

'The very same,' Carroll replied. 'He's a French fellow, over there they call him the father of photography, together with that Niepce chap. Anyway, that's not important. Like you say, he did invent the daguerreotype. Now, I'm sure we have all seen such things before, usually a portrait of one's wife or child or suchlike.' Carroll fell silent. I knew why, he and Pandora had suffered some misfortune with children, poor souls.

'Yes,' Metzer said, picking up the conversation, 'it really is a fascinating process, in which a single image is captured using a combination of mercury vapors and a highly sensitive silvered plate, treated with iodine, invented around 1838 I believe. Of course, it is not widely used much these days, William Talbot's negative and positive process is far more successful.'

Carroll was listening to this intently, but looked disappointed when Metzer finished so abruptly. 'Anything else? Please, there must be something more.' he said.

'I'm sorry, I don't really know what to tell you.' Metzer said.

'Have they been known to change?' Carroll said, the horror evident in the last word. He drained the whisky in one swig and drew closer to the fire.

'No, of course not. Moving pictures? Hardly.'

'Then perhaps you would care to turn your scientific faculties to this,' Carroll said and staggered across to his writing desk. Metzer and I exchanged looks, mine concerned, the scientist's merely curious. Carroll eventually returned and dropped what I recognized to be a daguerreotype onto Metzer's lap. I leaned in for a closer look.

'There, what do you see?' Carroll said, and poured another drink. He was getting steadily more inebriated, and also more violent. I could feel his hatred and fear for the image he had given to us, and with some trepidation I looked to see if I could find anything horrendous or disturbing.

'I'm sorry, I am not really up on architecture. Roderick?' Metzer said, turning to me.

'I see a daguerreotype, depicting a house,' I said taking it all in. 'The sun appears to be out, and judging by the oak tree on the left of the picture, it is Autumn. The branches look quite bare. The house itself is a two story affair in a recent style that I seem to remember is called 'Italianate'. You can tell them by that small, squat tower, called a 'campanile'. Look at the overhanging eaves and the windows with the capped pediments. Yes, a fairly standard house.'

'Anything else?' Carroll asked.

'Wait . . . . yes. How could I have missed that? There appears to be a young couple under the oak tree. Their house? I should think so. The husband looks like a clerk, the wife appears to be pretty, young. Yes, good, hard-working people, I would say. Certainly house-proud.'

'What if I told you that when I bought this at auction a few days ago it depicted a Queen Anne house, twice that size? I saw it, Roderick! The red-brick, the windows narrow and dark, framed by white wood.'

'Nonsense,' I said, fearing that Metzer and I had been lured into some practical joke.

'What if I told you that a few days ago the couple were dressed in a style not seen for decades, and the oak tree you saw was little more than a sapling!'

'Clive, stop! Can you hear yourself?' I said. I hoped that my friend was about to jump up and reveal the whole thing to be a jest.

'No, wait,' Metzer said, quietly. He had been intensely studying the picture whilst I had been arguing with Carroll.

'What's wrong?' I asked.

'It does change, very subtly, but it does change,' Metzer replied.

'Oh fine, so I am to be the victim of this hoax alone. Let's just get it over with.'

'Quiet, Roderick! What do you see, Metzer?'

'The young lady. Her waistline appears to be expanding,' Metzer, said, as if he was recording any scientific fact. Without bothering to ask the bachelor Metzer why he had been so transfixed on the lady I snatched the picture and saw for myself. As someone who had been on an assignment to sketch fashion features for the leading ladies' magazines I recognized that her dress had altered considerably. The waist was expanding, but only because the corset had loosened. She retained the same, slightly shy, smiling expression, but it was not just her outfit that was in flux. Her husband was now sporting a rather bizarre necktie that offended the eye. The true change however had come upon the house. The refined Italianate style had dissolved into a redbrick building, with the roof pushed backwards like errant strands of hair, and held back with a garret window. The oak was now in full summer bloom, and had seemingly grown a few more feet, now branching up to the second floor window.

'What the hell is going on?' I asked Metzer, who alone out of the three of us was calm and treating the picture with curiosity rather than unbridled fear.

'The tree, Roderick. Think of the tree. I believe we are seeing the passing of history in the frame of this picture.'

'Nonsense. You are so blinded by this, you cannot see what is going on!' Carroll said.

'Oh, and what that might be?' Metzer said, barely looking at my friend. The scientist no longer considered the soldier relevant, Metzer had found his grail and anything or anybody else was beneath interest. As for me, I could not think of anything other than what the daguerreotype would show us next.

'This is the work of some evil spirit, and before you dismiss this with your science, Callum, remember India. It is a country of mysteries and Porroh men who would curse my name for their brothers I placed beneath the earth. We have to destroy it now.'

'Why didn't you do exactly that when you first noticed the change?' I asked.

'I had to show it to someone else, someone else had to witness it. I'm not mad.'

'No, Clive, you're not.' I said. This seemed to bring some modicum of calm to my friend, but before we could progress Metzer cried out again.

'My God! It's changing again!'

'Why should it change so quickly now?' Carroll asked.

'Maybe it wanted a receptive audience.' Metzer said, and I felt like cursing him for a bloody fool. However curiosity drew me back to my seat and the daguerreotype. The house had indeed changed again, and it shocked me deeply. The roof had been cut off, and where there used to be the familiar sloping roof there was now a level plain. Bands of white encircled the front of the building in thick stripes. The windows had fractured and become many. Where one pane had stood, there was now fifty squares of glass. The door was a sinister, unnatural looking portal and the windows surrounding it a deep black, despite the obvious spring day and the new bloom of leaves on the oak tree, which now dared to grasp the rooftops with new branches. The man, thank Heavens, was still dressed in his clerk's grab, although something seemed to have happened to his hat—it was nowhere to be seen, presumably blown off by a breeze.

'Why do they never age?' I asked Metzer, but he had no answer. His pale eyes were transfixed on the young lady.

'Good lord!' he whispered. I looked at the girl myself and raised him an 'I say!'

Now as an artist in one of the most progressive areas in London I have had the pleasure of knowing some rather interesting and fascinating young ladies more than the equal of some men, but the daguerreotype female was of another breed entirely. The 'skirt' she was wearing was almost fiendishly tight, and barely cleared her calves. The color was dark, that much I could tell from the dim daguerreotype tint, but my primary concern was for the show of ankles and the obviously constricting dress. How could she walk in such a thing? Get out of a carriage? Take it off? I wondered, and at that last pondering felt my face grow hot with blood.

'Clive, you're right, this must be destroyed.' I said, and tried to tug it away from Metzer.

'No, you fool! Can't you see the importance of this? We have found a gap in the curtain that separates the present from the future. This is the most important discovery of the year! My place at the Royal Academy is assured.'

'My dear friend,' I hissed, 'if you require enlightenment that much, I know of places in Soho where you can gaze on just as brazen sights through a gap in the curtain for just a few pennies, you knave.'

'This is science!' Metzer said, and threw my hand off the heavy lead frame of the daguerreotype, his eyes fixed on it, not wishing to let a detail, no matter how salacious, pass him by. Against my better judgment I watched for the next ten minutes or so, Carroll silent in his chair, the only sound the crackle of the fire. I watched as the house became sleeker and smaller, and the hems become higher and higher. At the first glimpse of a well-shaped knee, Metzer gasped as if he had seen an eclipse. The gentleman remained solidly be-suited, save for a thinning in lapel size and the fact that he never did appear to find his hat. In a blinding flash the daguerreotype flared up in heat and light, and Metzer and I were forced to shield our eyes. When we looked back the house was gone and the tree had been reduced to a blasted stump.

'What happened?' I asked Metzer.

'I haven't a clue, some kind of fire?' he replied. The couple was still there, both wearing loose clothes, suited for comfort not morality. Despite the destruction of their home, they still smiled slightly, still appeared proud of their home. The reconstruction began quickly, with the skeleton of the house appearing first, then cladded with light stone. The windows fell back at unusual angles and shapes, giving the impression of a race of impossible tall, slim people inheriting the earth after the unknown catastrophe had destroyed the house. The door was now a cavalcade of shades, although all appeared different browns through the daguerreotype's tint. A piece of twisted metal was perched on top of the building like a piece of machinery. A lightning rod, I pondered, or maybe a weather vane.

Metzer was entranced by the siren in the shrinking skirt. I could tell that his science, like so many others, was born out of loneliness, and I thought of Louis Daguerro, and what it was that he might want to have captured forever in an unchanging form. The man's missing hat was joined by his waistcoat, and after a while he began to not even bother buttoning his jacket. His tie grew wider and wider, the designs more and more complex, until I could have sworn I saw some Babylonian whore painted upon it, reclining in luxuriant venality. I thanked God that my eyesight alone was sharp enough to pick that out, rather than the laboratory myopic Metzer. I need not have worried in any case, he was in some carnal trance. The girl, no longer a young lady, was degenerating at high speed now, the whole picture was picking up velocity toward the even more unknown future. Her face appeared darker, and I recognized the telltale signs of too much rouge, such as would be more becoming to an East End doxy. The skirt crept from the knee to the thigh with the hideous speed of a snake crawling up one's body. It was all moving too quickly now, the lower thigh, then the upper thigh, and then the blouse losing shapelessness, a young bosom pushing through. Her hair hung in swirls and eddies like oil on water, allowed to flow freely, unfettered by combs or hat, falling about the shoulders.

I heard a cry that I assumed must have come from the woman's husband at the sight of her lasciviousness, but had instead come from Carroll who, so appalled at the way things were progressing, snatched the daguerreotype away from Metzer. He moved towards the fire, the scientist right behind him, and made as if it throw the unnatural thing in the fire. With another cry, this time borne more out of lust and desperation Metzer snatched up the poker and brought it up with surprising force into Carroll's stomach. The daguerreotype fell to the ground where Metzer snatched it. He was obviously not going to give Carroll time to recover and risk another attempt to destroy his prize, and whilst I attended to my fallen friend, I heard Metzer run through the hall, throw the door open and then the soft pads of his feet pounding through the fresh snow.

III

Carroll and I decided that we would pursue Metzer the next day, rather than attempt to search for him in the dark. I was reassured by this decision more than I could say; Metzer's behavior had frightened me deeply, it seemed so unusual for such a dull man to behave with such passion as to attack and rob his friends.

Naturally his home was our first port of call on the search and naturally we did not find him there. Carroll was too good a huntsman to think that a quarry would return to its burrow, but we had to draw a line through the more obvious possibilities. Most of his home in Callender Square was a warren of small rooms filled with scientific apparatus of such strange design and bewildering intricacy as to the leave the laymen (of which Carroll and I proudly counted ourselves) almost physically ill with confusion. Metzer had apparently not employed any household staff and filthy sheets on an old bed seemed to be the only indication that anybody had called this place a home. The kitchen contained no food, but a confusion of chemical stains that had seeped into the woodwork. His few good clothes hung on a rail in the lavatory.

If Metzer's home was a testament to a life lived solely for work, then our second target, his laboratory at the university where he lectured, was a perfection of the idea. There were no personal effects in-between the riot of pipes, bottles and benches that filled the cavernous room. At the heart of the laboratory was a working steam engine making an awful noise and sending jets of vapor up to fight with frost on the high windows. It did not seem to be powering anything, and the one person in the room, a young man in a white smock, seemed to be caring for it with the diligence of a nursemaid.

'What's going on here?' Carroll asked him, pitching his voice above the machine.

'This is Professor Metzer's laboratory. You'd have to ask him,' the youth said. He did not seem troubled by the fact that we had just wandered in.

'You mean you don't know what this machine actually does?' Carroll asked.

'Well, no. My responsibility is to look after it, regulate the temperature and so on, whatever the Professor wishes to do with it is his is own business. I say, what do you want here?'

'We are looking for the Professor.'

'He's not here.'

'Obviously. Where is he?'

'I haven't seen him for days, sorry. I know he works from home a lot,' the young man said. He was stopped of divulging anything further by the crescendo of noise from the machine reaching a climax in a loud blast and puff of acrid smoke. When this had cleared we could see a panel hanging loose from one side of the steam engine. Immediately the young man rushed to the wound and began trying to push the metal back into shape. Carroll and I left, almost running into the quad outside in a rush to breathe the harsh winter air and enjoy the silence.

I broke it. 'Another possibility gone.'

'Yes, but he has to be somewhere.'

'Do you think he is still in the city?'

'Where else is there? He won't require much, just some food and water, some privacy so he can look at that bloody picture without interruption.'

'How far do you think it has come along? The picture, I mean,' I asked, knowing that this was the question both of us had been asking ourselves since Metzer had run out into the night. We were both drawn to it, compelled to look future in the face no matter how much it terrified us.

Carroll's reaction was silence, and lots of it. I began to think as we walked out of the university grounds that his behavior was even more alarming than Metzer's. He seemed more enthused with the idea of finding the daguerreotype than with finding our friend. Even though he had only met Metzer on a few occasions before last night, and they could hardly be said to have much in common, I hoped our first priority would be to him.

'Very well, Clive, I have a suggestion,' I said when we had finally found a hansom cab. 'If you think Metzer will keep his needs simple and he wishes to disappear from sight, let me consult my friends at Bow Street.'

'The police? To what end?' he replied.

'We shall obtain a list of the worst boarding houses the East End has to offer and search them cellar to ceilings until we find him.'

'And if we don't?'

'Then we shall try something else,' I said, and true to my word within half an hour we had a list of the more ill reputed houses in London and the onerous duty of questioning the landlords and landladies began. Carroll was good enough to bankroll the search, and spent a small fortune bribing the degenerate slumlords, mostly for useless information.

As the day drew on the shadows between the buildings seemed to grow deeper, taller, able to hide more. Our good clothes and conspicuous billfold made us a potential target for any of the disreputable types that frequented the East End.

Eventually our diligence paid off and in a building by the river so poorly built and so tall that it seemed it would collapse in a strong wind, we found him. The landlady clearly recalled a tall, thin man of nervous disposition who had taken a room late last night. He carried no baggage save for what looked like a picture frame clutched tightly to his chest. This queer figure had paid a week's rent in advance, then promised more money on the proviso that he was not disturbed. Only when Carroll had met and doubled Metzer's figure that we were allowed to squeeze past the considerable bulk of the landlady as she proprietarily tucked the notes between her cleavage. As we walked up the narrow, filthy staircase I heard Carroll whisper: 'Safer than the Bank of England.'

We did not talk again until we were at the highest landing, standing in front of the door of Metzer's garret room. Carroll appeared more nervous than I had ever seen him, his hands shook and sweat rolled off of his face. I motioned for him to knock, he refused with a violent shake of the head. I stepped forward, feeling peculiar at this reversal of our usual selves.

'Callum?' I said, knocking on the door. I repeated his name once, twice, knocking louder each time. Finally I reached for the door handle and pushed. Two things struck me immediately: firstly the intense cold of the metal handle, which was almost painful to touch. Secondly the door was not locked, but seemed to be blocked by something. A few more good pushes and it creaked open. I could see that the barrier that had impeded me was a thick layer of frost around the doorframe and as I looked further I could see a thick layer of ice covering everything. The source of this was, I am pained to say, my friend Metzer, crouched by his bed like a man at prayer, except with that blasted daguerreotype in his hand rather than a prayer book. His skin was an unhealthy mix of blue and white with sporadic patched of dead, black flesh that I recognized as frostbite.

I walked slowly into the room, the floor crunching under my boots. I would not have normally entered such a ghastly scene, and my mind screamed for me to leave and fetch the police, but another part of me was acting on its own volition, it was desperate to see how the future would turn out according to the picture. Carroll too had overcome his fear and followed me, and for the second time the three of us crouched around the picture. For the first time we did not see the couple, nor their house, nor the sky, but instead a pure pristine white covering the entire area. No discernible features could be picked out under the blanket of impenetrable cold that had killed Metzer by his own curious obsession and our own futures that lay in that unknowable, perfect nothing.

THE CRUELTIES OF HIM
Brendan Connell

When fishes flew and forests walked
And figs grew upon thorn,
Some moments when the moon was blood
Then surely I was born.

    –G.K. Chesterton

I

'So this is your third adoption from the agency?' smiled the woman, from behind her administrative desk.

'Yes,' replied Ruth, the Doctor's wife, 'we love having children around the house. I thought that when I mentioned the idea of a third to Donald he would say I was crazy. But not at all, he thought it was a wonderful idea . . . He's so understanding you know—about my ovaries,' she blushed.

Doctor Blanche patted her hand sympathetically. Yes, he could very well understand what it must have felt like to be an infertile woman. He himself was a sober individual. Yet his face showed that he was capable of shedding a few tears, should the appropriate occasion arise.

* * *

That afternoon they took home the third child, a baby boy, hands grasping innocently and mouth puckered with bubbling spittle . . . The nurses flapped their own paws, in his face, as an expression of parting, let their lips curl up in semblance of joy, and stood at the door of the agency, uniforms chalk blue, to watch the infant submerge in the Blanche family car.

II

Doctor Blanche was a well-respected physician. He had awards to his name and works of repute on the shelves of bookstores. Colleagues sought his advice. He and his wife were greeted with effusion bordering on sycophancy when arriving at a dinner party.

His receding hairline exposed a broad and intelligent forehead. The eyes in his head were a dull shade of green. They bespoke a calm and methodical mind; a potential compassion that lurked beneath the pink of his skin . . . Ruth was infinitely matronly. Old fashioned, neighbourly to near blessedness . . . It was seldom that her face did not beam, irradiate the warmth of a country hearth, the charm of Middle America.

It was said that she was a bit simple for the likes of her husband. But who can rightly discern the ways of the heart? Better to let nature's elemental laws of attraction work their will; and be happy when two beings find shelter from the cold of night in each other's embrace.

* * *

The Doctor let his knife wriggle through the roast, the weight of the slice of beef, infinitely thin, depositing itself onto the serving fork. His right hand lifted it onto the plate held by his left. This was his second helping, and the meat lay wrinkled in folds in the light violet of its gravy.

'So what do you think of the little fellow?' asked Ruth, a forkful of oven baked stuffing held in readiness before her mouth.

'He's a beautiful boy,' the Doctor replied as he cut through a portion of the brown, gray and red rainbow of flesh. 'Really, he is in much better health than the others were when we received them. You remember how sickly Pedro was. The way he ran through those diapers was awful . . . And Cynthia was not exactly a prize as I recall. Getting rid of that rash became a genuine trial.'

'It was hard alright,' agreed Ruth. 'But you did want to begin with healthy children.'

'Of course,' he said, his jaws stirring a mouthful of beef, 'with all the stress they were to go through it would hardly have been right not to root out those little ailments . . . It's funny they should give a doctor unhealthy babies though. If I were a differently motivated man I would have returned them.'

'Well, at least this one is fit.'

'Exactly.'

* * *

After dinner the Doctor climbed down the steps that led to the basement. He flipped the light switch and a battery of phosphorescents buzzed into play. The chamber was fully subterranean. Two tables, covered in coarse white fabric, sat end to end against one wall. Medical apparatus, often antique, hung from hooks and nails. Industrial sized mayonnaise jars lined the tables and other shelves, grim metallic objects bristling out.

There were syringes, obscene in their length and throbbing glint. Odd shaped scalpels lay about, the ends curved like the Malaysian tjaluk. Others glistened with the obscure complexity of the African mongwanga, or the ends of certain European halberds, such as the guisarme, chauves souris, or the Lucerne hammer. Many of the implements could be described as nothing less than medieval, primitive . . . It was an inspired collection that would have been the envy of any museum's chirurgical reliquary.

The walls of the room were of red brick, thus making them outskirts of shadow. In the center sat a doctor's chair, lamps stationed around, leather straps with buckles hanging loose from its body and arms. Off to one side, against the wall opposite the tables, were a series of cages. The smallest, in the forefront, showed mice, a gerbil or two, and various other rodents. A forlorn monkey strutted across a residence much too small for it, chicken wire, fortified with re-bar. A few yellow warblers, perched in a jail on a string, quite still, apparently asleep. The larger two cages, of seeming professional make, were adumbrated by the play of light through their very bars.

A faint motion was detectable from that direction. There was evidence of life manifest behind those fingers of steel. A gurgling whine reached his ears. Soon this unpleasant noise became blanketed by a bizarre twittering, a frantic mutilation of musical song.

The cage birds awoke, joined in with their more elegant calls, beat their wings against the surrounding net of copper wire.

III

Pedro was the first to come under their roof. Despite what Ruth might have said to the adoption agent, the Doctor was the primary advocate in all those acts of offspring collection. Whatever state his wife's ovaries were in was without significance; he needed children. Unformed minds, unformed flesh—these called to him; they were of vital importance.

The boy was sickly to be sure. Doctor Blanche, like many modern physicians, believed that environment could overpower atavism. He did not want the creature to hear nasty language—or any language. The ear is delicate. Our Doctor knew anatomy like few men. Others might have the ambition to restore, but he would take away. The stapes are the smallest bones in the human body, more minute than grains of rice. He removed these, thus severing the connection between the malleus and incus, or the hammer and anvil, and the inner ear. Sound could not reach those delicate labyrinths, the utricle, saccule and cochlea.

The monkey, a male mangabey, was named Chako. The first years of Pedro's residency were spent in near intimacy with him. They shared the same cage. Doctor Blanche made sure to limit his own contact with the boy to a bare minimum, making it clear to Ruth that she follow suit.

With Chako for a guide, Pedro learned to show his teeth, bob his head, and slap the ground with his hands. The monkey would groom the youngster and he, in turn, enjoyed picking lice from his mentor's fur, decimating them between his bared teeth. At feeding time Chako took charge, setting the larger portion of raw eggs, frogs and roughage down his own gullet, while leaving the little homosapien enough nutriment to remain relatively vibrant.

Pedro's hair and nails were left to nature. Without sun, his skin grew to cotton whiteness—apparent subsequent to his monthly washing down, via Ruth . . . Her husband was sensitive to ill odors . . . He was growing his own wild boy, but chose to be sanitary about it.

IV

The smudge advanced into the slashes of light, its mane hanging thick around the shoulders. He strutted back and forth on all fours for a few moments, his buttocks prone in the air, then lurched up, grabbed the bars and oscillated his trunk like one intoxicated, a hideous grin riving his face.

The Doctor however was not interested in Pedro's antics. Though they gave him some measure of satisfaction, they offered but small amusement. He had come to attend to the other, Cynthia.

She entered the glow of the family hearth a few years after Pedro. Her adoptive father had been plummeting deep into the alchemy of the flesh. From the principles laid out by Thomas Vaughn, he delved into the old Chinese texts of Black Taoism. He possessed an unknown manuscript in the hand of Robert of Chester, which offered vital hints, as well as the Arabic works of Jabin Ibn el-Hayyan and the Persian of Ghazali. Of course the branch of the art that truly interested him he found laid out in uncompromising detail in a series of unique pamphlets. These documents, of anonymous authorship, were written in cyanic script on pages of vellum. The language was a sort of hybrid Latin, a post-pagan vernacular, combining bare Imperialisms with quaint strands of Middle English. Certain lines read eloquent, poetic, so much so that a man such as William Dunbar could have composed them. Others were blunt and trim, grammatically perfect, pure Latin, in the style of Tacitus or Quintilian.

* * *

She was more timid and let herself be heard before seen. The chaotic whistling and clucking came from the shadows. The songbirds responded from above. Slowly the girl waddled out, her hair straight and golden, body sheathed in a banana colored jumpsuit, a strange and xanthic being, with pale blue eyes and a simply innocent forehead.

He had stitched up the sides of her mouth when she was a baby, cutting the width of the aperture in half, transmuting the orifice into a puckered bud. The Doctor and his wife never spoke a word to her for the first years of her life. The cage of warblers hanging above her quarters served as masters of elocution. She heard them and replied, listened and imitated.

He elongated her neck, using the ring method of certain African tribes, stretching the item a portion further with every quarter year.

The tibula was extracted and re-inserted at the pit of the leg. Of course he had to alter the base of the femur to make the operation mechanically sound. But her bones were supple, young, and responded well to the chisel... The fibula and tibia he turned one hundred and eighty degrees, snapping them into alignment with the patella. When these bones turned, the gastrocnemius, peroneus longus, all the minor muscles and the entire foot also turned. The result was a leg that swivelled in reverse... Her heels faced what she approached... In order to keep proper balance she became forced to tuck in her pelvis and stick out her chest... As this operation was performed on her when she was an infant, these postures became, if not natural, at least habitual.

When Doctor Blanche opened the door of her cage, she shied away from him slightly, tucking her head to her shoulder in a fit of modesty. The Doctor patted his knee and whistled. At this she sprang forward, attaching herself to his leg. He hoisted the frail creature into his arms and brought her over to the surgical chair.

From the linen covered tables he took a sponge, which he infused with chloroform. This he placed over Cynthia's nose and the button of her lips . . . The lamps clicked on, closed in, brightening that center of activity, that little sentient being . . . And the scalpel flickered in his hand.

V

The black disk spun, a band of light playing on its grooved surface. The mellow sounds found passage through a fleck of diamond, created a silvery atmosphere within the room, a guitar plucking away, Gabor Szabo's 'More Sorcery' album emitting its exotic, somewhat sensual melodies.

The Doctor sat in a leather armchair, a Gauloise cigarette burning between two fingers, a glass of rye whisky, half consumed, set on a coaster on the table next to him. One of the kidskin pamphlets sat open on his lap. He turned the pages with great care, reading over material he already knew by heart. These were the root texts of jester anatomy, the design manuals for the construction of court clowns, circus freaks and necromancer's toadies.

The rap at the door and the sound of his wife's voice were simultaneous.

'Dinner is ready,' she said.

The Doctor glanced at his wristwatch and, after extinguishing his cigarette in a nearby ashtray, rose with a sigh, depositing his precious copy on the bookshelf.

A large platter of fried chicken was just being deposited on the table when he made his appearance in the dining room. The miniature body parts had the rich hue of unadulterated gold. A crockery bowl of mashed potatoes steamed on a second trivet. The cobs of corn were cut in half, a few strands of silk still clinging to the kernels.

He sat down, settled a napkin on his lap and scanned the food spread out before him.

'Have you thought of a name yet?' Ruth asked, gnawing at a leg of fowl.

'Tarquin,' the Doctor replied coolly from across the table.

'Tarquin?'

'Yes. I believe that it is a suitable name for the little fellow.' He methodically buttered a cylinder of corn, running a thick pat over the rough surface with his knife. 'Lucius Tarquinius Priscus,' he continued. '... And then there is Tarquinius the Proud, Tarquinius Superbus, who came along a bit later ... Roman kings you know ... Tarquin.' The corn rotated between his teeth, manifold seed coats bursting, embryo and endosperm stripped from the cob, pureed together.

'And you'll begin soon?' she asked, her voice flavored with wifely concern, fingers setting a chicken bone down on the side of her plate.

'Yes.'

VI

Tarquin was his human clay. A ball of flesh, malleable; a satchel of blood, bone and brain to be transmuted.

Doctor Blanche tampered with the facial muscles, crippling the right side of the boy's mouth in an eternal grin, the left an unalterable frown. The lips formed a sideways 'S', the twisted neck of a swan ... Those eyes, gentle brown, became sockets of horror. He removed a generous portion of the skin at the height of each cheekbone, thus straining the bottom lids of the visual apparatus, pulling them so that the sheltered pink became prominent, the serous edge of the ball exposed ... By taking away the tip of the nasal cartilage, at a descending angle, he caused the nose to acquire a radical snub ... The result was morbid, forlorn, the countenance of a lost soul.

His scalp was cicatrised with a web like pattern. Hair would not grow from the scarified skin, but clumped out pell-mell from those blocks left untouched.

His feet and hands were regularly injected with a mixture of cayenne pepper, procaine and excrement. They became inflamed, numb and infected, bloated and cankerous. The Doctor was careful not to let the infections become too malignant, and made sure that they stayed local, though in the end the damage was permanent ... The hands and feet became of a cartoon character, those of a grim Mickey Mouse.

The boy became an amalgam of comedy and horror. To see him you might laugh, if your stomach was not flopping with disgust.

VII

The Doctor would have liked to have had his intestines put under the protection of the children of Horus—How fitting, with one bearing the face of an ape, the next that of a hawk, then the jackal, and of course man himself ... After his innards found themselves in protective jars, giving him the chance for a second life, his brain would be extracted, through the nostrils, then laid aside to dry.

Those seventy days swimming in liquid natron, skin taking on the greenish gray hue, the gloomy color of swamp water—Yes, that epidermal tissue would toughen, to an armour for defleshed bone! Sweet spice and natron, stuffed into him, through the convenient slits made in his fingers, toes, arms and thighs ... The skull, filled with a pâté, a preservative seasoning of plaster and herbs ... Gums and spices, natron and bitumen, pounded together, packed in the cavity of his chest and stomach, through a slit in the side.

The obsidian eyes, the fingernails stained with henna, the ornaments of gaudy gold ... And bandages! ... He could not help but think he had been born three or four thousand years too late. There were no high priests to officiate his desire.

'In the modern age one should be dull and expeditious,' he told himself. 'Prepare oneself for the pasteboard sarcophagus of the new era.'

VIII

Edward Kelly's The Theatre of Terrestrial Astronomy, the works of Elias Ashmole, and the Pseudomarchia Daemonium of Johannes Wierus sat on the most frequented corner of his bookshelves. His favorite recreational reading however was The Life of Heliogabalus. After opening a bottle of Chateau Latour, set aside for special occasion, he extracted this latter volume, to read once more.

The text itself lay amidst the stories of the other Roman emperors. Yet, in the study of Doctor Blanche, those others went largely unread. Catallus was of course interesting, the way he had boys swim in between his legs, calling them his 'little fish,' and the newborn babies he nursed rather lewdly ... But the old pervert was no match for Heliogabalus in matters of decadence.

The young ruler had momentum.

Camels' heels appeared on the menu as well as peacocks' tongues. He would lay back on cushions stuffed with rabbit fur and partridge down, eating sparrows' brains, flamingoes' brains and thrushes' brains. Him and his base entourage feasted on the heads of parakeets, pheasants and peacocks. Meanwhile the dogs were fed foie gras.

A smile played on the Doctor's lips as he read of this dish: Wild sows' udders and wombs stuffed with pearls.

Heliogabalus never had sex with the same woman twice. We know however that he was more consistent with his boyfriends.

On an evening he would bath in a swimming pool perfumed with wormwood, feast with his friends on a meal of six hundred ostrich heads, eating out the brains, and tie a number of beautiful naked women to his dogcart, cracking a whip in their ears as they pulled him around the living room.

That liquorish youth met an unpleasant end, as grim as his life was indecent... The jewel crusted court that he had had constructed beneath the tower, to meet his flying body when the time came, proved unnecessary . . . In the filth of the gutter his corpse was dragged.

* * *

The pages pressed themselves together and the book sat closed on the Doctor's lap. The blood coursed languidly through his veins. Blinking his weary lids, he arose, putting the volume aside.

With bare feet he strode to the bedroom. She was there, the thick, down stuffed duvet covering her to the chin. He smiled sourly. He knew it was a personal weakness to let his curiosity take hold of his better judgement, but those very failings were in fact the perfume of his life and genius.

Within an hour he had her somewhat plump figure strapped to his medical chair in the basement. She was well anaesthetised and would certainly not awake.

It had long been his fantasy to see her other than how she was. He would lie next to her, or in the embrace he jokingly referred to as love, and time and again the vision would flash upon him. It wormed its way into his brain, and he gradually found it delicious.

The instruments were arrayed around him, vicious and clawlike. He adjusted the light, took up a pair of callipers and made measurements of her cranium and neck, jotting down the figures in a nearby notebook. His palm glided over to a sawlike tool, of incredibly ferocious aspect, and he set to.

The operation was an incredible challenge. There was the entire vertebral body, which had to be readjusted, bit by bit, inside the living flesh, with all the intervertebral disks as well as the esophagus and trachea which needs not be over tweaked or deranged for fear of terminating the flow of oxygen—And then the axis of the brainstem (though he never thought she made much use of it) was vitally important to stretch to some degree, without however severing; and turning the spinal column while preventing it from corkscrewing, in order to mitigate the odds of utter disability—which would in no way serve his designs.

IX

During the week that followed he slept alone, and was satisfied with freedom of movement, being without one-hundred and eighty pounds of woman flesh pressing upon him in the night with an over abundance of warmth.

* * *

He fixed himself a bowl of muesli and yogurt for breakfast, washing it down with unsweetened cranberry juice and black coffee.

'She stirs,' he told himself as he heard the cries resonate from below, muffled and miserable.

He swallowed the last of his coffee, set his bowl in the sink, and proceeded down the steps to the basement.

'Donald!' she screeched, panic stricken.

'Coming dear,' he called and, with a show tune whistling from his pursed lips, flipped on the lights.

The songbirds, awoken, began to twitter with maniacal pitch and soon Cynthia was in motion, parading about her cage, lending the recital her own musical mutilation. The monkey, Chako, joined in with a furious cackle. Pedro rose to his feet and craned forward, jaw protruding, simian, salient, the boy's eyes marbled with unnatural ignorance. Though unable to hear the sounds, he could none the less detect the air of excitement, and began to strum the bars of the cage with his head, like a guitar. Tarquin kneaded his bulbous hands. The hair shocked out of his head like a sea anemone. A gurgling falsetto rose from his twisted lips—Though whether it was a cry of pain or pleasure was indeterminate.

'I care for you so much!' Ruth cried from the shadows. 'Donald, I care for you so much!'

Doctor Blanche laughed callously and stepped to Tarquin's cage. Toward the back, kneeling on a heap of straw, neck bandaged, body half covered by a white sheet, she groped, disorientated, unable to fathom the new twist to her anatomy.

'I know you do dear,' the Doctor said crisply, peering into the half-light of the cage.

'But why?' she sobbed, tears melting down her cheeks. 'Why this? ... I'm not the same!'

He observed her torso and back and how her breasts pressed against the wall. He was satisfied to see her face thus, chin saddled between shoulder blades, eyes staring in wonder down at the soles of her feet and fleshy flipside. An exhalation of breath, whining, almost like the bleating of a goat escaped from her lips and she looked up with an entreating gaze.

'Oh, don't worry,' he grinned savagely, delighted with his success. 'This will in no way impede our love making.'

LOST IN THE CROWD
Simon Wood

The film credits started to roll and Jane got up to leave, as did the most of the three hundred or so patrons who had paid eight bucks each to see the latest Hollywood blockbuster.

'What did you think?' Peter asked over her shoulder.

High priced disappointment, she thought and groped in the dark behind her and clasped Peter's hand. 'I'll tell you when we get out of here,' she whispered behind her.

'That bad, huh?'

Jane made it to the end of the row with Peter in tow, after clambering over two assholes that refused to move until they had seen every one of the people who had been involved in the film, including the guy who walked the director's dog. As soon as Jane stepped into the aisle, she was whisked away with the crowd and lost her grip on Peter's hand.

Jane snapped her head around to find Peter. She caught a glimpse of him, stuck at the end of the row waiting for a gap in the human traffic, as unseen hands forced her forward. He mouthed to her, 'See you outside.'

She tried to send a message back but Peter was already lost in a sea of faces and if she wasn't careful she was going to end up flat on her face. If she did fall, she doubted whether anyone would stop; they would keep on moving and walk all over her without a second thought.

Even though everyone was in a God-awful rush to get out, it still took over two minutes to traipse less than two hundred feet into the hallway. As soon as Jane was out of the theater, she was greeted by the blinding brilliance of the hallway lights and even more cinemagoers pouring out of the other theaters.

I thought these places were meant to have staggered timing to prevent this, she thought irritably.

Jane fought her way over to the opposite side of the narrow hallway, nearly losing her purse on the way. She stood underneath a poster for a forthcoming attraction—It Came to Feed. Below the title, a black beast cloaked in darkness was lumbering out of the shadows, only its baleful eyes illuminating its shape. She turned to examine the poster and realized that where she stood, it looked as if she was in the clutches of, It Came to Feed. She dismissed the appetizer; she didn't like monster movies.

'C'mon Peter,' Jane whined.

A constant flow of people continued to dribble past her towards the lobby exit.

Peter didn't appear.

After ten minutes, the people passing Jane were occasional and no one had come out of her theater in the last two. Peter had probably already come out and they had missed each other in the crowd. He was probably waiting for her outside. She cursed.

Jane broke away from the clutches of It Came to Feed and headed out the main exit. The lines outside for the next showings were minimal and most people leaving were already in the parking lot. Peter was nowhere to be seen.

'Everything okay?' someone called.

Jane turned and a ticket-collecting usher, wearing a loud vest, looked her way. 'I'm looking for my boyfriend. We got separated and I thought he was out here,' she explained.

'Well, I'm sure you'll find him,' he said.

'Can I go back in to have another look?'

'Not now that you've left the theater,' he said doubtfully.

'I just want to make sure he's not waiting. I'll only be ten minutes.'

The usher sighed, 'Okay, ten minutes but don't let anyone know I let you back in.'

Jane smiled and slipped past. Outside the theater where she had lost Peter, a red seatbelt-like strap had been stretched across the doors. Without any hesitation, Jane unhooked the strap and it whizzed back into its reel on the other side of the entrance. As Jane opened the door, someone called, 'Hey!'

Jane swung around to meet the voice. An usher approached.

'You can't go in there. The theater isn't ready,' she said.

'I'm looking for someone,' Jane said.

'Who?' the usher asked, coming close.

'My boyfriend. We lost each other and I wanted to see if he was inside the theater,' Jane explained.

'Well, I'm sorry, nobody's in there now,' the usher said.

'Have you been in there?' Jane asked.

'No.'

'Then you don't know,' Jane said, and started opening the door.

The usher slapped her hand on the door, slamming it shut again. 'But I do know. No one's in there.'

'Get the manager. I want to speak to someone about this,' Jane demanded.

The usher unclipped the walkie-talkie from her belt and spoke into it. 'Security, we have a—'

Before the usher could finish her message, Jane had torn open the door and rushed inside the theater. Ignoring the shouts from the usher, Jane sped along the twisting corridor and burst into the theater. Two further ushers, on clear-up duty, shot up from their task. Instead of sweeping up popcorn and picking up discarded drink cartons, they were mopping. Even with the house lights up, the theater was still in semi-darkness. But what they were mopping was unmistakable—blood.

Jane froze to the spot. Where the ushers were cleaning up the blood, was where she had last seen Peter.

Hands grabbed Jane from behind and snatched her back. 'Let's be having you, lady,' the security guard said.

'I told you there's nobody here,' the usher with the walkie-talkie said, sternly.

'But he was here,' Jane cried, as she was dragged back to the corridor.

'Well, there's no one here now,' the security guard said.

'We've got it contained,' the usher said into her squawking walkie-talkie then to the security guard, 'Get her out of here.'

'Tell me what you've done to Peter! Tell me what you've done!' Jane shrieked hysterically. Wrestling with the security guard she managed to release an arm and pointed at the blood the two ushers were poised over. 'That's his blood.'

'Clear that up,' the usher with the walkie-talkie snapped at the ushers. They got their heads down and did as they were told.

She came around to face Jane and the security guard stopped dragging her. The usher put her face close to Jane's.

'I would watch that mouth of yours. Talk like that could get you into trouble,' the usher said, like a cheap hood she had seen in one too many gangster flicks. 'There isn't any blood down there.'

The usher stepped back and pointed behind her, towards the blood and the other ushers. The blood was there but the ushers were gone and two further pools of blood were in close proximity to the first. All three pools continued to slide down the inclined floor.

When the usher saw the missing clean up crew, her tone changed from malice to fear. 'Oh, God. Not us!'

The usher snapped her head back to Jane. Her eyes were wide and a horror show played in them. She stared at Jane and the security guard as if they had just announced that they were taking over from where Charles Manson left off. Slowly, the usher shrank back towards the exits that flanked either side of the screen.

Suddenly, the security guard's arms released Jane and in that moment, she heard a ripping-shredding sound combined with a thick-heavy splatting like soup being poured from a great height onto concrete. Wetness splashed the back of Jane's legs. With the sudden release she stumbled backwards and stood on something—the security guard's peaked-cap. The cap was speckled in resin-thick blood, as were her legs.

Before Jane could scream, the usher beat her to it. Jane jerked her head up. The usher's hands clawed at the polished floor as she was dragged into one of the rows of seats, leaving bloody streaks behind.

Jane darted over to the usher's aid but by the time she made it to the row, she had disappeared and another bloody pool was all that was left. Jane's chin started to tremble and tears welled up in her eyes. She flicked a glance from one bloody pool to another but lingered on the pool that was Peter.

'Jane,' the voice boomed over the theater's sound system.

Jane automatically turned to the screen. The screen was black but if it was off, it should have been white. A pair of green eyes in the virtual distance of the screen came forward. The eyes became greener, as if charged with a radioactive isotope, and bigger until they filled the screen. But no face supported the eyes.

If the screen is working then someone is operating it, Jane thought. She whirled to see into the projector booth but the lights were off and the projector wasn't working. The voice deflected Jane's attention.

'No, Jane. Don't look for the obvious,' it said.

Jane turned back to the eyes on the screen.

'That's it, Jane. Now you can see me,' it said.

'What's going on?' Jane asked.

'You've stumbled onto something you shouldn't have. You've found me out,' it said, its voice coming from all the theater's speakers at once.

'What have I stumbled onto?'

'Onto me,' it said with a single voice from a speaker to Jane's left.

Jane cocked her head to the source of the sound.

'Onto us, onto Cinema,' it said from all speakers at once.

Jane couldn't believe she talking to this entity while surrounded with the remnants of five slaughtered people. And she was getting pissed off with the cryptic bullshit.

'What is Cinema?' Jane said sharply.

'I am. We are Cinema.' Cinema must have seen the unimpressed look on her face and continued. 'A hundred years ago we were created. Not invented. All the mechanics you see are purely window dressing to make you believe. We, Cinema, live!'

'You live,' Jane said astounded.

'Yes, we live. Just like you.' Cinema's eyes came even closer to the screen, stretching it, causing it to bulge into the theater confines. 'And like you we need to feed.'

'Feed?'

'Yes, feed, you stupid child. We made a deal with the Lumieres, Edison and all the others. We play their banal stories and they let us feed on the odd patron.' Cinema's eyes bore into Jane, 'Don't give me that whipped puppy look, you don't give a second thought to the animals or resources you consume in order to live.'

After hearing Cinema's revelation, Jane tottered over to one of the seats and used it for support. The images conjured up in her mind made her gut churn. Looking at the floor, she saw the untold number of bloody pools that must coat the floors of every multiplex in the world. She said, 'You ate Peter?'

'Was that his name?' Cinema said, disinterestedly.

'You bastard!' Jane screamed at the cold green eyes.

'Watch your mouth,' Cinema boomed through the surround sound.

'Why tell me this, Cinema?' Jane shouted back.

'I don't usually show myself but seeing as you found me out, I thought I should talk to you . . . before I consume you,' Cinema said calmly.

Jane didn't waste any time and started to back away from the eyes on the screen. A mouth-like hole the width of the aisle opened up at her feet but instead of teeth, a pair of curved rotary blades, like from an old cylinder lawnmower, spun. Spinning blades intermeshed, not leaving an inch of space that a person could slip between without being torn to shreds.

Jane jumped back from the whirring blades and Cinema's mower-mouth mimicked her move. The mouth contorted its shape as it slipped across the floor and chomping blades flexed seamlessly and the blades never clashed.

Jane knew she had to be fast if she were to get out of here alive. She turned tail and ran for the exit. Mower-mouth followed. With every step she could feel the blades snipping at her heels, her sneakers disintegrating by the second. The service cart the ushers were using to clear up was an obstacle blocking her path. She would have to slow to get past it but if she slowed she was dead.

As Jane came to the cart, she leapt to her right, landing onto the aisle seat's arm. Her shoes skidded on the smooth plastic and she fell, crashing into the row of seats but clung onto anything she could grasp and never touched the ground. The service cart bucked and convulsed as mower-mouth, too slow to react to Jane's leap, opened up underneath the cart.

Mower-mouth gorged with the cart, plastic trashcan and cleaning tools was unable to move to attack Jane. She jumped down from the safety of the seats with no time to nurse her twisted ankle and blazing shins. She saw the weapon she needed. Hobbling over to the rapidly disintegrating cart, she snatched out the broom complete with a freshly whittled tip, thanks to mower-mouth.

'You're not going to kill anyone else, Cinema!' Jane cried.

Jane drew back the broom and launched the makeshift javelin at the screen. With an accuracy she could have only dreamed of, the broom pierced the screen and Cinema's right eye. Blood pumped from the devastating wound and since it had no hands to remove the weapon, the broom wagged in Cinema's rotating eye. Mower-mouth stopped eating.

Cinema roared, its agony exploding in all directions in perfect digital sound. The floor rippled and Jane struggled to ride the waves. Mower-mouth started to whir and spat out the chewed cart as other mower-mouths opened up throughout the theater. Instead of looking for people to consume they vomited what they had eaten.

Jane took her chance and bolted for the exit corridor avoiding the blood geysers. She never looked back at Cinema's eyes, its screams were enough and the bloody spray raining down was no invitation to see what was to unfold.

The corridor stretched and contracted. The walls, floor and ceiling shrank and expanded. Sharp corners where the walls met the floor and ceiling blended, becoming intestinal. The corridor softened, becoming organic. Only the double exit doors remained unaffected and Jane, ignoring everything else, charged straight at them and burst through. Outside of the theater she did not stop and continued to run through the lobby as other people entered.

'Cinema is all evil,' Jane screamed over and over again to anyone who would listen.

The cinemagoers could only stare at the mad girl who burst out of the lobby and into the parking lot. Some were shocked, some were amused, some ignored her, but they all discussed her as they poured into the belly of Cinema.

THE DRAWSTRING
DF Lewis

She reached behind her and adjusted the drawstring. Clive couldn't see what she was doing because it seemed as if she were merely fidgeting. If he knew she was trying to signal to someone in the garden by means of the slightest movement of the curtains, he would have quickly moved her to another chair. As it was, she could barely reach the string and it had never properly worked even with someone standing up and giving it almighty tugs when the shorter evenings drew in. The curtains only worked by pulling them manually along the runners without the use of vertical pulley-systems.

Clive watched the pelmet shake. The girl was evidently creating this effect either by direct physical purchase between her and the curtain-rod or by mind over matter. The mantelpiece clock was shuddering nearer to the edge, threatening to fall off . . . but it always did this when it struck the hour. Clive had to re-adjust it every thirteen days before it could actually topple off. However, the coalscuttle had never before budged so significantly in the short space of time between him feeding the fire with more coal and the fire again threatening to go out. There must be a coal dust imp in there, he thought. All fairy tale stuff.

The girl had by now slipped her hidden fingers along the length of the drawstring after adjusting it short of obviously tugging upon it—then allowing it to fall back with the clatter of its dangling aglet against the glass of the window. Clive turned sternly towards her. On her lap was the kitchen cat looking plaintively up at him. The girl's eyes, though, were icy. The cat had just escaped from the coalscuttle, judging by the black smudges all over its white fur.

One of the servants stood in the open lounge door with a tray in his or her hand.

Clive couldn't actually see the servant—other than the shape—because of the shadows thrown by the firelight. The standard lamp cast one slanting beam right over the face. Meanwhile, the wireless at a barely perceptible volume tinkled in the corner, either with music or the high-pitched voices of a Home Service play. The servant, having emerged from the rectangular wreath of the doorway, declared a feminine bosom as the tray was posited squarely on the tea-trolley—which proceeded to roll forward through some hidden momentum.

'Anything else, Sir?' piped the servant as she minced back toward the welcoming folds of shadow by the doorway.

'No, unless you have forgotten the strainer,' said Clive a trifle hesitantly. He did not want to give the game away. The girl had sat unnoticed near the window; the cat was also still on her lap, purring in tune with the wireless in the opposite corner. Whoever the girl had been abortively making signals to in the garden would, by now, be subsumed in the afternoon fog, fog that was fated not to lift until late morning tomorrow. Dusk was earlier every day—ad infinitum it seemed as the evenings continued to draw in—and he went over to pull the curtains together; but they stuck halfway.

'Let me do it, Sir,' called the servant bravely, it appeared, from the hallway, having no doubt heard the throaty catch of the curtain ring upon the rod. It sounded like a different servant from that distance. Clive shook his head absentmindedly, convinced in his own mind that such a gesture was tantamount to an answer for someone out of eyeshot. It worked—for the servant failed to turn up again. The cat scuttled from the girl's lap and decided to preen itself in front of the dying warmth of the fire.

Something was riffling the inner layer of net curtains as it walked along the window ledge. He shuddered. In the garden with you, he mouthed. And with a flourish, he managed to tug the curtains together upon the grate and grind of a friction that should have swished along upon a coat of linseed oil. He had hated the cod liver sort when he was force-fed it as a child for the good of his health. He sighed as he blotted out the night and whatever haunted the garden. Houses, these days—even old-fashioned ones like this one with lit consoles masquerading as ancient wirelesses—could not countenance being haunted. Ghosts were too far fetched. Only the outside world, Clive believed, could harbour the shudders and fears of yesteryear. And now he had blotted them out with one clumsy curtain call.

The girl had followed the cat towards the dull embers of the fire that lit the room like one huge crazy-paved eyeball.

He decided that he would have to put the light on in the room if the tea tray of goodies were to be shared out upon and into individual items of crockery.

With the fire out now, who was coming down the chimney? Soot falling into the grate like droppings. Or something had been tugged up the other way through the flue. Clive shivered. He felt a chill working round him. It wasn't just sickness. The girl had left for the kitchen: where she must work as an oven cleaner or cook's assistant when she wasn't dusting or acting as chambermaid. Light footsteps from the wireless gave the impression she was still in the room. Clive poured the tea with a gurgle more like oil than a scalding hot infusion of refreshment.

Servants were far and few between in these days of modern living, where both men and women worked all hours God had given simply to earn a crust—or a roof: or at least one slate per week eventually to make a proper roof one day. He could hear far off scrabbling as if workmen were erecting scaffolding above the house itself: to mend his roof. Builders from hell, the TV often claimed. Strange they should still be working during this season when evenings drew in so quickly . . . upon God's drawstring.

THE PENATES
Donald Murphy

Pietro Coletti—gaunt, pallid, trembling Coletti—a St. Anthony painted by Masaccio, a weathered fresco of a man, had always seemed about to tell me something. When he finally did (we were boarders in the same pension, and both of us insomniacs), I realized all at once how important it was for him to go over it again, to relive it in the hope that this time he would understand better what it meant. For if it seemed incredible to anyone, it was to Coletti himself, and not even the steady ingestion of watery wine which went on for most of the night could calm his uneasiness as he recounted it to me. What can I say? I was moved. I told him that someday I would write it down for him, and he thanked me. But when, two years later, I came looking for him with the finished tale, no one could tell me what had become of him. He had people in Liguria, perhaps he'd gone there, or perhaps he was dead. I left a note with the woman who ran the place, our only common acquaintance, but I've never heard from him again. If he has indeed left this world, I hope he is finally at peace. I suspect, however, that he is still with us, and again telling, in some room as shabby as that one, to some other listener, the story from which he cannot escape.

It must have happened about thirty or thirty-five years ago. Coletti was a student at the time, and living in the Roman neighborhood of San Lorenzo. It seems he was also suffering bitterly from a broken heart. He didn't give me any details about this but said that, according to his usual habit, he had gone to his best friend, Utto Spezzi, for advice. The levelheaded Spezzi had simply told him: 'Excursions, and lots of them!' Coletti begged his pardon, and Spezzi explained. He meant that Coletti should spend as much time as possible visiting museums, monuments and ruins, and in this way distract himself from his pain. Such needless suffering was, swore Spezzi, not only unproductive but by nature transient, and until it went away of its own accord his broken-hearted friend would do better to fill his mind with culture and stop boring other people with his problems.

The plan seemed like a good one to Coletti, who dutifully made a list of the wonders that lay within a thirty-mile radius and resolved to see them all, ashamed that he had lived his whole life in Rome without ever making this effort before. And now that she (we'll call her Gisella) was gone, what did it matter if he used up his weekends in this way? He felt that he might even be on the threshold of some great adventure, one that would change his life forever. A strange excitement took hold of him as he imagined the possibilities. And so one Saturday, equipped with a new pair of walking shoes, a plastic raincoat and a Michelin guide, Coletti set out bravely to conquer both the Eternal City and the dank swamplands of his own emotions.

Within a few months, he had exhausted the Vatican and Capitoline Museums, the Thermae di Caracalla and the Circus Maximus, the Catacombs and the Palatino. He had explored every cubicle of the Coliseum, knew the statues in the Villa Borghese as if they were his own flesh and blood, could identify with ease each of the successive dynasties represented in the Augustinian Forum. Alone, at all hours and in all sorts of weather, he prowled the Jewish Quarter, the Gianicolo and the Appian Way. He fought with aggressive tour groups, stood in countless queues, endured the pranks and screams of unruly brats on school field trips. He returned home from these outings dead-tired and often fell into bed fully clothed, but always with the same thought in his mind: Gisella. It was time, he decided, to look further afield.

An overnight stay in the Pontine Islands proved a cold and wet ordeal that he did not care to repeat. Tivoli he found unbearable for the number of like-minded day-trippers. He was getting weary of this excursion business, he admitted, and it still had not restored his peace of mind. Another cathedral, another aqueduct or *palazzo*, and he would have to tell Spezzi that it was no use, that he would be better off suffering than wearing himself out so pointlessly, and neglecting his studies into the bargain. And then one day, just as he was about to give it all up, something made him circle 'Ostia Antica' in his Michelin.

The ancient Roman port stood a mere twelve miles from the capital, curiously inland now, as the coastline had moved two miles further west to Lido. According to the Michelin, a visit to these well-preserved ruins was '... an experience one will never forget, a time machine capable of magically transporting the visitor to the very heart of classical antiquity.' He had, of course, nothing to lose and so the following Saturday he took an early train from Termini Station to Magliana, where he waited among a crowd of noisy teenagers and handholding lovers for the connecting train to Ostia-Lido. He carried with him a shoulder bag containing his lunch (a ham-and-cheese *panino* and a box of dried figs), a bottle of mineral water, his Michelin and, in the event of afternoon showers, his folded-up raincoat. The second train was crowded and he had to stand, but this he didn't mind. He leaned in the doorway and daydreamed as a leafy quilt of farms and orchards went flapping by in the opposite direction. Of *her*, yes, but he noticed that in proportion to the distance he traveled into the bucolic west, toward the salt air of the Tyrrhenian, the memory of his failed romance seemed to cause him less and less grief. He was just on the point of letting her go for good when the tiny station popped up at the window, gaily ornamented in blue and white tile, and with 'OSTIA' set in large letters over the platform. Below this a smaller, hand-painted sign read: 'Ruins this way'.

Nothing in the Michelin could have prepared him for Ostia. He'd had no idea of the scale of the place, of its crumbling magnificence, of its ability to project into the mind a vast panorama of life in ancient Rome. It was not a roped-off graveyard like the Forum, but a real city, abandoned to the sky and the trailing ivy, where one wandered freely along broad boulevards and tiny lanes; through palaces and shipyards; into temples, bathhouses, cemeteries and slums. Spezzi had been right. Immersed in the phantasmal world of Ostia, no other thought was possible. This was what he'd been looking for, and for the first time in months he felt his aggravating heartache retiring to some high, distant shelf where, for the moment at least, it was incapable of tormenting him.

The entry road led directly to the center, where Colleti began his explorations. It had been the commercial district of the busiest port in the world, and was still more or less intact. At times it was hard to believe that those hundreds of shops and *tabernae*, empty since the 5th century A. D., would not be re-opening for business as soon as the holidays were over. In the Piazza della Corporazione, the great imperial marketplace next to the harbor, he read in mosaic images the professions of its former stallholders: a pair of crossed oars for a shipbuilder, a sheaf of wheat for a grain-seller, a goblet for a wine merchant. At the fishmonger's, a stained chopping stone still showed the hatch-marks of its attendant's knife. One had the eerie feeling that everyone had just stepped out for lunch or for an extended siesta.

Coletti said he stumbled along open-mouthed, stupefied, at first following the route marked out in his Michelin but soon abandoning that to the pleasure of chance discovery. And so, without knowing what was coming next, he peered into ancient bakeries, tanneries, forges and mills; followed the course of canals and sewers; sat in the carved thrones of prelates and senators. How many years would it take, he wondered, to see it all?

He spent most of the morning in this urban nucleus before wandering, quite by accident, into the residential area, which lay slightly to the southwest. He found himself suddenly alone (none of his fellow tourists seemed interested in those deserted suburbs), and unable, even with his Michelin, to get his bearings. But it was an enjoyable feeling; and it was there, among the mansions of the rich and powerful, that he was to make the greatest of his finds.

They were really no more than skeletons of houses; time had removed their top halves, and vandals had long since stripped away everything moveable. But enough remained for Coletti to reconstruct their interiors in his mind, furnishing them as he pleased and populating them with characters extracted from his readings of Martial and Ovid. As if in a dream, he paced their marbled patios, explored their mysterious recesses and chambers, seemed to hear the splash of long-silent fountains as he watched the clouds glide serenely across the sky. He could have spent hours in some of them, but so many others lay waiting among that knot of twisting lanes that he found himself hurrying on, eager for what the next would bring.

Several times that day he had spotted two enormous white columns rising up impressively from some structure in the distance. Thinking that they must be part of an exceptionally fine dwelling, he decided finally to investigate. It was already late afternoon and the heat was overpowering. He would rest and have lunch there, he thought, and then it would be time to head back to the station.

The columns, it turned out, graced the inner courtyard of the most beautiful house he had seen all day. They stood on either side of a long rectangular pool, tiled in rose-colored marble, and with a writhing sea-dragon inlaid on the bottom in blue stone. The row of pedestals along the edge of the pool had once supported statues of some type, but these were gone now, leaving only their slender footprints behind. There was a wide platform of some darker stone at the end of this, from which a flight of steps led down to a lower level. Coletti mounted the platform and then descended the narrow staircase. He found himself in a sort of well or cistern, still half-full, though the surface of the water was covered over with a scum of algae. He lit a match and studied the clammy walls; the tiles were still in good condition. He remembered reading in his Michelin that the most prominent citizens of Ostia had had private wells dug inside their homes. What splendors this house must have contained! He thought, picturing the great bronze censers, the tapestries, the silk divans, the tables encrusted with jade and mother-of-pearl...

He was still dreaming of these riches when he came back up to the patio and discovered that he was not alone. A girl sat on the step above the pool, her chin resting on her knees and her arms hugging her shins. She turned her head slightly to take in the image of Coletti, as if she were capturing him in a mental snapshot, then went back to her contemplation. Next to her was an Alitalia flight bag, with an unwrapped sandwich lying beside it.

Coletti, a bit self-consciously, made a further show of examining the patio and the empty pool, feeling like a fake archaeologist, he told me. The truth was that the girl's presence had disturbed his dreaming, and set some old wounds to aching. When he looked again she was smiling, and he noticed this time how really pretty she was. Her hair was dark and tangled; her eyes round and brown. They registered everything, pulled at him like glittering magnets.

'Hello,' he said, approaching the step. 'What a place, eh?'

They talked for a few moments about the magnificent house, which enclosed them, about what it must have looked like when the pool still held water and the surrounding walls had been intact. He told her about the well he had discovered and she responded that at the other end was the kitchen—you could still see the stone ovens. Next to that was an indoor toilet. 'This house must have a name,' said Coletti, and opened his Michelin to a small diagram of the ruins. No, nothing—that district of Ostia was not detailed in the guide, nor were there any important landmarks in the vicinity. She only shrugged her shoulders and smiled again, in the most charming way, it seemed to him. They talked then about the heat—he noticed that a sheen of sweat stood out on the girl's upper lip, and on the back of his own neck he felt the sting of sunburn. Yes, this was the hottest hour of the day, he remarked. Eyeing her sandwich, he explained that he was just thinking about having lunch himself. As if it were the most natural thing in the world, she invited him to join her.

Her name was Daniella. She seemed to be a northerner, although he didn't ask where she was from. Something made Coletti avoid personal enquiries as they talked; his recent disappointment in love had taken the conqueror out of him, and he could not bear the thought of playing that tiring game with this stranger, who it seemed was genuine, kind, and refreshingly uncomplicated. She appeared not to expect it from him anyway, was not coquettish, nor distant, nor devious. What a relief! thought Coletti, and he found himself talking to her unaffectedly and with a surprising self-assurance, about the ruins, about the ancient world, about flowers and trees, about the weather and a variety of other natural phenomena. It had never been that way with Gisella, although Coletti did not think this. He had forgotten, he told me, that there had ever been a Gisella.

They finished their lunch and then Colletti mentioned something about leaving. According to his Michelin, he explained, the ruins closed at 6:00 and it might take them a while to find the exit. Daniella quickly outlined three alternative routes for him. 'I come here every weekend,' she laughed. 'So I know my way around, I suppose.'

She was also going back to Rome, and so they were able to continue their conversation in the train. Not that Daniella talked much. She wasn't shy, just unconcerned about any obligation to keep the patter flowing. Coletti even apologized at one point. 'I don't know what's gotten into me. I must be boring you to death,' he said. 'No . . . ' she replied. 'But you don't have to say anything, you know. It's not important.'

Coletti was impressed. He was not innocent, and liked to think that he had had his share of adventures; but this unassuming, child-like young woman astonished him, even made him feel that he was the child and she the possessor of some deeper, more elemental wisdom.

At Termini he suggested having something cold to drink and she agreed with the same disarming simplicity. She said yes when she meant yes, no when she meant no—a rarity among women, thought Coletti, and reflected that so far she hadn't said no to any of his suggestions. They had a beer in the Via Vicenza, then an ice cream in a shop on Palestro. The streetlights were just coming on and the hulking edifices of the Policlinico were looming blue in the twilight. She loved Rome, she said. Coletti said that he did, too.

He remembered then that he'd bought groceries the day before, and so he boldly invited her to have dinner at his apartment. Not surprisingly, she said yes.

To dispense with too many unnecessary details (Coletti didn't give them to me, in any case), he and Daniella had dinner, drank a great deal of wine, and ended up making love on his tweed-upholstered sofa-bed before he'd even served up the sticky *tiramisù* he'd promised her for dessert. And somewhere in the course of those unexpected and delicious events, it seems he fell desperately in love with her.

In the morning, he woke with a pounding headache and found to his surprise that she was gone. He searched the rest of his apartment but saw only that she had made herself a cup of coffee before she'd left and had used his toothbrush. How could he have slept so soundly? He wondered. Worst of all, she had left no note, no indication of how he could contact her again, nothing. And of course he hadn't asked. He fell back into bed, feeling a black hole gnawing through his heart. Is there no end to it all? He moaned, burying his face into the pillow where her head had lain, inhaling over and over its rich scent of lilacs.

She did not call and somehow Coletti knew that she had not copied down the number from the front of his telephone. It was clear that his only chance of meeting her again lay in going back to Ostia, and for this he would have to wait until Saturday (this, and Coletti's subsequent adventures, coincided unfortunately with his mid-term exams). But how could he know she would be there? It seemed out of character for her to be playing games with him. Perhaps she was even simpler than he thought and, not needing the emotional torture he continually subjected himself to, would be content never to see him again. Every hypothesis led to the same wall of doubt. He asked Spezzi for advice, but his friend was no longer sympathetic. 'You're a real piece of work, you are!' said Spezzi. 'I give you a perfectly good recipe for curing a broken heart and look what you do! Don't tell me anything more because I don't want to hear. You're hopeless, Coletti—*hopeless!*'

Saturday, when it came, was hardly a day to be visiting ruins. All morning, gusts of cold wind howled through the streets, flinging raindrops against windowpanes and setting a thousand doors and gates to banging. In the Piazza Venezia, pedestrians scurried through the tangled traffic, their umbrellas turned into strange inside-out creatures by the chilling blasts of wind, while the clouds that rolled over the city like tumbling bales of wet laundry promised no relief from the blustery weather. It was a day to be inside, in bed, savoring the warmth and idleness that one craves on Saturday mornings like these. Coletti, of course, was not in bed, but shivering on the platform at Magliana, warming himself with swigs from a thermos of hot tea and thinking of Daniella.

Ostia had an altogether different aspect from that of his first visit. Soaked with rain and washed of its color, it seemed less the enchanted city he remembered and more a vast, wet archaeological dig. Coletti said that in the beginning he had difficulty orienting himself, but wait! There was the amphitheatre, and the forum . . . He flipped through the now-soggy pages of his Michelin; the residential zone should be just there, bordering the Necropolis of Via Ostense. He tramped through the mud, cursing himself. She would not come, of course. On a day like this! The only other visitors he had seen belonged to a hardy German tour group, determined to stick to their rigid itinerary regardless of the weather. In thirty minutes they would be sipping cappuccinos on the boardwalk in Lido, and he would be alone. But he could not give up; not now, not when there was still the slightest of possibilities. He passed a public latrine that he recognized; the rows of ancient stone seats had a cozy, social look about them. Yes, and there was the first of the imposing mansions he had visited the week before. He was getting warmer, but his excitement could not dispel the anxiety that he felt growing steadily inside him.

He went on retracing his steps, picturing with total clarity the two massive columns of the house where they had met. That she should be there and not in some other house was perhaps the vainest of wishes. Did he expect her to be waiting for him? In any case, no matter how hard he looked, he could not locate the columns, nor catch the slightest glimpse of them, as he had the time before without even trying. A miserable hour went by, then another, and finally three. Luckily, the rain had almost stopped; it was only the constant wind that continued to drive the chill into his bones. But long after he was exhausted and felt he could not take another step, a desperation bordering on panic was still pushing him on, and crowding out the image of Daniella in his mind was a new uneasiness: if the house existed, then why couldn't he find it?

Coletti noted that he was on the verge of tears. He blamed this on the miserable weather, on his aching feet and general fatigue. What he needed was a moment to rest and collect his thoughts. A building that still displayed a section of roof above its dilapidated walls offered a bit of shelter from the wind and so he ducked into it, feeling that whatever was going to happen had slipped irrevocably beyond his control.

The house was another of Ostia's great showplaces, perhaps not as elegant as the one where he had met Daniella, but bigger and more complicated in its layout. Under the roofed section was a honeycomb of tiny cubicles, some of which opened onto small patios of their own, turned now into interior gardens by the exuberant vegetation. The rooms themselves were dank and gloomy, and there was an acrid, moldering smell in some of them. A few had mosaic patterns of mythical beasts and astrological symbols covering their floors. Coletti wandered through each one, staring into their dark corners, absently reading their layers of multi-colored graffiti. As he did, he felt his mind growing numb with exhaustion and despair. Finally, he collapsed onto what had been a windowsill and closed his eyes in the darkness.

Coletti could not remember how long he sat like this, aware only that the wind, amplified by the million nooks and recesses of the ruins, was still howling outside. But after a while he began hearing a faint rustling sound somewhere inside the house, followed by two or three unmistakable metallic clicks. A moment later, the smell of freshly lit tobacco came drifting towards him through the gloom. It was not Daniella, unless she had taken up smoking in the last week. Footsteps began to echo in the corridor. He got up mechanically and went towards them, making his own resound loudly so that he would not frighten whoever was there.

The woman was not startled, nor did she seem surprised to see him. She stopped and stood very still, examining him from head to toe with a gaze that seemed hardly to move but nevertheless sized him up quickly and mercilessly. And right from the beginning, he detected on her lips that smile that was not a smile, which beyond its faint suggestion of mockery was in fact impossible to decipher. Other details came later: gray raincoat, black boots, wet stringy hair... A comment about the weather stuck in his throat—he knew somehow that she would not have it, or any other triviality.

It was her who finally spoke, at the same time exhaling a cloud of blue smoke into the shadowy space between them.

'Looking for something?'

Coletti found that he had no response to this. Only a handful of precise words would do, and among all those at his disposal the majority had suddenly been made empty and meaningless. It was not that the woman was so intimidating, he said; perhaps it was all he had been through up to then, or his long fruitless search for the white-columned mansion that made it so difficult for him to put his words together. She, the stranger, who didn't suffer as he did, who was not looking for a lost love or a house that no longer existed, and who had stepped into this one merely to have a pleasant, windless smoke by herself, was in absolute control of the situation, and by extension, of poor, confused Coletti. This he did not mind, strangely enough. He told me he felt like running to her, taking refuge in her presence as a child hides in its mother's skirts.

He could see her more clearly now. She was tall and blonde, had an angular face, with high cheekbones; like a model's or an actress's, he thought. Her eyes were a snowy gray, and they held him in a cool, unwavering grip.

'The servants' quarters,' she said suddenly, as if he had asked, 'or perhaps a kind of harem. Slaves were property and could be used as their owners saw fit. All the same, it seems they lived pretty well.'

She knew something about the ruins then. He was on the point of asking her about the house he'd been searching for, but felt ridiculous; how could he explain his reasons for wanting to find it?

'In fact,' she went on, 'after legislation in the 3rd century introduced 'testamentary manumission'—that is, the freeing of slaves once they'd reached a certain age—a large number of them chose to remain servants. Why give up all this, and six square meals a day? The life of a freed slave was not an easy one, believe me.'

Coletti complimented her on her knowledge of ancient history, and she said it was her hobby, the continuation of a university education that had so far proven completely useless. Ancient history, yes, no better description than that. Now she was a typist who hid away in the ruins at the weekend. 'What's your excuse?' she asked him. Coletti seemed to hear something like a challenge in her voice, but dismissed it as an acoustic phenomenon, an effect of the echoes that bounced their voices around inside the labyrinth. She laughed when he began stammering out an explanation. 'Forget it,' she said. 'It's none of my business.'

They both agreed it was a foul day to be exploring the ruins, and Coletti found himself inviting her to have a coffee somewhere. 'Well, there's nothing open here,' she said, ' . . . *ever!*' Coletti said that he had to be getting back to Rome anyway; maybe she'd consider . . . She responded by looping her arm through his, then leading him out of the house and all the way to the station. She did not let go until they were both standing on the platform, huddled together with their collars turned up against the wind.

In the train, Monica, as she introduced herself, dried her hair with her scarf and illegally lit another cigarette.

'Do you often pick up girls in the ruins?' she asked him.

'No,' said Coletti. 'Not often.'

He and Monica had coffee under the colonnade of the Piazza della Repubblica. Then, at her suggestion, they went back to Coletti's apartment, carrying with them the bottle of *grappa* that she had insisted on buying in an *alimentari* on the Via Tiburtina. This time there were even fewer preliminaries; Coletti had never had a great tolerance for strong drink, and he was stretched out on the sofa in a cold sweat when Monica appeared before him gloriously freed from her garments, and with the same implacable expression in her owl-grey eyes (she was the most beautiful woman he had ever seen, he told me, with a sincerity that made me turn my eyes from his in embarrassment). Again Coletti's account of what happened was sketchy, but it seems he was able to respond to her advances, more than once, and with each of their exquisite clinches he felt himself falling into a vast lake of fire, where he regretted having only one eternity in which to burn for her sake.

The next morning he was very ill and (need we mention it?) Monica was gone. Twice he'd done it, and he was now twice as hopelessly in love. He felt, in fact, that he would die if he did not see her again, but like Daniella, she had left no note. As he waited for his dismal hangover to subside, he replayed it all in his mind. He dreaded the thought of going back to the ruins, but this he would have to do. These two women had cast some abominable spell over him, that was certain; and he was sick at the thought that he could love both with such simultaneous passion. Along with this, the memory of the house he had not been able to find began to disturb him deeply. And the second house, with its gloomy servants' quarters and worn mosaics—its location was not at all clear to him now; what if he could not find it either? To lose two women that one loves is bad enough, but to lose two enormous mansions—there would really be no explanation for it! He began blaming it on the Michelin. If that worthless book had contained a decent map, none of this would have happened, he thought, and he threw it across the room with a force that crumpled one of its corners into a tiny accordion of pleats.

On Monday morning he scoured the bookshops along the Viale di Termini, looking for a superior guide to Ostia. He was convinced that this was just the ammunition he needed, and only the very best would do. A clerk at Feltrinelli's suggested one that indeed looked complete. It was called 'Ostia: Past and Present' by Dr. Giancarlo Campanini, and the dust-jacket proclaimed it ' . . . the ultimate guide, written by the world's foremost authority on these incomparable ruins . . . ' It was expensive, but had a color-coded pullout map that showed in amazing detail the very neighborhoods he had spent so many hours wandering through. In the shop, and later under the light of his desk lamp, he identified several houses that might have been the ones he sought. It was not possible to say for sure, but he grew more and more confident that with this map he would find them. He told himself that he no longer cared about Daniella or Monica; there was more at stake now. He dreamt about them both, however, and woke to find his pillow wet with tears.

By Saturday the good weather had returned. Again the train was crowded with picnickers and beach-goers, the countryside shimmering and green. Coletti took a window seat and lost himself in Dr. Campanini's book. The home, it seemed, if you could afford to build one as lavish as had existed at Ostia, had been in its own way a temple for a people whose gods comprised a sort of magical sub-population within the bustling material one. If, as one of the ruling class, one had ships, slaves, land, houses—then why not one's own gods as well? There had been almost a surplus of them, and none provoked any undue notice in a world as multi-form and cosmopolitan as that of ancient Rome. And so each family had had its private deities, its household gods, esteemed and pampered more devotedly than those of the official religion. Coletti mused for a while on what it must have felt like to be a pagan; how the trees rushing past his window had once been inhabited, how the rivers and lakes had been the domain of naiads and water sprites. And, he thought, with a sigh that turned a few heads in his direction, how godless was *our* world in comparison!

At the station, he began to feel nervous. But, gripping his book tightly, he made for the ruins with a firm determination. The layout of Ostia was imprinted in his mind and, with Dr. Campanini's map to clarify the fine points, he was sure that not a corner of the place could escape his detection.

Entering at the visitors' gate, he carefully followed the main street, the Decumanus Maximus, along the edge of the Necropolis to the point at which it was intersected by the Via Semita del Cippi. Turning left on this grassy avenue, he continued past the mills and the Temple of Ceres until he came to the House of Fortuna Annonaria, the grand structure that had served as his landmark on his last visit. From here he entered the residential zone, and he thrilled to see how closely the two-dimensional city he held in his hand conformed to the real one. Everything was there, every path, every wall, each public square, fountain and sewer, all painstakingly drawn in and numbered. He hurried on to each of the buildings he had circled, and found that he recognized every one. The white-columned house, however, and the great honeycombed structure, were not among them. He slowed down and studied the map more closely. He would take his time; a careful, methodical search was sure to be rewarded.

He had covered all the major avenues and most of their side streets when he realized that he was going over and over his own steps. The neighborhood was not infinite; he saw that it was not even as extensive as he'd thought and that there were no more than twenty houses big enough to be the ones he was looking for. These he went back to again and again, as if they were capable of transforming themselves while his back was turned. But no, in none of them did he find those features that he remembered so clearly. Coletti felt sick and confused; if he could not rely on the solidity of brick, mortar, and marble, on the immobility of houses, then on what could he rely? This could not be happening, he told himself, but it was. The two houses were simply not there.

Coletti kept up his search for the entire morning. The hours passed as if they were repeating themselves, and as the sun reached the top of the sky, he was still stumbling along, not seeing or hearing, but remembering, and feeling very sorry for himself.

Then, as he turned once again into the Via Semita, he noticed an old man hobbling along with a cane some thirty meters ahead of him. Not in the mood for conversation, he turned down a small lane that he had already explored a dozen times and came out into a wide, weedy plaza. He sat down on a block of lichen-covered stone in the center of it and opened his map again. The House of Marcus Aupuleus, the House of Praxitelus Livy, The Temple of Cupid and Psyche, the Baths of Neptune . . . He went through them methodically, despondently, and was only interrupted when the stranger spoke.

'I see you have *the guide*,' said the voice.

He looked up and saw that it was the old man, who had approached without his being aware of it and now stood over him, leaning on his walking stick and stretching a thin-lipped smile across his yellowed teeth. The man's appearance was startling; he was so old that he seemed on the verge of drying up completely and blowing away. His face was flecked with brown liver spots, and his filmy eyes were recessed deep into their sockets. Even so, they contained a faint but definite spark of life and this, for the moment, was fixed firmly on Coletti.

'What? Oh, this. Yes, it's good, I suppose,' he replied, not eager to pursue the subject.

'Good?' said the old man. 'It's the best there is, boy. And I should know. I wrote it.'

Coletti squinted up at him. 'Dr. Campanini?'

'At your service,' said the old man, offering his wrinkled claw in greeting.

Coletti was about to muster up some sort of praise for the book, but did not have the chance; Dr. Campanini was one of those elderly gentlemen who feel that their longevity should serve as an inspiration to the young, and so he went on:

'A life's work, boy, a life's work! And do you know how old I am? Take a guess. No? Eighty-two—that's right, eighty-two!'

Coletti would have guessed ninety or more, but the man's weathered complexion was surely due to the years he'd spent out of doors, poking around in the ruins. And despite his fragile, hunched-over appearance, there was indeed a sort of spryness about him; or perhaps he was merely excited to have someone to expound his vast knowledge to. Whatever the case, Coletti was happy that no participation was required from himself.

'This was a local market,' explained Dr. Campanini, waving his cane, 'something like the 'general store'. Those niches in the wall there held grain; fruits and vegetables were laid out here, on woven mats. Sunday was market day, and it was a social event. Both sexes mingled together, made their secret rendezvous, flirted. The servants carried home the groceries. Under those arches, the *vinarii* served bowls of wine, usually mixed with hot water.'

Dr. Campanini had begun wandering across the square as he described it and Coletti got up to follow him. The old man seemed lost in the scene he was conjuring up, as if he were seeing it all spring to life again behind his viscous eyeballs.

'Come with me, boy. This is really extraordinary . . . '

Together they crossed the square and peered into a narrow alley, like a corridor and lined with broken slabs of marble.

'A secret passageway to the baths,' said Dr. Campanini. 'To the mixed bathing section. They were no prudes, of course; but the formal baths were strictly segregated. One had to enter by this path to reach the 'special' area, where anything went. Petronius was very fond of it, and based one section of his Satyricon on the adventures he had here.'

For the next two hours, Dr. Campanini led Coletti on a tour of Ostia that few tourists have ever had. In the baths, he pointed out the exercise area (the *palaestrum*) and the great tiled changing rooms (the *apodyteria*); then the successive pools into which the bathers had plunged (first the steaming *caldarium*, then the *tepidarium*, and finally the icy *frigidarium*). They went on to inspect teetering *insulae*—hi-rise apartment buildings once filled with poverty and disease—and squat *domae*, the lower and more luxurious quarters of the landlords. Dr. Campanini showed him the deep pits where urine had been stored for the treatment of cloth and leather, and the warehouses that had held the loot of a hundred far-off kingdoms. Coletti's head swam with this exotic merchandise: ivory, amber, silks, papyrus, incense... No less astonishing was the variety of religious cults that had been available to both rich and poor, the most popular imported from Egypt and Persia and represented in lavish temples to Isis, Mithra, Attis, and Cybele. Before long he knew, through Dr. Campanini's encyclopedic descriptions, the exact occupations exercised in all sixty-one stalls of the Corporazione, the number of spectators that could be accommodated in the amphitheatre and what they had worn on feast days, how many cubic liters had flowed through the city's aqueducts into the municipal fishponds, and so on, and so on.

Yes, it was fascinating, but at the same time Coletti found his attention wandering. Ostia, in fact, had never seemed to him more dead and abandoned. Dr. Campanini himself was not long for this world, reflected Coletti, and one felt he would be happy to soon join his city of specters and memories.

A circular route led them back to the market square, and they sat down together on the great block of stone. The doctor was visibly worn-out. He passed a handkerchief over his spotted forehead and stretched his legs, then propped his hands on the head of his walking stick and wheezed quietly to himself.

Coletti felt ridiculous to ask it, but it had to be done. It was a harmless enough question, and only the most essential details were necessary.

'Dr. Campanini,' he began. 'I wonder if you have ever seen a house here that has two white columns inside it, and a pool with a blue dragon on the bottom, and at the end of this a platform and a flight of steps leading to an underground well...'

The old man stared blankly through his ancient, runny eyes.

'... or another house, with a section of roof still standing, and a maze of rooms below this, with patios connecting them, and mosaics on the floor...'

Dr. Campanini let out a 'bah!' and the blood seemed to be rushing into all the tiny capillaries of his scalp. 'Columns, dragons, mosaics...' he sputtered. 'You'll have to be more specific, boy... Do you know how many houses there are in these ruins?'

His voice had more than its usual quaver, and he seemed upset.

'Forget it,' said Coletti. 'It's nothing. A dream I had . . . '

They sat for a while in silence, and Coletti fell into a deep melancholy. There was not a cloud in the sky, nor was there any breeze; everything, past and present, seemed far away; all still and hushed. And then suddenly he felt the doctor's bony fingers digging into his forearm.

'Where did you see them?' croaked the old man. 'What happened?' He had a look of terror on his face that was frightful to behold.

Automatically, without his being able to stop it coming out, Coletti told Dr. Campanini everything—about his solitary excursions around Rome, about his first visit to Ostia, about the house, and Daniella, and then his return to the ruins, and the wind and the rain, the dark labyrinth, the *grappa*, and Monica . . . He did not omit anything, and almost ashamedly he found himself telling Dr. Campanini how desperately he loved them both, those two women who had loved him, however briefly, and then abandoned him—Daniella, Monica, Daniella, Monica . . .

He realized then that the old man was weeping softly at his side.

'My God!' exclaimed Coletti. 'Do you *know* them?'

Dr. Campanini lifted his face from his hands. Tears were streaming down his cheeks.

'Know them? Do I know them? Boy, why do you think I've spent three-quarters of my life in these damned ruins? And I've never found them again! Never! Not since then, since that summer. How long ago it was—*how long ago!*'

Coletti did some quick mental calculations, which turned his blood to ice. For several minutes neither of them spoke. It was Dr. Campanini who finally broke the silence.

'Describe them to me,' he whispered.

And so Coletti described them, as much for himself as for the defeated old man, described everything he could remember, everything that had not already slipped away into oblivion: the music, jarring and sweet, of their laughter; their inscrutable smiles; their freckles and moles; the way each had walked, talked; the sound of their voices; the way they had captured him with their stares and destroyed his will; how they had wrapped themselves around him and dug their nails into him; the warmth of their bodies; their moans and bites; their smells; their taste of brine and mist; the rushing of their breath; the pumping of their hearts; even their absences—Daniella's like the end of summer, Monica's like the spaces between the stars. What he had of them was so little, so fleeting! He searched through his memory for more, but there was nothing left; everything gone forever...

Dr. Campanini listened with reverence to Coletti's description and gave a soft, rheumy sigh when it was over.
'Incredible!' he said. 'They haven't changed a bit!'

LAST BUS HOME
Andrew Roberts

'Bitch!'

Jimmy stamped his feet against the cold. He took a last drag and flicked his cigarette against the chemist's window. It bounced off the glass in a flurry of sparks. The man with kebab on his shirt smiled at him.

Jimmy blew into his hands. He checked his watch. It was three minutes past. A while yet. The bus was due at five past, but it was invariably late. Sometimes only five minutes if you were lucky. Twenty-five if you weren't. He pushed his fists into his armpits and wriggled his toes inside his boots.

He said it again: *'Bitch!'* You tried not to think about them like that. But sometimes they just drove you fucking crazy.

Then he blinked. The bus was a hundred yards up the street—large as . . . well, *a bus*. His hands dropped to his sides. He raised his left arm again and checked his watch. The unit number shuffled over from a three to a four.

'In-*fucking*-credible.' He fumbled in his pocket for the saver-card he knew was in there.

The bus pulled away from the junction and headed across the roundabout towards him. It looked new. In the light from the streetlamp as it pulled into the kerb, he saw it was. A shiny new red—like blood. There was no number on the front. The destination window was blank—just a clear black rectangle.

The door *whooshed* open before him. He let Kebab-Man get on first, pulled himself up the steps and offered his card.

'Can't use that.'

He looked up at the driver. The man had slicked back hair and the beginnings of a Spanish beard. He was in his mid-thirties. Not the usual old fart you got.

'It expired yesterday.'

Jimmy looked down at the card. Hell, the guy was right. He tried to think back to when he had bought it. It wasn't like him to make such a stupid mistake. And, anyway, he had used it on the trip out here. Still, there it was—yesterday's date.

He shrugged and fumbled in his pockets for change. His coat threw up thirty-seven pence. He patted his jeans—empty. He hooked a finger in the watch pocket and came up with nothing. He looked at the driver and shrugged.

The driver smiled. Grinned, even. He hooked a thumb down the length of the bus. 'Have one on me.'

He might have had a generous nature, Jimmy thought, but the man drove like a lunatic. The bus was usually all but empty for the first ten minutes, but they were outside the old bingo hall in under five.

The crumblies. It was sometimes difficult to believe they were out at this time, but here they were—large as life and twice as wrinkled. Eleven-fifteen sharp every week. It seemed they'd be more at ease congregating in the afternoon and then shuffling home while it was still light. Anyway, it was eleven-ten this week. Still, they were all there. Had probably been there for the last twenty minutes in that old folks' just-in-case type way. Besides, twenty minutes in the cold would give them something to moan about.

Jimmy and his friends had joked about being beaten up by these old hooligans—the used-to-be big-but-shrank kids. They had even come close on one or two occasions. A jab of a walking stick, a thick calloused hand with tendons like rusted ship's cables around the back of the ear for cheek or riding late-night bicycles on pavements. Sometimes just because the OAPs felt like it.

Had that stuff really been two or three years ago? And here you were now at seventeen, spending your weekday nights waiting in the freezing cold for the last bus home, a girlfriend you fell out with every other night and still no sign of a proper job. Well, this time that was it, he decided. He was going to ring her in the morning and tell her it was all over. And not like the last three times. Life was too short.

The bus pulled in a little past the stop. Jimmy saw the driver's fingers come down on the cash tray and start drumming while they waited for the oldies to walk the extra five yards.

They boarded the bus as orderly as possible, flashing their cards and dropping a concessionary and exact 30p into the tray before they moved down the aisle—their steps made a little more certain by the alcohol they had consumed while they were trying to cover four corners, one whole row or a complete   card and then did that little walt old folks do when they seat themselves anywhere stand, sit, stand, change, indicate seat, assist someone in, check everyone made it, lean across and chat to someone you should have sat ne t to in the first place.

It made you wish for the heady days when the bus company could afford to run double-deckers. Better to be upstairs inhaling the piss and the vomit than watch this routine time and time again.

Jimmy saw the driver had acquired a cap from somewhere. He was doffing it as the pensioners climbed aboard:

'Thank you . . . thank you, ladies . . . thank you, gentlemen . . . thank you, one . . . thank you, all . . . thank you!'

Jesus Christ, was the guy on drugs? Or just extracting some serious piss?

'Ding-ding.'

Drugs.

The bus pulled away sharply. The last old woman was still standing. She flew backwards and smacked into the metal of the seat hip first. There would be a nasty yellow-black old person's bruise there in the morning.

'Steady up!' one of the men called out as the bus picked up speed.

The driver replied, but it was lost in the rising pitch of the engine as it began to ask for third. It had sounded a little like *fuck you.*

Jimmy checked his reflection in the window. It was smiling.

A couple in their late forties got on at the next stop. The driver hung out of his seat and leered at the woman's rear-end as she made her way down the aisle. His beard looked a little longer. He ran a hand through his hair and brushed it back from his face. His eyes glittered. As they pulled away, he began to whistle like a 1950s' milkman.

Two stops later it was a group of fifteen- and sixteen-year-old girls excited to be out this late. The driver whistled then threw his head back and howled at an invisible moon. 'Ladies, ladies—climb aboard. Room for one more on top! And might I add those are particularly delightful skirts you're wearing tonight! Nothing like a glimpse of inner thigh on a cold and rainy night.'

The girls giggled loudly, already rehearsing their discussion of the incident for the following morning. Jimmy noticed the windscreen wipers had been switched on. They moved back and forth out of sync, the left one falling briefly into beat with the right every third sweep. He pressed his nose to the window; if it was raining, it was pretty fine drizzle. The girls didn't look any the worse for wear.

The driver tapped fingers across his ticket machine like a movie actor pretending to type and a roll of tickets appeared. He picked up a pound coin and flipped it. '*Heads*, that's all four of you—who's first?'

The girls giggled again. Jimmy thought at least two of them looked as though they had lost the toss of a coin before. One of them mumbled something about *dirty bastards in uniform* and a third round of giggling broke out.

They must have been hitting sixty by the time they approached the lights of the city. It was the town crew next. The ones who were too drunk or too skint to make it to a nightclub. They climbed aboard in fours or fives or on their own. Sometimes they were in courting pairs, the males in black trousers and white shirts whatever the weather or season, the females in skirts that were too tight, make-up that was too orange and contrasted noticeably with their chip-pan-fat legs.

Then, the bus was sailing past the shelter, leaving those waiting to stare after it in drunken disbelief. A man who looked as though he had one foot nailed to the ground, his head nodding at the floor like he had dropped his wallet there but didn't quite know how to go about picking it up, tried to turn with an angry fist raised and promptly fell over. A tray of food splattered the window and dripped what looked like yellow curry down in front of Jimmy's face.

He grabbed for the back of the chair in front of him as the driver slammed the brakes on. The bus squealed and screeched to a halt fifty yards past its stop. Amazingly, there was smoke rising from the tyres. The drunken mob began to run towards them in a cloud of witticisms and abuse. Those already on the bus offered their own protestations, then clammed up as they saw what the driver was doing.

He had climbed up and was now standing on the half-door that doubled as cash receptacle. His hands were at his waist as he pulled his belt free from its buckle. He tugged the zip down and dropped his trousers and underwear in one fell swoop. His backside was red and completely hairless. He wiggled it at the angry faces outside.

A fist appeared out of the mob and began to hammer on the door. It was joined by others. Pneumatics breathed into action as someone hit on the idea of using the emergency door switch. The doors folded open and the bus began to move again. Trousers still dropped, the driver turned himself around and grinned at the people outside. He pushed a stray strand of hair from his eyes and took hold of his penis. A stream of dark yellow urine arced through the air and out into the night.

Who's operating the pedals? Jimmy thought. He watched as the white-shirts began to move after the bus. What was wrong with them? Wasn't one faceful of piss enough? They gave up the chase as the bus began to pick up speed.

The man with kebab on his shirt stared after them. 'Fucking hell.'

The driver's stream sputtered twice and began to die. He shook the last few drops off, tugged up his trousers and hopped into his seat.

'Hey!' one laconic pensioner shouted just in front of Jimmy. 'What's going on?'

The driver's head appeared around the edge of the cab. It was as red as his arse had been. (*It looked red when you got on,* Jimmy thought. *In the cab-light. Only there wasn't a cab-light, was there?*) His lips parted to reveal a perfect-toothed white grin. And his beard! His beard was growing visibly as he spoke. Short to long and back again like some strange special effect.

The man spoke up again. 'What are you playing at?' His wife grabbed his arm.

The driver tipped his cap back on his head and scratched his temple. 'My friend—who's driving this fucking bus, me or you?'

Silence held firm.

The driver tugged his cap back down. He stroked his moving beard. 'Exactly. Now, let me . . . CONCENTRATE!!'

He wrenched the wheel sharply to the right as a Post Office van loomed in the windscreen. The bus mounted the kerb, bounced and settled, came to a halt.

The driver leaned out of his window. 'MANIAC!!' He looked down the bus again, speaking to the pensioner. 'Now, look at us! Jesus, we're on the wrong side of the *road!*'

He looked back in front and pulled away. The side of the bus scraped the length of a parked car as they moved across to the left-hand side of the road and picked up speed.

People were glancing around at each other now, not knowing quite how to deal with the situation. Those who knew their neighbours, whispered short sentences to each other. Those who didn't, looked around for someone to tell them everything would be all right, they weren't really in the hands of a madman. The young girls had gone unnaturally quiet.

Kebab-Man reached into his pocket and drew out a single cigarette and match. He struck the match with his thumb and held it to the jittering cigarette.

'Hey, mac!'

Mac?

'Can't you read, mac?' The driver was indicating a NO SMOKING sign. His arm stretched the length of the bus until it found the cigarette. *That's twelve feet,* Jimmy thought. *Oh, Jesus—I'm trapped on a bus with some lunatic version of Mr Fantastic.*

Kebab-Man's eyes were wide as saucers. The fingers flexed in front of his face and snatched the cigarette from his mouth. The arm shrank back to its proper length. 'Fumes, don't you know?!'

The bus was really struggling now as it climbed the hill that led away from town. Gritty, black smoke clung in a cloud as it left the exhaust. The engine had begun to growl and rattle. The smell of oil and diesel hung heavy in the air. It felt as though they were riding in some 1920s' boneshaker. Then they breasted the rise and the juddering eased off a little as they pulled into the next stop.

A couple in their early twenties climbed aboard. They wore leather jackets and tight jeans and from the back they could have been twins. The girl dropped two pound coins into the tray and stated her destination. There was an awkward pause while she looked at the driver.

'*Give me the right goddamn money!*'

The girl frowned. Her boyfriend looked drunkenly on.

'*Jesus—you people! Do I look like a fucking bank?*'

The passengers sat like tight-lipped zombies. Jimmy wondered if it was the hypnotic beat of the windscreen wipers. What made you sit in silence when you wanted to scream *Run, dammit, run! Can't you see the situation here?* Fear? Fear of what—suffering alone?

The doors folded closed. The driver waved a dismissive hand. '*Christ—just sit down!*'

The couple found a seat as close to the back as possible. On his way there, the boy shrugged a comic shrug that under other circumstances would have drawn a response. No one acknowledged him. He dropped into his seat and looked at his girlfriend as if to say, "I don't know. Do you know?"

No one had spoken for more than ten minutes. Faces were grey, mouths dry, lips drawn tight.

They screamed through a red light and under the bridge. The curve and the stonework had hidden the road ahead from them and now they could see again.

On the other side of the road a blacked out bus was heading towards them (*it's on its way to the depot*, Jimmy thought ridiculously). They were all conscious of how wide they had taken the last bend and now the inevitable was going to happen. Their thirty-minute nightmare ride was about to be brought to a final and dramatic halt as it collided head-on with something of equal size and mass.

The bus loomed and loomed. Then both drivers were twisting their wheels in opposite directions as they headed for space. A huge *YEEEEE-HAA!!* erupted from the cab. The interior darkened as the other vehicle careened alongside them. There was a terrible crump and shatter as the window of the emergency exit door exploded.

Jimmy jumped back and brushed desperately at his head and shoulders. His eyes had closed shut and he examined them carefully before easing them open. No blood—good. 'It hit the wing mirror,' someone said stupidly.

Up ahead the alarm was beeping just in case anyone had missed the incident. The driver had won his fight with the bucking wheel and they raced down the white line now, straddling it perfectly. His face appeared in the aisle:

'Anyone had a heart attack, yet?'

He ducked back inside the cab and then reappeared. A grin to shame an American game-show host smeared his face. 'How about a little singsong?' Then his voice struck up:

'Show me the way to go home . . .
I'm tired and I want to go to bed . . . '

Jimmy moved along the seat, away from the broken glass. The wind chased itself in through the starburst hole and swinging door. It had been closer than he thought. There was a painful looking dent in the metal. It was buckled badly. The lock hung in its frame, ruined. He checked his clothing for more shards and pulled his collar tight around him.

The lady who had grabbed her husband's arm was standing out of her seat. She was looking directly at him. 'Can't you stop him? Please, can't you stop him?'

Jimmy looked at her. 'Lady, you must be fucking kidding.'

The woman sat down as if slapped. 'At least get his number,' she said, almost to herself.

But Jimmy didn't want to do that. He was afraid he might already know what that number was. He thought it might be the number for the Australian police. The number a child called Damien had had stamped on the top of his head. Six-six-six. Six-double-six. Double-six-six. Any way you rolled it, those numbers added up to one thing: *El Diablo*. How else did you explain a red arse and a beard that lengthened at will?

He leaned across, tapped the woman on the shoulder and heard himself say it again:

'Lady, you must be fucking kidding.'

Suddenly, the driver's voice broke off mid-line. They could see him standing on his seat, peering into the night. He bounced up and down, bending at the knees like Yosemite Sam riding a camel.

He turned towards them. His eyebrows wiggled up and down. He looked back at the road. 'Would you look at this? It's the contest we've all been waiting for—man against cat. Or should we say man and bus against cat?! Here we go, folks! Eight and three quarter tons of pure steel against eleven pounds of spit and fur. Who will win this titanic battle, brains or brawn? Join us after the break.'

He dropped into his seat and leered over the wheel. The radio crackled into life: *'One-four-four-five? One-four-four-five?'*

He reached up and plucked the entire unit from its housing, 'Christ, I hate that thing!'

He held the metal body in one hand, the talk-box in the other. He pressed the send button and spoke into the dead mike. 'Bandits at three o'clock, Red Leader! Scrag those bastards! *Thokka-thokka! Ee-ooo-mm!! Duh-duh-duh-duh-duh!!!* One-four-four-five, over and out.'

He launched it through the window, his hair flapping madly in the breeze, and looked up into the mirror. 'Now it's just us, people. No one to spoil the fun. *Here, pussy-pussy!'*

It was impossible for them to see. Only the mounting enthusiasm from the cab indicated what was about to happen. One minute they were rattling down the middle of the road (they weren't in a boneshaker, now. No, they were inside the belly of the last dinosaur as it lumbered its way to the tar pit. If this were a cartoon a huge, red tongue would be lolling from the radiator, the wheels would look like the limbs of a crawling man, beads of sweat would be oozing from the ocular headlights), and the next they were swerving sharply to the right.

The screech to end all screeches filled the night, and then the driver was leaning out of the cab, one hand on the wheel, the other scooping down beneath his dangling body, plucking something from the road.

He held it up, proudly. 'Round One—*the Steel Bomber!!'*

He smelled the dead cat like a man inhaling the scent of a rose or a line of quality-cut cocaine and tossed it over his shoulder. It fell into the luggage rack and stared lifelessly at the advertising strip above it. Its guts were pink and steaming, its skull a battered crimson pulp. Someone vomited. Jimmy saw it was Kebab-Man with no surprise at all. An old and cracked voice offered its summation: 'Oh, God! Oh, God!'

The driver leaned out of his cab. 'What do you expect for thirty pence—a side of beef?'

Jimmy wondered if it was smoke or steam that seemed to be floating off The Horned One. He had been smelling sulphur for the last couple of minutes.

One of the young girls got to her feet. Speechless, Jimmy saw it was the one who had expressed doubts about both the driver's cleanliness and parentage; she of the loudest giggle. *Ask him if he can drop me off too*, Jimmy thought. *Tell him I have to finish with my girlfriend.* He felt himself sink into his seat as she stepped cautiously towards the front of the bus.

The driver appeared. There was a sign in his hand. It was written in script, with gothic stems and large, ornate capitals, and perfectly legible:

> DO NOT DISTRACT
> DRIVER'S ATTENTION
> WHILE VEHICLE IS IN MOTION

The girl stopped and looked over her shoulder at her friends. She turned back to the driver and raised her hand as if pulling up the right words from inside herself. 'Please?'

The driver propped the sign against the windscreen. A crack of lightning shot out from his extended finger. It hit the girl and engulfed her in its orange flare. Her body began to melt. She folded in on herself and ran onto the floor, liquid now.

Jimmy gagged. He sensed the rest of the bus was doing the same. The orange liquid (it looked like candle wax) dripped into the stairwell by the doors.

'Shit!' the driver yelled. 'Now look what you made me do.' He addressed himself directly to the puddle, as though it might speak to him. Bubbles rose from its surface.

Hysteria took hold. In the pandemonium, softly and from the front of the bus, the sound of singing began again.

People were weeping all around him. Every so often there was a high-pitched whine that was cut off almost as soon as it began. Someone had been saying the word *god* over and over again for the last fifteen minutes.

The night was dark now. No streetlamps lit the outside world. No on-coming vehicles illuminated them briefly. Even the bus's own lights had started to buzz and flicker. One fluorescent had exploded over Kebab-Man. He was sleeping now, curled on the floor like the world's biggest, drunkest baby. Every so often the orange goo would run towards him across the floor and disappear beneath his chest as it rose and fell, seeping out again as the cant of the bus shifted.

As far as Jimmy was concerned, the darkness was fine. He didn't think there was anything out there he would recognise, let alone wanted to see.

In the cab, the driver was muttering constantly to himself like some crazed fairy-tale character.

He was sitting in the broken glass now, close to the ruined door again. It had lodged itself into its frame and no longer flapped in the breeze. One good shove and it would swing out into the night. The road would be rushing beneath him, only too eager to reach up and grab his body, unforgiving in its solidity. But that was okay. Rather that than what lay before them.

It reached into the night, glowing red. Its walls seemed to have been accreted rather than made. They rose slick and wet into the night sky like a brooding fortress. The light that illuminated them seemed a part *of* it—inherent, innate, like a radioactive crystal. It bathed the bus interior in its rubric glow. There was a large entrance in the wall facing them. The light inside was the same as out, visible only as a subtle shift in tone, a maw of more redness.

The bus shifted down a gear as it made its approach. Jimmy looked at the door. There was a sign above it:

> WE TRY HARD TO GET THINGS RIGHT
> *Occasionally, we don't quite make it*
> *We want you to enjoy travelling with us*
> *If you experience difficulty or have any comments about our service please telephone to speak to our Customer Satisfaction Team—0666 666666*
> THE REGION'S FAVOURITE.

Their speed dropped as they hit the final twist that would straighten them out. Jimmy felt tears sting his eyes. He shoved.

There was blood dripping from a wound on the side of his head. He had been unconscious, but didn't know for how long. His watch was intact from the fall, but its liquid numbers flashed continuously on 00:00.

Walking now, he began to count. He reached two thousand and then stopped. It was as long again before the darkness began to give way to a faint line of brightness ahead of him.

His pace remained even and the line became a strip, the strip a band. Until, eventually, it filled three-quarters of his view and he realised he was inside it now, this blessed light. The darkness was behind him and he had no desire to turn and see what it had become in the brightness.

He began to recognise things. Trees and clouds that jarred his senses and dizzied him like a look over the edge of a very high cliff. And then a bird, tiny and brown as it flitted from one place to another. He looked at his watch and the last nought twitched over to a one.

An hour after he saw the bird, he looked down and found he was on a road. It was narrow and there were no markings, but it was made of asphalt or tarmacadam or whatever it was they used to make roads in the world he was used to. He wept.

Later, he discovered he had been hearing a noise for a while now. He listened and recognised the distant hum of traffic, far away but there, worshipfully and irreclaimably there. It grew louder as he walked.

And then he was standing at the edge of a hill overlooking a city. And even though he had never seen it from this perspective, he knew it was *his* city. His people, his buildings.

There was a telephone-box and he stepped inside and watched his coins rattle on the steel shelf. Thirty-seven pence. He dropped what the slot would take into it and dialled. It was a while before someone answered.

He lifted the receiver closer to his mouth. 'Suzanne, I don't think we should see each other any more.'

He stood with his head on the glass wall, the phone to his chest.

Finally, he hit redial. 'I'll see you tonight, okay?'

THE CATACOMBS OF OSIMUS
Alastair G Gunn

The following particulars were recently recounted at a college gathering which I had the pleasure of attending. The narrator was a Dr. Ernest Jardine, reader in Renaissance Art at St. Andrews, a man I had not hitherto met, but whose integrity and motives in relating the story could not be faulted. I have managed to examine for myself the diary around which Jardine's account was based and there can be no doubt that some intrigue surrounds the events that I shall presently relate.

Some months prior to our meeting, Jardine had read, in *L'Osservatore Vaticano*, the obituary of one Monsignor Giuseppe Landini, a long-standing curator of the Pontifical Commission for Sacred Archaeology and a recognised authority on early Christian cemeteries. Jardine was a vague associate of the priest, having received, on several occasions, his generous hospitality at the Academy of Science in Rome. On reading this obituary, Jardine was immediately taken with an inexplicable impression that the obituarist had omitted more fact than fiction concerning the lamentable passing of the cleric. Indeed, the tone of the praise was strangely apologetic, dismissive and incomplete. By happenstance, the Dr. had occasion, the very next week, to be in Rome and was reminded of Landini's death when passing the ancient cemetery of *St. Callistus* on the *Via Appia*. He decided to present himself to Landini's successor in order to show his respects and offer his condolences. Travelling to the small town of Montignoso, not more than fifty miles from the capital, he came to the ancient catacombs of Osimus, of which Landini had been curator and chief conservationist.

The new curator, Monsignor Bartoli, welcomed him. Following a midday meal with the priest, Jardine questioned him concerning the cause of Landini's death.

The obituary had not made mention of it and Landini had been, Jardine knew, a young and vital man. Bartoli became very agitated, saying under his breath 'triste' and quickly making the sign of the cross over his cassock. He explained that Landini had been found, expired, in a chamber in the deepest part of the catacombs beneath the town. Bartoli could offer no explanation. But there was more disturbing news. It seemed Landini had an associate with him on that fateful day. After pressing the priest further, Jardine ascertained that an English scholar, on sabbatical leave at the Florentine University, had accompanied Landini into the labyrinths. The Englishman had also met with his death and a similar ignorance as to the cause troubled Bartoli's face as he related the atrocious events. Jardine was perplexed, but, since the priest was by this time visibly shaken by the memory, did not press him further.

But Jardine himself was very intrigued, and not a little troubled, by the story of two untimely deaths in the ancient catacombs. On his return to Rome, he enquired of the British consul about the Englishman's death. He thereby discovered that the man in question, Prof. David Hewitt, was an archaeologist visiting Florence from the Victoria University of Manchester. The consular office informed him that the Italian authorities had performed an inquiry into both Hewitt's and Landini's deaths, but that the results of the investigation had not been made public. They too were completely ignorant of how the two men had come by their deaths. Jardine made further enquiries with the Vatican authorities, specifically with the Pontifical Commission and the State Secretariat. They were most adamant that the English scholar had, in fact, not died in Montignoso, though they could offer no explanation of the man's whereabouts.

Mystified, Jardine returned to England shortly afterwards. He then contacted the late scholar's faculty in the hope of ascertaining the circumstances of the deaths and was thus put in touch with the scholar's widow. She informed him that her husband had indeed died in Montignoso, but that both the Vatican and Italian authorities had offered no explanation and had at first denied the incident. Her husband's body had been returned through diplomatic channels but she had not received his many possessions from Florence. Incensed with this state of affairs, Jardine called upon his numerous contacts within the civil service to pressure the Italian authorities for the return of Hewitt's possessions and an explanation of his death. The latter was not forthcoming, although, after protracted wranglings at the highest level, Hewitt's possessions were returned. It was by these means that Jardine came by the diary of which I have spoken.

The volume is a plain leather-bound manuscript book of the kind used by artists for their jottings. Hewitt had used it both as a personal diary and as a record of his thoughts and discoveries in the field. The pages are scrawled over with untidy plans of archaeological sites and notes of inscriptions and excavations. The final section of the diary details Hewitt and Landini's investigations in the catacombs of Osimus, far beneath the town of Montignoso. I believe it offers a consistent explanation for their unfortunate deaths, though I have great difficulty in accepting the fantastic conclusions that must inevitably be drawn.

Diary of Prof. David Hewitt.

15th May. Tomorrow I am meeting Landini in Montignoso to begin the next phase of our exploration in the lower chambers. I have managed to identify this area in a single ninth century pilgrim's itinerary in Turin. We only discovered the exact location last summer although Marucchi had indicated its approximate whereabouts in 1902. No basilica or chapel was excavated covering this site, as is common at the enormous Roman vaults, and the galleries are generally of a poor, rural form. It is undoubtedly a very early cemetery, probably first century, and quite possibly undefaced in parts. We shall see.

16th May. The day was hot when we arrived at the cemetery and the sandy depression in the ground that gave entrance to the underground vaults was reflecting the sun with a torturous ferocity. We took some refreshment beneath the shade of the olive trees by the road before descending into the darkness. We followed the stairway down the thirty feet or so to the first level of the vaults. We passed through the main gallery and down another level to the later excavations. This level consists of a main corridor perhaps thirteen feet in height but only two or three broad. There are over a hundred passages leading off the main corridor and along the length of each are hewn several burial chambers. The sidewalls of all the passages have horizontal tiers of graves cut out of the rock, usually five or six high, and there is also evidence of graves cut into the floors.

We came to the place where we had ended our initial exploration in February. From here the main corridor continued on and further passages led off to the right and left. We continued onwards, Landini lighting the way ahead and I noting down the sequence of adjoining tunnels as we went. I counted another thirty passages before we suddenly stepped into a wide chamber. It was an impressive vault and may have been constructed for a family of some importance, perhaps even senatorial. We spent the following few hours measuring the new passages and making brief notes on interesting burials to which we would return.

On this, the first day of our return to the vaults, I am beginning to feel again the excitement of discovery. Although the work is enthralling, it still makes the hairs on my neck stand as we scurry along these dingy passages, the bones of countless people entombed in the rock closing in on us. It never ceases to amaze me that we are likely to be the first men to walk the corridors for 1500 years, perhaps even more. The enormous span of years that has passed since these people were interred in their sacred networks is inspiring. Their lives and loves are forgotten, only commemorated by the odd, fading inscription. As we work, I often wonder about these people's lives and achievements. It is the saddest aspect of my profession; unearthing remains and monuments that long ago were the focus of whole communities. I pray that they perceive the respect that I hold for their resting-place.

17th May. This morning Landini and I had a difference of opinion. The priest thinks the terminal chamber we discovered yesterday is enigmatic. He reminded me that no such cubicula has been found in any of the Roman catacombs. He insisted on a closer look at the room, suggesting that we may have missed something important in its location or construction.

On our arrival we carefully measured the space and sketched its general features. It is rectangular in shape, the main corridor entering on a shorter side. There is no central sarcophagus but niches about one foot deep are carved out of the walls. These are not obvious entrances to further burial chambers although they may have been intended for that purpose. The niches are faced with marble but bear no inscriptions. I made some sketches while Landini inspected the chamber in the minutest detail. As I scribbled, Landini suddenly spoke.

'Guarda!' he said excitedly, pointing to the niche that faced the entrance to the chamber. He invited me to inspect the rock that abutted against the marble slab. He brushed away a layer of encrusted sand and the cause of his excitement became obvious. Ancient tiles, set in a rough mortar, could be seen protruding from behind the marble. The corridor did not end in the chamber at all. It continued, but had been blocked, the huge sealing rock cemented to graves hewn into the sidewalls. We looked at each other in astonishment. It seems there are further vaults and tunnels awaiting our exploration. They have been deliberately concealed from us.

18th May. Landini and I first debated yesterday's discovery. It is curious that the passage should be blocked. Landini suspects a high ranking family lie in the vaults beyond. But something bothers me about it. The tunnel was blocked after burials were entombed along the passage walls. If the vault had meant to be sealed, why were graves cut where the sealing stone would be placed? We decided to break through the sealing stone into the passage beyond to attempt a solution to the mystery.

This afternoon we took our tools to the chamber. For three hours we worked, scraping cement from the edges of the rock to gain a foothold for the levers. We arranged a system of pulleys so that we could pull the rock free but prevent it from falling once it had been loosened. As I was working at the marble block I suddenly noticed some depressions in its surface. It was an engraving, extremely worn and covered with loose sand. I called Landini over and we laboured to clear the inscription of debris.

After some time we revealed the roughly scratched words; *Cave Diaboli*.

'Misericordia!' Landini exclaimed, shock clearly visible on his face. I agreed with his sentiment. Such a warning I have never encountered before in all my researches. The very use of those words is an anathema in a Christian context. We passed over the discovery with few words between us, avoiding each other's reservations. But I quietly felt a breeze of trepidation pass over me.

By early evening we had rigged our equipment and loosened the stone from its position. It hung towards us and was held fast by our system of pulleys. We decided to leave the removal of the stone until the morrow. Strangely, neither of us felt the urge to thrust a torch into the gloom beyond and take a peek at the newly opened passage. I must admit I was uncharacteristically keen to make our ascent to the surface today. Some urgency seems to have gone from our endeavours.

19th May. On returning to the large chamber today, we proceeded to pull the stone from its moorings. Fortunately, it had not been secured with mortar or tenons, simply placed perfectly into the diameter of the tunnel. Gradually we lowered the huge stone to the floor; its top coming to rest in the middle of the chamber. Again, I felt an odd reluctance to proceed.

Our dim lights did not penetrate into the tunnel beyond. I grabbed a wick and stepped up onto the stone, about to see what we had uncovered. The strangest feeling took me just then. I felt an urge to turn away and leave the discovery to someone else. Rather than the anticipation of new mysteries, I felt only a sickening repulsion from the dim corridor before me. It wasn't the blackness, or the dank smell, but a foul wind of ill seemed to brush past me.

But necessity pressed me on. I jumped onto the floor of the tunnel ahead of me and beckoned Landini to follow. Quickly, we discovered that the tunnel did not continue into other labyrinths; after a few steps we entered another chamber, twice as large as the previous, with no other exit. The area was clearly the vault of an important family. But there was hardly any decoration or obvious interments; as if the room had been prepared but then unused.

Landini and I proceeded to measure the enclosure and make notes on its contents and construction. I searched for carvings and found some long-worn and unreadable characters in one of the many niches surrounding the chamber. In another of the niches the stone had been gashed deeply as if during the cutting of the rock. But underneath the scar there was unmistakable lettering. At first I thought the carving was the chrism, the monogram of Christ, roughly cut in the red sandstone. But on closer inspection the talisman was not that distinct. It was very worn but seemed to consist of two over-scored letters, perhaps a family monogram. Then, beneath it, very worn, but still readable, lay the inscription;

SEVERA
QVI VIXIT ANN. IX. MENS. V. D. XIV DEPOSIT IN PACE KAL MART
DVLCIS IN AETERNUM

The niche was the resting-place of a young girl, Severa, only nine years old. I was suddenly smitten by an intense sorrow at reading this inscription. I had seen many like it before, but the solitary and forgotten nature of the place, combined with a tangible grief in the atmosphere, made me feel quite faint.

20th May. Today I sent word to our friend and colleague, de Baglio, at the *Biblioteca Apostolica Vaticana*. I have the feeling that the sealing of this chamber represents something of importance in the history of the Osimus catacombs. I asked him to research, in any way possible, the history of the early Christian communities around Montignoso. It will be a difficult task. I have uncovered nothing relating to Osimus in three years of diligent study, but de Baglio's resources and skill are far superior to mine. Perhaps he can throw some light, however dim, on what led the leaders of this community to separate the grave of a little girl from the rest of her kindred.

21st May. Landini and I today continued our investigation of the terminal chamber. Its importance seems to warrant a detailed study. We have been cleaning the many years of debris from the floors and walls of the crypt. The construction is indeed of high quality; the marble facing stones are exquisitely cut. But we have found no evidence of interments other than the young Severa. Except for those unreadable characters in one of the niches. I spent some time looking at this area. The marks are not natural, but do not seem to be related to the stone's dressing or placement. I am sure that there may have been an inscription on the rock, but it looks like it has been deliberately scored over. It is perplexing.

22nd May. I am becoming concerned that there are areas beyond our knowledge involved in this work. The discovery of that dismal chamber has unnerved me somewhat. Its purpose and history are not within the realms of my usual experience. The atmosphere there seems unholy somehow.

I have also noticed a distinct change in Landini's manner. He seems distracted and irritable. Today, as we worked at opposite ends of the chamber, I got a terrible shock. It was Landini, exclaiming as if a cat had jumped out at him. I ran over to see what had surprised him but he brushed me off with a shrug of the shoulders as if nothing had happened. But he had had a fright, no doubt about it. He was sweating more than the confined space usually caused and he was trembling slightly. I imagined it was symptomatic of the confined, grim enclosure and continued with my work.

23rd May. I am now even more concerned for Landini's well being. Today, after we'd been working for several hours, I noticed we were running short of wicks. Fortunately, I had left some with our supplies on the upper level. I left Landini to continue his scraping, and went to retrieve the items. On my return to Severa's chamber I thought Landini had disappeared. But then I noticed him in a dark recess; his back firmly pressed against the hard stone. He was looking, glaring in fact, into the centre of the chamber and seemed unaware of my arrival. I shuffled towards him and he was shaken out of his trance.

'Are you alright?' I asked. He looked at me for a moment and then simply nodded. His face was ashen, the blood completely drained from his features. He swallowed dryly and returned to his work.

I let the incident pass, but am convinced there is some conflict affecting the curator's mind. He seems distant and troubled. Although I too feel claustrophobic, an oppression borne of rage, anger and fear, I am fearful that Landini may become unhinged by the odd place. I will keep my eye on him and have resolved to speak of this if there is no improvement in his constitution.

This morning I received a note from de Baglio. He refers to a discovery that we may find interesting, but does not say what it is. He promises to send word by the weekend. Perhaps he has found something relating to our explorations. Hopefully, it will help in restoring some composure to the troubled Landini.

24th May. My sleep has been troubled of late. Sleep comes easily but never seems to refresh my spirit. I am not haunted by nightmares, though on waking, I feel a conflict has been raging about me during the darkness hours.

Before we retired to bed last night, Landini made a startling admission. He referred to his odd behaviour on my return to the chamber yesterday. I was right, something quite extraordinary had happened. With difficulty, he explained that while I was away, he'd been taken with a sudden feeling that he was not alone. Rising from his inspection of the floor, he turned to see, in a corner of the chamber, a shadow, or patch of darkness, growing and pulsating. To his astonishment, the shadow transformed into a human figure, an eerie greenish light forming in its interior and radiating to fill the apparition. It was a small girl. Landini broke down, sobbing, as he described the hallucination.

'She turned to face me,' he said, 'her eyes were forlorn and tearful. She was frightened beyond comprehension, pleading with me. Then she began to circle, her arms outstretched, as if looking for some escape from the dark chamber.'

I have no explanation for Landini's experience. I tried my best to reassure him, but for some time he was distraught and cried uncontrollably. He insists the apparition was not self-induced but I suspect the sad chamber has indeed unbalanced him. This exploration has had a disturbing effect on both of us and I am unsure whether we should continue under the circumstances. Some rest may clear our minds of these grim imaginings.

27th May. de Baglio has triumphed, though his letter adds to my concerns for Landini. In a forgotten recess of the Vatican archives, he tells us, he came across an eighth century manuscript. It had been copied from a much earlier source and makes several references to the Osimus catacombs. They are all quite cursory and indefinite remarks. In one extract the book tells of the tragic death of a young girl of a senatorial family. It even names her; Severa. Reference is made to the construction of a new family chamber for her interment. But there is a more disturbing aspect to de Baglio's research. Vaguely, the book speaks of another burial, a person unnamed, but who was guilty of some unmentioned atrocity. A final indistinct passage speaks of the sealing of a lower chamber of the Osimus catacombs. The explanation is again unclear but de Baglio implies that one of the tombs became regarded as spiritually unclean. What is meant by this, I cannot imagine. de Baglio has not sent me the Latin text, so I cannot speculate as to how these facts relate to our investigations.

28th May. I am abhorred and do not wish to proceed with this infernal excavation. I have seen enough to convince me we are dealing with something unwholesome, though I am still convinced that it is merely a sickness of the mind, induced by that hateful place, which infects us.

We have spent the last several days in the welcome light of the sun. I have made excuses for our remaining on the surface in order to relieve some of the stress on Landini. Hopefully, these awful delusions will evaporate with the heat of the day. His *and* mine.

de Baglio's letter put me in a quandary. I didn't wish to add to Landini's troubled mind, but I felt he should know of the librarian's findings. I resolved to discuss them with him before we started out for the labyrinths once again. A greyness descended over his face as I related the facts, but he was not put off returning to the grim chamber.

We returned there after lunch today. The recuperation gained during our break from the excavation dispersed immediately. The place was still infested with that sick oppression. We looked at each other, uncertain as to what should be done. Landini looked troubled again. He turned to me.

'David,' he said, 'this place is not right. There are things here beyond our understanding. We can only guess what the sad history of this chamber may be. But whatever it is, something here seeks our help.'

'Help?' I asked, 'help for what?'

'There are troubled souls here,' he replied, 'we must offer them salvation.'

Without another word he began walking around the perimeter of the chamber, brushing his fingertips over the dusty marble walls. He came to Severa's resting-place and knelt by it, kissed his hand and pressed it to the inscription. He made the sign of the cross.

Just then a breeze seemed to rush through the enclosed space. And to my amazement, it carried with it the sound of a girl's voice, faint and echoing, as if rising from a deep chasm. It was a pained cry, a muted call for help, unimaginably sorrowful. I was stunned, my bones chilled to the core.

But Landini seemed totally unconcerned with the ethereal cry. He stood, closed his eyes and held out his hands, as if welcoming the child to be comforted. Again a breeze floated over me, and this time it bore a sigh, something like contentment, but wavering with a fearful uncertainty.

'Gloria Patri,' said Landini, 'et Filii, et Spiritus Sancto . . . '

As he spoke, the air changed. It moved again, but was no longer a ghostly breeze. It was turbulent and ill. The impression was no longer of a child's emotions. Instead it spoke of anger and distrust.

'Sicut erat in principio,' Landini continued, 'et nunc, et semper . . . '

Now a tumult began to rise all around us. At first I thought an earth tremor, not unheard of in this region, was shaking the small chamber. But almost at once, I realised it was not the ground that shook, but the very air around us.

'Et in saecula saeculorum . . . '

The rumble grew in intensity and I flung my hands over my ears. But it did not lessen the ferocity of the sound. Landini was unperturbed, his eyes still closed, his arms still open. Then, rising out of the cacophony, there seemed to be the murmur of a voice, growing in clarity. There were no recognisable words, only a hideous, guttural growling like that of a trapped beast. A pain shot through my head, sharp and deep. The growl echoed through me, its anger searing my very soul. I think I screamed as Landini, only now succumbing to the hideous evil, dropped to his knees, shielding his head from something grasping at him from within the storm of hatred that enveloped us. I too dropped to the floor.

'In nomine Patris, et Filii, et Spiritus Sancti,' Landini went on, enduring the torment. The rage grew and grew till it seemed we stood amid a tempest. My vision became blurred, the pain in my head unbearable.

'Stop!' I screamed and made a grab for Landini. He was unconscious.

I cannot recall how we reached the safety of the surface.

29th May. Today, we did not go underground, but spent most of the day discussing the best course of action. Landini is now convinced that some spirit, or spirits, infest the crypt. He believes he did, indeed, see the apparition of the young girl entombed there, and is further convinced that some entity has held her in unending torment since her untimely death. De Baglio's research perhaps offers some credence to the idea, but I am uneasy with such a fantastic and supernatural explanation. However, the evidence of my own senses has left me confused and apprehensive. I don't know what to think any more.

I suggested we re-seal Severa's chamber and move onto different parts of the labyrinths, trying to put events of recent days behind us. But Landini was adamant that whatever presence inhabits the vaults must be given peace. He insists that it is his duty to offer guidance and redemption. He wishes to exorcise whatever evil presence may lie beneath our feet, and will not rest until the attempt is made. I could see no cause to refuse Landini this option and with some reluctance offered my help in the ritual. This evening we prepared the items with which the ceremony is performed and go now to bed with the hope that the new day will bring peace and calm to the girl and her antagonist. Tomorrow, we shall see.

This was the final entry in Hewitt's diary. He and Landini were found dead in the chamber on the following evening, after they did not return to the surface at the usual hour.

Jardine ended his story with the news that the lower levels of the Osimus catacombs have been sealed off and there are no plans for further investigation of the ancient labyrinths. The Italian authorities continue to remain silent about the events at Montignoso. It is tempting to believe Hewitt's diary offers an explanation, but, as Hewitt himself believed, the inferences are too fantastic to contemplate. If such conclusions can indeed be drawn, my only hope is that the poor Severa achieved eternal rest by the endeavours of the courageous and pious Landini, and the unfortunate Prof. Hewitt.

CHARNEL WINE
Richard Gavin

When Finnegan dreams he dreams of the spaces between. His sleeping mind does not blossom with images of people or places; no muddied symbols percolate up from the depths of his Id. When Finnegan drifts off he dreams only of voids. Fabulously intertwining abysses that wind and open unto vast and varying textures of nothing. And when he rises the next morning, teary-eyed and spiritually feeble, he often has to pinch himself to ensure that he had not lost all form and mass and merged with that dreamscape of nihil. It's a fairly recent affliction, this. Sometimes he takes lovers into his bed as a hopeful remedy. I am one of these. I say one of because I know Finnegan too well to be fooled into believing that I'm either the first or the last woman to lay down with him.

His is a strange and fitful love. He often says our relationship is psychical rather than physical. We've yet to fully consummate our urges, instead we indulge in more unique exercises of intimacy; long and wordless exchanges that come from staring deep into one another. Studying every inch of our body and souls. Finnegan admitted to me that although our romance is still quite young, he feels as though he's known me forever.

I felt him jolt upright in bed next to me. His breathing was heavy, panicked. I propped myself up on one hand and stroked his back with the other, hushing him, trying to banish the terror. His eyes darted about the unlit room and it was clear that he found no comfort in these familiar surroundings. I drew his face to mine and kissed him, and for the first time Finnegan's response was one of genuine passion. Our bodies poured back onto the bed and at long last we made love. I could sense a curious hesitation on his part, as though he was second-guessing his desire, but in the end he followed his bliss.

Our passion evolved into whispered pillow talk and by dawn our whispers had succumbed to exhaustion.

Several hours must have passed before Finnegan shattered my slumber with a wrenching shriek that faded only when he ran out of breath. I tried to comfort him but his sweat-slick body continued to convulse like a live wire beneath the twisted sheets. After a frantic eternity, Finnegan began to settle; a broken man crouched in the fetal position; muttering, sobbing, so hopelessly bewildered.

'Finnegan?' I stroked his matted hair with the temperance of a warm breeze.

'Horrible.' He spoke the word like a mantra. 'Horrible, horrible.'

Our discarded clothing was strewn like tiny islands upon the ocean of carpet. Rain splattered upon the window glass.

'Tell me,' I whispered through a kiss.

'Bodies. Rotting bodies everywhere. God, it was so horrible.'

'It was only a dream, Finnegan. It can't hurt you.'

'I was in some kind of crypt; locked inside with all these corpses. And every time I tried to escape they would surround me. Then they held me down. I could taste their rotten fingers as they pried my jaws apart. One of the corpses, a woman, came before me holding an old-fashioned bottle, like a wine bottle. She took it and poured this bitter fluid down my throat. I was choking on it... and then I woke up.'

A gnawing terror exploded in my stomach. I tried to mask my concern with further words of consolation.

Nights melted into days and the whole of our lives was spent together in my single-room apartment. The idea of venturing out into the world beyond, of walking those grimy streets, smelling the people, hearing the cacophony of urban life, had grown unbearable to me. As for Finnegan, he didn't seem to even notice that there was anyone else in the waking world except for him and me.

'I should really think of going home soon,' he said to me one afternoon, quite unexpectedly. I looked up from the book I'd been reading and saw Finnegan standing like a misplaced totem in the center of the living room.

'Why?' I asked. 'You can stay with me as long as you want.'

His gaze was one of disorientation.

'At least stay until the nightmares end,' I suggested.

He reluctantly agreed, but the nightmares were unceasing.

Night after night after night; shrieks and teary embraces and rants about walking cadavers, abominable wine. When calming words grew futile I resorted to restraining Finnegan with Mysticism.

The first time I uttered the incantation he fell immediately into a sleep that was so deep I feared I'd inadvertently bled the lifeforce from him. But Finnegan did awaken—three days after my spell had been cast. I prayed that Finnegan wouldn't question me, and in an act of merciful strangeness, he never so much as mentioned it.

Now when he sleeps by my side I can feel him stirring. I have no doubt that he is still assailed by the unfathomable night terrors, but he no longer wakes from them. Words of crypts and charnel wine go unuttered.

* * *

I don't know how long he stood above me, watching me as I slept, but when I opened my eyes I saw Finnegan staring accusingly at me, the bottle of Life's Blood clutched tightly in his fist. Tears streamed down his face, the graying flesh of his cheeks.

'Please,' I whispered, 'Please understand, Finnegan. Please listen.'

'Send me back, Jessica,' was his only reply. 'I don't belong here anymore.'

'No,' I sobbed. 'I can't let you leave me again.'

'It's the way things are meant to be.'

We returned to the cemetery and crept back into the crypt I had plundered several weeks prior.

I performed the necessary ritual, banishing the nightmares, which, in truth, were but memories of an agonizing resurrection. My months of research, toiling over strange oscillators, transforming my tiny kitchen into a mad alchemist's lab, all of it done to steal Finnegan back from the grave. But Death, it seems, is far more adept than I at snatching souls.

The elixir bled out through his pores, framing him in a rancid pool. I clung to my lover until his shell grew cold once more.

There are no nightmares for Finnegan, only the sweet maw of oblivion.

THE MAESTRO AND MONIQUE
Martyn Prince

It is difficult to describe those fleeting moments as sleep departs. One can never adequately recall what was dream and what was reality, save for that which remains throughout the waking day. And there are so many questions you would ask, if only you had the time. Yet there was an air that night . . .

I watched the warm-up acts with unexpected interest. London's own Tommy Catchpole was the unrivalled master of the ventriloquial art, late of both the Empire and the Alhambra in Leicester Square. Josephine de Sévigné, resplendent in feathers and silks, was the most elegant dancer I had seen in many a year, though the trenches had provided little in the way of attractive females. And as for the comedic genius of the American Ballsworth Twins—well, who could ask for more?

Things had much improved in Music Hall while I had been away, and the concert parties I organised in the Somme were tame by comparison. Variety was a joy, and the atmosphere at the Tivoli was gay and heady—a far cry from the old Song and Supper Rooms of my father's day. But like everyone else in the theatre, it was the legendary Maestro himself I was waiting to see.

Señor Cervantes was a true master of his craft. The consummate illusionist; a hypnotist extraordinaire. His name was known throughout the civilised world and in every music hall across the land. And those that missed the show, or those that couldn't afford a ticket, would clamber for the papers the following morning to read the undoubtedly rave reviews.

'Stupendous!' the headlines screamed. 'Bravo! Wonderful! It is a joy to behold such magnificent skill.' And none more so than Phileas Bender's Monday review, which I was already looking forward to with excitement.

And then, of course, there was Monique. Ah, Monique; that name as fluid in its sound as the French beauty's own movement. Even Señor Cervantes' mastery was dwarfed when it came to the charms of his lovely assistant, and the Spanish flamenco rhythm with which he tripped around stage was so easily overshadowed by her undeniable grace. And though she did little more than enhance the Maestro's performance, there was always a presence that would touch many a male heart. I, as a man long since removed from female company, save for that of nurses, was eager for that touch, and to see those eyes that so many had reported.

If only I had known.

* * *

It was the young nurse in the hospital who told me that the Maestro was in town.

'Your goin' home this weekend, aren't you sir?' she smiled one morning over a tray of breakfast.

For a moment I toyed with the idea that this charming cockney sparrow enquired out of some interest in my personal life, and that I might venture to ask her around to my humble Ludgate rooms for supper one evening. She would be the first girl to speak with me on matters private since before the war. Pretty girl she was. So caring in her manner.

Never mind.

'Only I saw this advert, sir,' she continued. 'Seems that Maestro fella is on at the Tivoli on Saturday. And seeing as how you said you were in the concert parties and the like, I thought you'd probably want to be goin' along.' She punctuated the sentence with a fresh-faced smile that brought a warmth to my face.

'Thank you, my dear,' I said. 'I'd imagine tickets to be scarce at such late notice though.'

I took the crumpled scrap of paper from the girl's hand. It was such a nice thought, so considerate. Though I do wish she hadn't pulled away so sharply. Surely I don't look that ugly. The iron plate over the side of my face must have looked a little shocking, I grant you, but what do they expect when you've taken a bullet to the skull? I needed it there to hold everything together, as it were. Shouldn't she have understood that, what with her being a nurse and all? I was grateful nevertheless.

'You ought to ask Old Jack,' she ventured, trying to regain her composure. 'You know, the porter. I've heard it said he knows where to lay his hands on a few tickets, if you catch my drift, sir.'

Smiling as warmly as one can with only half a face, I thanked her and asked if she would send the fellow my way later on.

When she left I read the advertisement. It had been carefully clipped from an edition of the Illustrated London News, no doubt with a pair of pristinely kept surgical scissors. So thoughtful.

Saturday March 8th 1919
THE MAESTRO ENTERTAINS
Señor Cervantes *and Monique*
- ONE NIGHT ONLY -
The Tivoli in the Strand
3d—2/6d—boxes available

The advert said little, nor did it give away the content of this particular performance. But it was enough. And when I showed it to Old Jack later that day and handed over a ten-shilling note (more than enough to cover a tout's leverage and a percentage for the porter's trouble), he duly disappeared to obtain a ticket for me. Finally I would see the Maestro!

* * *

At last, with warm-ups departed, it was time for the highlight of the evening. There was neither announcement nor drum roll as one might expect. Instead just a patient silence, broken only by a single, progressive note from the orchestra pit, cast out over the audience on a violin of such sweetness that one wondered how they managed to confine such musical talent to the realms of the theatrically unseen.

The note drifted, slowly touching everyone until all noise in the theatre had ceased. Not a chair squeaked. Not a programme rustled. I swear the audience hushed even their breathing as they waited those last few seconds.

And then it began.

As the note began to fade, so Monique drifted onto the stage as if propelled by nothing more than a breeze, and with a liquidity of movement belonging more to ballerina than showgirl. I'd heard in the Times that she was always the first to appear, cloaked in modest blacks and paving the way for the Maestro's entrance shortly after. But I was ill prepared for the full beauty of the creature that stood before me. That exquisite china face—so white, so smooth. With iridescent eyes so fierce against the darkness; with hair so raven black. And with lips so utterly, utterly red.

Perfection, I thought.

Suddenly I realised how privileged I was to have a seat in the eighth row, and I offered silent thanks to Old Jack at the hospital.

And yet, for all the beauty of this femme fatale, there was a carnal quality about her—lasciviousness in her gaze, some hidden desire in those lucid eyes, eyes that never once left the audience. A Siren but for the sea lapping at her feet and a hundred splintered hulls beneath the waves.

Slowly, and as the violin's note drifted into final silence, she raised her arms and threw back the heavy cloak that had been drawn around her. In one motion the audience was presented with her bounteous female form, with all the curves and roundness we had been led to expect.

She wore a single-piece bodice of softened leather, drawn tight with laces at her side and lined with gatherings of soft lavender fur. Its cut was low—luridly low—and was alone the catalyst of the heat beneath my collar. I wondered just how the modern risqué press had been so guarded with their descriptions. Her legs too, their abundant length was bare but for a shimmer of glitter and the high pointed shoes upon her feet.

Graciously, and savouring the moment with a yearned-for smile, she bowed toward the audience. I caught my breath on her expanse of cleavage, coughing and spluttering my embarrassed approval.

Rounds of applause for Monique's astounding appearance were only halted by the arrival of the Maestro himself. But he seemed happy for our attention to be distracted by his lovely assistant. There was little ceremony in his entrance. He slipped quietly onto the stage by way of the darkened wings and drifted to Monique's side, using this inconspicuous moment to wheel the famous gramophone onto the stage. And there he waited, meticulously stacking his collected shellac disks at the front of the stage, patiently listening to the sound of our heads gradually turning. And turn they did, to his black cape and top hat, to the white scarf about his neck and the ruffled shirt beneath, to his long musician's fingers that could express is every whim.

'Isn't she lovely?' he announced in deep, booming tones that held no more than a hint of his Spanish accent.

The audience, myself included, erupted into spontaneous applause, the appreciation of a voice previously heard only in our thoughts. Quite elegant, quite mysterious. A masterful and magical voice; one that could turn a man to sleep with scarcely a word, one that could usher in a change of spirit with little more than a phrase. At last we heard it.

'Bravo!' we called. 'Bravo!'

Monique smiled in warm acceptance of the Maestro's adulation and, for a moment, she turned her unrelenting gaze toward him. It was only then, by a chance flare of a smoker's match and an unlikely flurry of hair, that I noticed the leash, and the silver chain about her neck to which it was attached.

My heart lost a beat that moment, as surely as if it were clasped between her fingers. But I suppose I was more curious than concerned, more confused than troubled by this strange apparel. And with that questioning eye I followed the leash's line as best I could, past the pleasurable contours of her body, past the folds of her cape, all the way down to the floor where it curled out across the boards and lost itself in the darkened areas of the stage.

And it was there, amongst the shadows and the ruffles of curtain, that I received another shock. There, in the darkness, half lost in theatrical gloom, stood a hunched figure, dressed in blackened garb to better hide his presence and weighted down with eccentric gestures and queer mannerisms, and with a great pile of sacks draped over his arm. I wondered if this bizarre figure, this hidden addition to the performance, held Monique's peculiar leash. But my answer came as Señor Cervantes raised his hand to take a flourished bow at centre stage and I saw the other end tied securely about his wrist.

I should have left then. I most definitely should have left.

Monique, at the Maestro's silent behest, took a record from the small pile at the front of the stage and placed it on the waiting gramophone. She cranked the handle vigorously (not necessarily a suitable job for a lady, I thought, but then again one appreciated her involvement at any stage). And as the revolutions increased so the sounds of 'A Wandering Minstrel I' began to echo around the theatre. It was a scratched and crackled recording, more so than any other I'd heard and certainly not one that did justice to the Mikado's Nanki-Poo repertoire.

> *I remember Captain Rigg had a copy in the Somme. He'd played it so often that its tune had grated upon an entire company of nerves, and that even the first few bars could ensure his utter privacy. No-man's land had become an absurdly preferable leisure.*

But this was a different version to the traditional Gilbert and Sullivan, and the

Maestro's gramophone bore small likeness to the Edison Standard of Captain Rigg. The tune possessed a backbeat; soft and gentle. A dull throb, if you will, out of place with the music emerging from the horn.

Monique, finding no shortage of enthusiastically skyward hands in the audience, summoned a young couple up onto the stage. She gestured for them to sit, manually positioning them cross-legged upon the floor beneath the imposing figure of Cervantes. The Maestro, seemingly content with Monique's choice of volunteer, began to study this somewhat ebullient couple. Carefully he scanned their expectantly wide-eyed faces, occasionally brushing his long fingers across their brows or rearranging a misplaced strand of hair. Then, to everyone's astonishment, he began to dance, tripping a flamenco step around the stage in time with the wholly inappropriate operatics.

It was a disarming sight to behold. Such originality, such theatrical skill, such bravado! And as the young couple began to sway and nod, as their bodies were spirited by the throbbing sounds and the strange dance before them—as they themselves became part of the show—so they fell willingly under the hypnotic spell.

Soon they were fast asleep, and the Maestro went to work.

He spoke softly at first, to a level where his language was indistinguishable as either English or Spanish. But as it steadily rose in tone to a crescendo, each word was as surely tne Spaniard's native tongue as my own mother's English. And I gave thanks that my scholar years at Oxford had not been entirely misspent. I'd managed to pick up a little Spanish. Bad Spanish, I'll admit, but Spanish nevertheless.

'Sueno,' he said. 'En el fondo—el pájaro!'

'Sleep, at the heart—the bird!'

Then he stopped, bending down to whisper something in each of the sleeper's ears. The audience was silent. Not a breath was taken. There was surely not one among us who did not try to hear those final words. But to no avail. The Maestro, his singular, secret magic retained, stood back, helping Monique gently to her feet.

And slowly the squawking began.

It was as if the young couple believed themselves crows. Each flapped at the other with featherless wings, rivalling for some unseen perch. It was a stupendous sight to behold, and one that made me realise the reviews of the Maestro had not been overstated. 'Bravo!' I cheered. But that was not the end. Up they leapt and began chasing one another about the stage in demented flight, mimicking birds with every turn, screeching and swooping. It was an abandonment of all that it is to be human. 'Bravo!' I cheered again. And as the Maestro snapped his fingers and returned the couple to normal, I said again, 'Bravo!'

And so it went on, feat after indubitable feat, the audience heralding their approval with every turn of will and suggestion. It was a never-ending parade of the subconscious, a spectacle of suspended reason. And such variety too: a man more than twice my age turning a flamenco step around the stage with castanets of air; an old woman suddenly transformed into a giggling schoolgirl; and as rugged a sailor as ever you saw singing high like a choirboy and extolling the virtues of theatre acoustics. A true wonder.

After nearly an hour of such entertainment, the theatre fell silent, lulled into quietude by a Schubert lullaby.

'Señoritas y Señores,' he began solemnly. 'Ladies and gentlemen, esteemed patrons of His Majesty's finest theatre, let me take you upon a journey of peace and tranquillity.'

Abstracted sounds of bemusement arose from the audience. Soft gasps of air charged with apprehension and excitement. And though I was part of this audience I felt somewhat wary. The Maestro was known for such audience involvement, that much I'd heard, but still I felt the faint tinge of unease.

'Let me, dear people, take you to place where sleep is a welcome friend and the joys of rest are tenfold. Sueno; en el fondo. A siesta, if you will. A joyful slumber in the arms of . . . Monique.'

Monique, with showgirl flourish, placed another record on the gramophone. Slowly the music began to play. But it was a different tune to that which we'd heard before. No recognisable notes this time, or operatic semblance. Yet there was a familiarity to the music, a subtle warmth that leant itself well to thoughts of comfort and sleep. All about me I could see the audience begin to sway, drifting from side to side as they drank in the qualities of the sound. I too was swaying, though it took me a moment to realise just how much, enveloped as I was in the purely hypnotic.

And then it started.

I could feel it in my head at first; a dull pulsating throb that seemed to accompany the music as it swam around my skull. Thump, thump, thump it went; harder and harder, penetrating. Yet there was no pain or discomfort, no wincing or grimacing. The pulse was a velvet glove about my mind that gently squeezed away my consciousness, enshrouding my head with the music and the pulse, with the Maestro's words and the remembered sights of Monique. Somehow, though I cannot explain it, Señor Cervantes was in my mind.

All at once I swam with a unique delirium, unable to resist the sleep, unable to resist the myriad dreams that began to fill my head—the Maestro dancing about the stage, his fingers before my eyes, the skulking figure in back, Monique and those heavenly eyes. And words too; more of the Spaniards foreign rhetoric. But in that fading sanity they were unfamiliar; Monique, efusión de sangre; buen provecho.

Oh how I slept.

It is difficult to describe those fleeting moments as sleep departs. One can never adequately recall what was dream and what was reality, save for that which remains throughout the waking day. And the ghosts I saw about the theatre had just such a place in my mind. Those that sat and watched, those that stood in the wings—they were mine for just a moment, halfway between life and death, perched on seats and hanging from gargoyles, lost souls who had seen it all before and could tell you so much if only you could linger long enough to ask. And he who stood in darkness, the hunched figure in black—he saw them too, for I could see him trying to push them away.

As suddenly as it had started, it was over.

I awoke with a start, that much I remember, jerking my head back and drawing a sharp breath as if roused from a train journey by a sudden shunt. Immediately I began to look about me for signs of transformation. I was fully prepared to be confronted by an audience full of squawking birdmen, or at least some semblance of group hallucination that the newspapers had promised. But I saw nothing, no furore of jubilation, no metamorphosis for Phileas Bender to describe in the Monday Review. Instead, just row upon row of silent people, eyes expectant upon the stage. And it was only when I had sensed the change, and furiously pounded the shoulder of the gentleman to my left, that I realised the trance-like state they were in.

Then why not I? What prevented me from entering this communal slumber? I scratched my head and received the answer. This plate—this ghastly iron helmet that holds my head together—it must have stopped the Maestro taking hold, prevented all but that brief moment's sleep. But why would he do it? There was no enjoyment to be had from an audience incapable of applause; no joy in waiting for an illusion if waiting was all you did.

Yet there was something else, something I should have seen approaching. And at that moment I prayed for sleep like I had prayed for nothing before. As the audience enjoyed their quiet slices of death, as all but I contentedly drifted through dark comfort, so Monique was unleashed.

Perched on seats and hanging from gargoyles, lost souls who had seen it all before and could tell you so much if only you could linger long enough to ask.

* * *

Señor Cervantes carefully unhooked the clasps about her neck and I saw the thin line of leather fall to the floor. All at once she was free, bounding away from her master, back and forth across the stage, running and scampering like a puppy let off its lead for the first time in the park.

And then she was down, down from the theatre's well-trodden boards and out into the waiting audience.

At first she just stood there, perusing the quietly unquestioning clientele with eyes that flared with every movement. They seemed jaundiced now in that half lit gloom between stage and seat; not the pearlesque charms they were. The music had gone too—the gramophone long since dead and Monique's only accompaniment the squeaking leather of her bodice. Her mouth was open and her breath strangely visible, though I felt no chill in the air. And like that same dog in the park—the puppy let off its lead—she panted, almost uncontrollably. If she'd had a tail then I swear it would have wagged.

And if I'd had the nerve, if I'd had the presence of mind, I would have run then, at that moment, before . . .

* * *

It started with a burly young man in the third row. He was the first. A tall and imposing figure, he cast considerable shadow across his neighbours even without the benefit of his hat. Yet for all this manly stature he seemed unaccompanied. No woman clung to his arm in comfort; no companion leaned his way in close consultation. And with Monique's eyes upon him he was a surely alone as any in the theatre. That was how she wanted it, how she'd been taught. And so she moved upon him.

With silent steps she clambered. First, standing on the legs of a woman in the front row who was far too old for such treatment. Then up, perching on the back of her seat without quiver or waver. Then with steps as deft as any gymnast she pranced from chair to chair. Sideways, forwards; sideways, forwards; until she stood above the tall young man. And then down, in a single movement upon his lap. Half kneeling, half sitting. Though I was too far back to see clearly, too scared to move my head anything other than a fraction lest the light reflect, I imagined how her pointed heels jabbed at the people next to him.

> *—There was a moment, just before it happened, when things became suddenly clear. For that moment the show became complete, all parts seen to me at once as if my seat were privileged with a better view. The Maestro on the stage, the skulking figure in black who hovered unseen but for the ruffles in the curtain, Monique with her heavenly form; the audience captive beneath. All at once there was a unity, as if this was all the show had ever been, all it ever would be. Everything else simply building to this moment, a painted backdrop to all I surveyed. Nothing more—*

She slipped her hands lovingly across his face, tilting his head from side to side with such gentleness, such care. Then, with teeth more animal than human, she sunk low upon his neck.

I wretched. Silently though, with a restraint born more of fear than manners and self-control. It was a ghastly sight. I watched though. For all the sickness I felt, for all the disgust and the nausea, the bile and the loathing, I watched. I watched every moment of this unspeakable act. Fear and abhorrence engulfed me. Incomparable disgust.

And yet this dreadful sight was not the end. Like the jackal her eyes betrayed, she had the taste. And soon she was up, perched high upon the backs of chairs, caring nothing for the bloody man she left behind. Her eyes sought out another who sat alone.

But this time an innocent girl. Alone she sat between two others, who leaned towards their men and left her cold. It was unmistakable; an unavoidable solitude. In but three strides Monique had crossed the gap between them, so fast I swear I could not have released a warning scream even if my paralysis had allowed it.

But I wanted to scream, to shout and to bawl, to do something, anything that might prevent the act.

And as the girl's head fell backwards, as her throat was exposed at the touch of Monique, so I saw her face. That pretty face, those caring eyes, the kindly demeanour of the young nurse from the hospital, the one who had told me about the show, the one who had so carefully clipped the advertisement from the Illustrated London News.

And then from the wings emerged the hunched figure in black: he who skulked, he who carried the sacks. Like an old man he walked, stooped low and with little haste, as if the very weight of his load was too much.

But old bones or no, he clambered from the stage, wafting the cold, unfriendly spirits from his path as he went. Then to his duty.

Picking his way along the silent rows, he journeyed towards the remains of the burly young man. But not so burly now; wasted somehow, enough that an old man with a slow pace might lift the emaciated corpse with but a single arm, and drag its lifeless form to the aisle where a sack was duly waiting.

And all the time the Maestro looked on, content in his position on the stage, content with his minions beneath.

My God, I thought. This has to stop. This simply has to stop!

Braving the unknown, swallowing my fear in one fateful gulp, I stood. And in that moment she saw me. Monique's eyes turned upon me like the fox that sees the rabbit, like the cat that sees the mouse. Blazing yellow they were; no half-lit jaundice now. Jackal eyes, piercing.

But they held me. Oh God, for one awful moment they held me, gripped me with a hideous passion that I could barely resist. But I'd seen too much to be taken so easily. There was a fear in my heart far stronger than any spell of magic she could weave. This creature. This phantom. With blood licked from her sharpened teeth with scarlet tongue. I fled. Oh how I fled.

Up and over the backs of seats I clambered, my boots finding ground against the faces of the stricken crowd. But there were no screams of pain to hinder me, nor did I look down to check the injuries I inflicted. I had a goal: I had to get free and warn the outside world of what was going on. It made no difference how. No difference at all.

At one time I felt the frail bones of an old women crush beneath my feet. I knew she would never awake from the hypnosis. And then a child, a helpless young boy with eyes still hopeful upon the stage and the wondrous performance to which his mother had taken him—another who would wake to pain and disfigurement. There was still no choice. I had to get out, had to find help or we would all be damned.

But Monique was close behind, her stiletto heels spearing the faces of the audience as she careered towards me. There were no such pangs of guilt from her, nor did she care for the extra work she made for he who carried the sacks.

Pounding she came. Stabbing. Stalking. She the huntress, I the hunted.

And I was just a few rows from the back when she caught me.

I stumbled against the body of a tall gentlemen, one who defied my desperate attempts to scale him with a paunch that too easily gave way underfoot. All at once I felt her warm breath against my hair, an icy hand on the back of my neck, its nails slipping deftly beneath my collar, digging in to my flesh. Blood splattered warmly down my shirt; a sickly sweet torrent.

But it propelled me. Like the spurs driving deep into the horse's flank, it thrust me forwards. Up and over the tall gentlemen I climbed, past the next, and the next, not stopping until I had cleared the final row.

And headlong to the floor I fell, surely splintering the boards as my metal-clad head crunched against them. Arms and legs spread wide, I sprawled at the feet of a stricken usherette, though she would no more know my plight than I could have suitably explained it.

My nose had broken too, twisted against the metal on my face, and there was blood pouring from the wound on my neck. But that would make my explanation to the police all the more convincing. As if the ranting of an iron faced madman would not alone be enough. I was sure they'd waste little time in clawing there way back into the theatre with a vengeance.

Past the oblivious usherette I crawled. Then up, staggering as best I could through the doors into the foyer.

The doorman looked at me strangely. 'Everything all right, sir?' he asked.

'Of course not, man!' I screamed, my voice all but giving out with terror and rage. 'Look at my damned neck, will you? Call the police at once!'

I didn't wait for his response. I bolted straight through the double doors, crashing them against the pillars outside with enough force to shatter three panes of glass. Out into the street I ran, shouting and screaming, thrashing my arms about me to draw what attention I could.

But the night was cold and fogbound, and the Strand was little more than deserted. Not a soul to be seen.

The station, I thought. If I could get to the station there was bound to be a policeman! Stumbling, half blinded with fear and pain, I began to run in the direction of Charing Cross . . . and straight into the arms of a constable.

'Everything all right, sir?' he said calmly. 'You look a little flustered.'

'For God's sake help me, man!'

I could see him staring at the metal plate across my face. I could see his questioning eyes. But no matter, he would have to believe me and that's all there was to it. The blood would alone be enough. Surely the blood.

'Calm down now, sir,' he said. 'Take it easy.'

'Never mind that!' I shouted. Then less coherently, 'The Tivoli—people dying—just get inside, man—and call for help too!'

I turned on my unsteady heels and charged back through the half splintered theatre doors, hoping the constable would follow me with whistle blowing, and that we might save some of the audience before it was too late.

And follow me he did, yet it was with one hand firmly on my arm, painfully bending it back behind me.

'Now then, sir, what's all this fuss about, eh?'

'What?' I blurted. 'What in God's name—'

'We can't have you disturbing the Maestro on his big night, can we? Not when he's got Miss Monique to look after, if you know what I mean, sir?'

He thrust me forwards. I stumbled, rolling over in pain, not stopping until my head came to rest against the doorman's polished boots.

'Are you sure you're all right, sir?' he said. 'You look a little out-of-sorts if you ask me. What do you think, miss?'

Monique, eyes aflame, teeth bloodied and sharp, appeared above his shoulder. One hand gently caressed his cheek whilst the other reached down towards my throat.

* * *

I watch the warm-up acts with unexpected interest. London's own Tommy Catchpole is the unrivalled master of the ventriloquial art, late of both the Empire and the Tivoli in the Strand. Josephine de Sévigné, resplendent in feathers and silks, is perhaps the most elegant dancer I have seen in many a year. And as for the comedic genius of the American Ballsworth Twins—well, who could ask for more? All this, and yet the Maestro and Monique are still to come.

The house is full tonight, and the touts outside in Leicester Square are making upward of five shillings a head. Yet I am privileged in my position. I need no ticket. And I am no trouble to the young lady who shares my seat. She can't see me, nor the others who sit and watch, nor those that stand in the wings, perch on seats or hang from gargoyles. And I could tell her so much if only she could ask.

> *It is difficult to describe those fleeting moments as sleep, or life, departs. One can never adequately recall what was dream and what was reality, save for that which remains throughout the waking day. And there are so many questions you would ask, and some that might even save your soul. Yet there was such an air that night . . .*

***

Illustrated London News, March 10th 1919
BRAVO SEÑOR!
The Monday Review
by Phileas Bender

Once again the magic of Cervantes comes to town, and it is a magic I judge worthy of attendance for I have seen many a moribund performer dwindle before the limelight who tried to convince me of his prowess with the mind. Conjurors hold little interest, tricksters less so, and a cad is a cad, I will hasten to add. But this is an armada of a man, who navigates the audience as if it were a private flotilla doing no more than his own true bidding. With feats so exasperating, so unquestionably sound as to make you wonder just how much we really understand about our world.

But I am only human, and 'tis with only so many words I can delay my praise of the Maestro's beautiful assistant, Monique. Ah, Monique—a mere critic's locution cannot suitably enlighten. She is mystery, a star-crossed child of the boards illuminating the modern Music Hall stage with her scintillating presence. And that costume! Be still my aching heart.

And this magic, if that is what it truly is, comes our way via no wires or trickery. There are no stooges in the audience (no theatre would dare press such an advantage where I am concerned) and little help on hand but for he who skulks in the background with gestures belonging to the demented and a history no doubt steeped in illusionary tradition.

And yet for all this there was still an empty seat next to mine when the curtain fell, though I admit I was too engrossed to notice them leave. But then again, with such feats performed on even the audience then perhaps I noticed but never remembered? It makes a poor critic wonder what lengths the modern performer must go to in order that a house may be full, and stay full!

But regardless of those who refuse to be entertained, even when handed such lavishness on a plate, I say, 'On with the show!' And further more, 'Bravo Maestro. Bravo!'

IN MEMORIES
Lucy Fryer

I don't know what persuaded me to move to the country; I was a city dweller and had lived in cities all my life. In my inner-city apartment, I was safe in the knowledge that should I be robbed, mugged, stabbed, or any number of happenings, I would be but a few minutes away from the nearest hospital or police station, and mere seconds from another human being.

I was moving to a small cottage in the middle of nowhere, surrounded by rolling hills, sweeping valleys and blue, blue skies. Trees silhouetted the cottage and loomed at one side, while the other opened onto a vast fenced garden, a field really, in which I was told I could keep horses, if I liked. Not a bright neon sign or cosy alleyway in sight.

Actually, it was my aunt who found the place, on one of her regular rambles through the local greenery as she searched for these healing herbs, or those berries to make her cups of tea. My aunt was a strange woman who believed avidly in long forgotten remedies that most Gypsies and Witch doctors would readily shy away from. She said she knew every remedy for every illness that ever ailed, courtesy of her precious herbs, though proof of this was not often in evidence.

I hadn't thought her mad until more recently. Her belief in herbal cures and the power of nature was not the cause of my concern over her mental health—the talk of ghosts, however, was. My greying, wispy-haired aunt, with her oversized jumpers and long, sweeping skirts, had firm faith in the existence of spirits—ghosts, to be more precise.

I had scoffed at first, thinking this was another twisted blathering from the mind of a lonely old woman. But she sat me down, a tray of her rather delicious home-made flapjacks in her hands, and convinced me to listen.

At 4-years-old she had been sat on her bedroom floor, drawing with the leftovers of her dinner, when a woman in white had walked through her door. Nothing unusual about that, I had said, except, she told me, that the door had happened to be closed at the time. I dismissed this as a distorted childhood memory, but she told me it wasn't the only occasion, and went on to detail the four or five other times later in life when she had been similarly disturbed.

I drove down the winding country lane, away from the bright smoky lights of the crowded city I happened to love. I glanced out of the window of my scarlet Chevy. Maize swayed lazily to both sides of me, their golden heads reaching up to touch the buttering sun, while fat bees droned fuzzily over the heads of the flushed pink weeds that clamoured for attention.

A twenty-minute drive later, I arrived at the old house, and found my aunt waiting at the gates. She pulled at the wrought iron and I slid the Chevy through, smiling wearily in response to her enthusiastic wave. From the driver's seat of my car, I let my eyes rove across the impressively large house and its grounds, before jumping out as my aunt crunched across the gravel behind me.

The cottage was distinctly old, but really rather pretty, whitewashed walls having taken on a faintly aged colour and the thatched roof in need of repair. Large bay windows downstairs and smaller, cross-framed ones upstairs needed another lick of paint, while the vines and creepers of what looked like ivy pushed obstinately at the window panes, demanding dominance over the front door. I felt a challenge staring me in the face, and I had never been one to back down from a challenge.

'I left you some food in the cupboard,' my aunt interrupted my attention.

'Thank you,' I said, grateful, though I wasn't actually hungry.

'I suppose you'll be wanting to get on and make yourself at home,' she added. As per usual, she was wearing a cream jumper; the sleeves dripping off her fingers, and a long corduroy skirt the colour of my car, when washed. Her mousy hair was pinned roughly up in a bun at the back of her head, grey wisps swaying in the gentle breeze. Poking out from beneath her skirt was a pair of grubby brown army boots, hefty enough to endure her long walks across the often-rugged countryside.

I nodded, glanced at the house, and then turned back to my aunt for just long enough to say, 'Thank you, for everything. I didn't realise I'd feel so at home here.' I was rewarded with a satisfied smile, before I let my aunt get on her way. I didn't offer her a lift home, because she'd much prefer to walk back, the way she had arrived.

I spent the remainder of the morning and much of the afternoon 'making myself at home'. Three vans of furniture and possessions arrived—the fourth would have to wait until tomorrow—and my belongings were loaded into the old cottage, thankfully avoiding the expected scrapes and scratches. The deliverymen treated my furniture as though it was sacred, though secretly I wondered if it was perhaps the ancient house they were afraid of damaging.

By evening, I had a living room complete with a sofa and armchair, and four dinner chairs I didn't know what to do with, because I hadn't anticipated there not being a dining room in the old place, like there had been at my apartment. The kitchen was cosy and old-fashioned, but I thanked the stars there was an electrical socket where I could plug in my microwave—without it, I was pretty much lost.

The bedroom had a bed already, though the springs in the ancient mattress were long past repair and had to be replaced by my own somewhat more comfortable pad. I had mirrors, cabinets, cupboards and drawers for my clothes and bookcases for my books. My pine desk was, for the moment, sitting quite happily in a disused room downstairs, which I was considering turning into a dining room, as there was already a desk in the study upstairs. It was aged and the surface scored deeply by numerous pens, but it worked and held a dated charm for me that matched exactly that of the house.

I wrestled boxes of clothes and china and even my typewriter upstairs, having to abandon my PC as there were no power points that I could find yet. I found fresher clothes in a bag I had brought with me in the event that my belongings didn't turn up, along with a toothbrush and a few other essentials, and changed into them before going back downstairs.

Evening was bringing the day to a rather rapid close. I stood at the bay window of my new living room and admired the view, surprised at how little of the day had caught my attention. The sun was disappearing over the maize-etched horizon, changing the sky to a palette of dusky blues, purples and gold, and the brightest star was just beginning to show, though the moon was yet to be seen as more than the spectral shadow of some far distant orb.

I wandered away into the kitchen, my stomach, now with nothing to concentrate on other than food, reminding me that I hadn't eaten since my cornflakes at breakfast. As promised, my aunt had left food in the cupboard; a fruitcake, some buttered bread, now a little off, a quiche in cling film, salad, and some now-cold tea. There was also, I discovered, the beginning of a stock in the other cupboards, and in the larder. Stacks of tins—peas, beans, and fruit—greeted me with winks, and jars of beetroot, peanut butter, and a few of jam.

I grabbed a slice of the cake and routed around for something to drink. Apart from the tea, there was nothing, so I poured it from the Thermos and drank it, a wry expression contorting my face. I kicked myself a few minutes later, when I discovered two bottles of sparkling water and some squash and cola under the kitchen sink.

By a rusty teapot, which I promised myself I would throw out as soon as possible, I found a pad on which my aunt had written a list of numbers, one of which, I noted, was for the vicar of the nearby church. I ripped off the first sheet, stashing it in a drawer, and wrote myself a shopping list. The nearest shops were a five-minute drive down the winding road.

A yawn caught me by surprise and I finished my fruitcake before heading again for the living room, where I settled in my cosy armchair. I wouldn't sleep there; just rest my eyes for a while until I had gathered enough strength to drag myself up the stairs. But I was more tired than I thought, and soon the darkening world faded to the peaceful blackness of my sleep.

I was walking through the house, the lengthy corridors seeming so much longer than I had last remembered, tailing away into the darkness. Every room was pitch black, gaping mouths that yawned like forever, to either side of me. A cloaked figure stepped out of one room—its face was hidden in the black of its hooded robe, only its eye visible. They weren't the glowing red seen of demons in horror movies, nor the black sockets where human eyes once lay.

They were the eyes of a child.

Those big, beautiful eyes stared imploringly from their captive black shadow of a face, begging for release. Wide and white and afraid, they bore to my very soul. I tried to back away, but the all-too-familiar feeling of wading in treacle grasped me like the terror I was beginning to experience. I couldn't turn, just stand helpless as the spectre's arms raised to me, in one hand a piece of torn, ancient parchment, one corner dog-eared and charred, and in the other hand was held . . . a scythe.

The spectre started speaking, low and quiet, in a language I couldn't make out. I shook my head, rooted to the spot, not able to understand what the creature started screaming. The sound was becoming deafening—I lowered my head and raised my hands to my ears, but looked up just in time to see the figure raise the scythe and bring it down around my shoulders, as I looked on in abject terror.

'BONG!'

I awoke with a start, shaking with unjustified fear, to listen to the grandfather clock in the hall outside my door chime away into the night. All around me it was pitch black, and I shrunk back into the comfort of my quilts, pulling them up above my ears. I lay beneath their soft safety for what seemed like an eternity, thinking about the haunted soul that had caused me the first nightmare I had suffered since I was a child. Sleep was a long time in coming.

It was half past ten, and the sun was streaming into my room through the delicate white of my lightweight curtains. All darkness I had found last night was gone, banished by the shimmering rays that danced across my eyes, dappled by the leaves of the apple tree outside my window. I stretched; rapping my knuckles smartly on the iron bedpost I had to learn to get used to, and rose, a good three hours later than usual.

I poured a glass of squash and made myself some breakfast—actually, it was another slice of my aunt's rather delicious fruitcake. I was secretly disappointed that she hadn't slipped a few of her flapjacks in with the supplies. I sat out on the patio as I ate, enjoying the feeling of the warm sun, and looked out over the horse-field, as I had dubbed it, though I doubted I would ever get to have a horse in there.

The fourth and final van arrived around midday, bringing with it the last and most important of my possessions, which I had missed quite significantly last night—my books. I usually read before sleeping, and I reasoned that my nightmare, which was this morning vague and uncertain, had stemmed from a busy day and no relaxation before I slept, which is what I found in reading. I would therefore read every night before I slept, and keep the strange invaders of my sleep at bay.

I stacked my bookshelves and put away the last of my clothes, leaving the piles of papers and files in the study alongside my typewriter for assortment at a later date. Though, I had never got round to 'sorting them out' when I lived in the apartment, so there was little likelihood of it getting done here, either.

About two o'clock I got in my Chevy and drove to the nearest town, Demie. It was a nice little place, a small community where everyone knew everyone else and it took the postman five hours to do his rounds because he was stopped for a chat by all who passed him. I would have liked to buy a house there, but there were none for sale, and nobody anted the countryside digging up to make room for more. While it was a pleasant place, Demie looked as though it was stuck thirty years in the past, with no place to go.

I found the grocer's after a bit of driving round, and stopped to stock up on fresh fruit and vegetables. Carrots, lettuce, potatoes, apples, a good supply of grapes, which I considered brain-food for the busy writer, and a dazzling array of coloured foodstuffs went into my basket, and I received a surprised but nevertheless friendly smile from the grocer as I hauled my purchases up onto his counter.

'Buying for a feast are we?' he asked, vaguely amused.

'Not really,' I replied, finding money. 'I've just moved near here, and it's too far to come every five minutes for food.'

'You'll be the one that's moved to White Lilies then?'

I nodded, not really surprised that everyone would know about my arrival with Demie being such a small town. 'I'm quite busy, so it's more convenient to stock up, you know?'

The grocer nodded and passed me three carrier bags of food. 'I know exactly what you mean. Got four kids at home, one of them at Uni, one at college now. It's a handful keeping up with them.'

I handed over my money and waited for change.

'If you need anything over there, just pop in and I'll get one of my lads to deliver to your door.' He gave me my change and smiled.

'Thank you,' I said, surprised by this offer. These people were friendly, that was not up for debate.

'Just be careful you don't upset the spirits,' he gave me a joking smile, and I left with a questioning look, which I took great pains to hide from him.

Spirits, I tutted at mere thought of anything so ludicrous. I dropped the grocery into my car and found first the butcher's then the Post Office. I got warned the same thing as I bought sausages and stamps, then got given a very strange piece of advice in the middle of poring over a tempting cream bun outside 'Bet's Bakery':

'If any of them ghosts give you hassle, come down here and tell Bet. I'll give you my best cake for nothing, and you can wave it the face of them ghosts.'

Why a cake would have any effect on the supernatural, I didn't know, and even if I did believe in anything so absurd and ghosts I wouldn't frighten them off with cake. Was everyone in the world like my aunt, or was I the only person who could run into a town of Ghostbusters?

I was driving through the town, looking for the last place on my list—the stationers, where I could buy paper for my books and ribbons for my typewriter—when I noticed a large, ancient building that looked like it had been there longer than the town. Intrigued, I stopped outside and read the aged plaque by the door: Demie Public Library and Record Office; Opened 1846 by Mayor Douglas Quentin.

The Library inside was a mixture of aged and refurbished; there were new chairs around old scarred tables, ancient books stacked in pristine pine shelves, and while the service desk gleamed with polish, the lady behind it was crinkled with age, like a soggy page.

'Can I help you?' she asked, rectangular glasses on the end of her nose and grey eyes greeting mine over the dusty glass. I didn't know what I had come in for, curiosity had drawn me, but now I was here I might as well make the most of it and do a little research.

'Have you any public records about White Lilies Cottage?' I didn't give directions; she would undoubtedly know where I meant.

'Of course,' she said, shuffling out from behind the desk. She wore flat black slippers. I followed her to the other end of the storey; what seemed to be mostly old men and women sat around the tables in the middle of the floor, reading silently or to young children.

'Here we are,' the librarian announced, stopping before rows of cabinets, an outdated filing system that had probably not been sorted out since the library opened in 1846. A bit like my study, really.

'Will this take long?' I asked, sure we were about to get lost in files and papers as she unlocked and opened a drawer. No sooner had I spoken, she pulled a hefty file out of the drawer and landed it on the table behind me.

I must have looked surprised, because she frowned and said, 'I have worked in this library for thirty-seven years. Of course I'm going to know where everything is,' and she stormed off back in the direction of her thirty-seven-year-old post. I tutted at myself—fine impression I was making; move into a town and upset everyone you meet.

I sat down on a surprisingly comfortable padded chair and pulled the file open. Page after page of scrawled handwriting met my eyes, a hundred-and-fifty-five years of the town's history compiled by its residents, and much of it, if I was reading correctly, telling the tale of the family that first lived at White Lilies Cottage. A family who died on the premises. I read on.

Daniel and Mary Emerson first moved to White Lilies in 1854, from a town by the coast. Daniel Emerson was a farmer, and quite a handyman. Although the cottage was relatively new when they took up residence, he painted it to its whitewashed glory, gave the windows beautiful cross-frames and made elegant chairs and a table for his family.

Mary Emerson was expecting a child, and gave birth to a healthy daughter six months after the move. They named her Demie, after the town that had so warmly welcomed them to their new home.

Daniel brought pigs, cattle, sheep, and even a goat to the cottage, and he raised them for food and milk, every now and again selling meat to the town in exchange for other items the Emerson's might need.

A year later, the cottage was fully renovated and beautifully rural, set amidst the rolling green hills. As a finishing touch, Daniel built a fence around the house, with a gate at the front that opened onto the path that led to the cottage. The fence incorporated a large area of land to the left of the house, which the animals were moved to.

Another month passed, and Mary gave birth again, to twin boys, a rarity and cause for much celebration in the family. Half the town attended the party the Emersons threw in honour of their sons, and it was a night to remember for both the townspeople and the family at White Lilies.

Two years passed happily, with Daniel bringing in a fair income through meat trade and selling the furniture he fashioned from wood, which was in plentiful supply thanks to the forest that backed onto the house. Mary again was with child, and had another daughter in the autumn. With all four children alive and healthy, and a comfortable home, the Emersons were lacking nothing.

Then, one day in the summer nearly ten years later, Daniel Emerson arrived home and religiously slit the throat of his eldest daughter, Demie, who was found by her mother on the upstairs landing in a pool of scarlet blood. Mary cried out in the pain of seeing her beautiful daughter dead, an anguished wail that was heard by a man leading his cattle to the town market, who scurried past in fright of the ungodly sound.

Daniel Emerson proceeded to murder each member of his family, stabbing his sons, strangling his youngest daughter and finally beating his wife until she fell down the stairs and broke her neck. Daniel was found, drowned, in the water trough behind the house, stained with the blood of his family.

I took all of this in, a lump in my throat and hot stinging behind my eyes when I thought of the anguish of Demie Emerson, and Mary, and the other children, whose names I couldn't find, and I wondered what had driven Daniel Emerson to murder his family.

I drove home slowly, in a daze, almost afraid to enter the house where so many people had lost their young lives. When I drew up outside the old cottage, the dusk was turning the walls silver-blue and gold. I contemplated staying in the city for the night, thinking over whether I should stay at White Lilies. But I shook the idea away—this was my house now, and the memory of a long-dead family was not going to scare me away. I didn't believe in ghosts, anyway.

I spent the next four days dusting, polishing, washing, painting, and I even tidied the papers from my study into the two filing cabinets I placed either side of my beautiful antique desk. I also gave the window-frames that Daniel Emerson had constructed a fresh lick of paint. It may just have been the fresh air on my skin as I climbed the ladder in front of my house, but as I touched the aged wood, the hairs on the back of my neck prickled.

The ivy that had for so long dominated the sidewall was trimmed and tied and told where its place was. The trellis at the back of the house was planted with Virginia creeper, and I even got down to do a little planting, just to add the touch of personalised greenery I had never had the chance to watch flourish in my city apartment. Pot-plants were slightly out of my reach, as yet, as they seemed to die quite readily whenever I bought them.

There was a long archway at the back of the house as well, made of wood that had lasted surprisingly well over the years, and atop it was a cross-lattice that was laced with more creeping ivy and some beautiful roses that were no in full and glorious bloom. I didn't dare tangle with those.

I spent almost an entire day messing around outside, investigating every inch of my new home, and I was grateful to note that the trough where Daniel Emerson drowned was no longer there.

My aunt visited a week after I moved in, though this time she was a little more neatly attired. The hiking boots were gone, replaced by some black, much cleaner shoes, and the long red skirt had turned into... well, a long grey skirt. The jumper was the same cream polo, but at least she had made an effort with her hair, which was in a neat bob that settled on her shoulders.

'Nice to see you've done something with it,' she said, admiring my handiwork as I led her round the house, one arm linked through hers. 'You'd never know someone died here.'

I turned to her, mildly outraged, but not surprised. I seemed to be getting good at hiding my astonishment. 'You mean, you knew? And you didn't tell me?'

She chuckled and sat on the archaic swing I hadn't got round to moving. I sat beside her. 'Do you think you would have agreed to move here if you'd known?' she asked, and I had to agree with her logic. 'Besides, I knew you'd find out sooner or later. It'd make a good story, wouldn't it?'

'That's not the point,' I argued, but finally submitted. My aunt was firmly right, as always.

'I brought you something,' she announced, and rose suddenly, and moved off in the direction of her car. I continued to sit on the swing, rocking gently back and forth, listening to the sound of . . . silence. Nothing but the breeze moved, and I slowly stopped swinging. Why was it so quiet?

'Are you going to come and see?' my aunt called from the front of the house, and I almost jumped. I went to meet her, glad to be away from the deathly silence of my back garden.

'Here.' She handed me an old woven bag, heavy with the promise of her flapjacks. At least, I hoped it was her flapjacks. I opened it, and peered inside and was met by several freezer bags filled with leaves and grasses and flowers. They all looked dead. I looked up questioningly.

'They're medicinal,' she explained, clearly annoyed that I had failed to recognise her trademark herbs. I smiled gratefully at her, intending to go inside and throw them away without a second's hesitation. 'I've left a pamphlet in there,' she continued. 'It tells you what to do with them.'

'Thanks aunt,' I said, shouldering the bag. 'I'm sure I'll need them.'

I kissed her goodbye and made to go indoors, when I heard her say, 'Watch out for spirits tonight, there's a feeling I've got you might see a couple of them.' With that, she turned on her heel and strode off down the road.

Baloney, I thought, dumping the bag and its contents on my breakfast bar and rifling through the pack. My aunt had clearly spent a lot of time finding and sorting and packaging these herbs for me, so I felt they didn't deserve throwing away. Besides, I had just found a covered tray of my aunt's flapjacks at the bottom, and they were fair compensation. I read the 'pamphlet' my aunt had written and chewed luxuriously on a sweet treacly flapjack.

I was shaken out of sleep that night, not by the nightmare, which hadn't plagued me again since I started reading before bed, but by footsteps along the corridor outside my door. I swallowed hard and picked up the nearest thing that came to hand—the hefty book I had been reading, a collection of poetry by Edgar Allen Poe.

Not wanting to startle what could be a burglar into fleeing before I could give him a fright, I left the lights off and wandered cautiously onto the landing. There was no burglar. I looked left, then right, then peered over the banisters to the pitch black below. I turned the lights on, illuminating the house, and searched it, satisfied there was no-one intruding on my property, then went back to bed, turning off lights as I went, and vowing to buy a proper lock for the front door as soon as morning came.

I did exactly that. At 8am I rose, dressed, grabbed a bowl of cereal and was out of the door and headed into town by 8.30. I bought a bolt for the door, locks for the windows, smoke detectors (just in case) and spare battery for my mobile phone. I hadn't needed to use it yet, which was surprising, as I used to spend hours on the thing, but I decided it would be useful now, seeing as I was so far from the nearest person. I also decided on buying a torch.

With my house now secure, I started to relax, and sat at my typewriter for the first time in weeks. I finished the article I had been working on for my newspaper and then went on to furiously type away on an idea, one of many that often popped into my head. I rose twice during the afternoon, once to open the window and once to go downstairs, stretch my legs and dig out a lettuce. I ate the whole thing, uncut and unwashed, without realising it.

Again, night fell over White Lilies, and I hadn't even noticed the day. I finished my writing sometime in the night, when only the light from my lamp glowed in the darkened house. I had bolted the door earlier, so there was no need to go downstairs again, and I stacked my newly typed papers on my desk and decided to sleep.

Footsteps again were heard on the landing. I sat bolt upright, eyes wide, and dropped the papers from the desk in my haste to get up and scream blue murder at whoever was in my house, terrorising me night after night. But when I stepped onto the shadowy landing, there was no one in sight.

I grabbed my torch and shone it down the stairs. Nothing. The bright beam penetrated the black to reveal only the four walls around me that seemed to be closing in. Floorboards creaked, though not beneath my feet, and the sound of whimpering breath made me whip around and stare into the yawning blackness around me. Then something knocked the torch from my hands.

'Who's there?' I yelled, comforted a little by the hollow echo of my own unnecessary shout. When there was no reply, I backed into my study and threw on all the lights, then ventured back out onto the landing to retrieve my torch. Behind me, the study lights went out. 'Leave me alone!' I shouted, shocked by my own reaction to what had to be a series of unrelated events caused by the age of the house, or perhaps the weather.

I shone the torch at the landing—to my horror, a figure was stood there. I yelled in surprise and resisted the temptation to throw my torch, and only source of light, at the intruder. But after a moment, I noticed it wasn't a burglar, nor even a person. My torchlight shone through it, as though it was a delicate lace cloth.

She was pale and intangible, hair as black as a raven's wing floating down her back. She wore a dress, thin and fragile and faded with age, and soft house shoes. Her eyes were blue and sad, red from crying, and a thin-welted line ran around her neck, just above the locket that settled on her chest. A vivid green jewel on a silver chain, it seemed out of place on the pale apparition, and sparkled with a light of its own.

'Who are you?' I managed to ask, my voice betraying me as I whispered and shook. She moved her head side to side slowly, like she didn't want me to know. I wanted to reach out, touch her pretty face, reassure myself that this little girl with pained eyes was real, that I could talk to her and ask her why she was in my house. But she seemed as empty as a dream. One touch could banish her, like a finger through a wisp of smoke.

Recollection of events from then on was dulled, and the next morning as I woke I found myself wondering if all of it had been a dream. But my torch lay on the landing, flickering painfully as its batteries slowly died.

I went into the city for a few hours during the day, bought new batteries at Mick's Hardware Dept and visited a couple of friends, just to let them know how things were going and ask if they wanted to visit sometime. I didn't mention what I had seen last night. I was beginning to doubt that I had even seen it, putting it down to an overworked imagination or my aunt's crooked influence, not to mention her herbal remedies. I had made a cup of her herb tea and gagged before vowing never to put my body through that kind of torture again. Perhaps, I reasoned, that was what had given me nightmares of the little girl with raven-black hair and mournful eyes.

I drove through the streets of the city, just after midday, a hotdog in my hands as I looked out of my window at the old haunts where I used to write my books. The park called to me, with its rainbow of cultivated flowers, flat green lawns and well-kept fountains, the benches inside the safety of its iron railings where I would sit and write and watch the population of the city walk by.

I passed the department stores where shoppers quite happily handed over their well-earned cash, the cafés where I spent many a happy hour with friends or business associates, discussing matters over cups of coffee. The grey sidewalks were dominated by real people, pushing prams and trailing behind eager dogs—there was not a hill or field or cow or cottage in sight.

It was early evening when I returned to the cottage, a bit of shopping in my car boot and the promises of visits from friends in my mind, but the sky was still lit and the sun was only beginning to show signs of sinking. Breezes stirred around me as I went inside the house, unloading batteries and bags and the notebook I took with me everywhere I went, in case an idea sprang unbidden to my mind. The house seemed so much friendlier in the daytime, with the golden rays glittering through the windows to dance across my wooden kitchen floor, or dapple over the shadowy cupboards.

I ate my dinner out on the patio again, and promised as the sun went down that tonight I would not be intimidated by phantom creaks and hollow cries. This was my house, and no figment of my spooked imagination could persuade me that it wasn't safe here.

I exchanged my torch batteries for heavy duty ones, dragged my comfy armchair up the wooden stairs and made myself a flask of hot chocolate. I had saved the last of my aunt's flapjacks as well, to my own surprise, and brought them up to the landing so I could eat them as I watched. I would wait until dawn if necessary, sat in my armchair on my landing, with my hot chocolate, in my house, until I saw the pale little girl again, or was convinced she didn't exist outside my mind.

I set up camp by the grandfather clock outside my bedroom door, where I had been standing the last time she appeared, whether in reality or simply in my dream, and I waited until it got dark before switching on my torch. The back of my chair to the wall and the grandfather clock to my right, I felt more protected now from whatever plagued me.

When nothing had happened by the time my clock struck 11pm, I was all ready to admit I was crazy and troop to bed. Then, from the corner of my eye, I saw movement. I swung my torch around and couldn't see anything for a moment as my eyes adjusted to the light. Then an apparition formed.

Slowly at first, my pale girl took shape, and stood at the side of the stair, the same place she had been the last time. I wouldn't have rubbed my eyes to check I was awake, but I dared not even blink for fear she would vanish. She looked delicate enough to dissipate on a breeze. I stayed absolutely still.

My heart was pounding so loudly in my ears that I barely heard myself say, 'Who are you? Why . . .' I couldn't finish the sentence, I didn't know what to say! What does one say when faced with what I can only, unfortunately, term a ghost? I rose slowly, the torch shaking in my quivering hand.

I reach my free hand to her, slowly, not that I could have moved fast if I had wanted to. She seemed to shy away; her eyes shimmering with unshed tears. Then she disappeared, faded from my sight, like a memory you desperately, hopelessly grasp at, before all is lost.

I swallowed and looked around me, shining my torch into hidden corners, convincing myself that she was gone, that there were no others. I reached for my mobile phone on the arm of the chair behind me. The chair bumped the back of my legs; I sat down hard, breath escaping me faster than I could draw it in. I was cold with fright and hot with excitement. I phoned my aunt.

'Hello?' she said, a sleepy voice greeting my ear.

'They're here,' I whispered, eyes darting around, hands shaking and stomach full of crazed butterflies. 'They're in my house.'

'I told you they would be,' she sighed, 'Didn't I tell you they would be?'

My aunt walked round the next day, and found me in quite a state. I had slept little during the night, and when I did briefly drift off, I dreamt of the little girl and her scythe.

'I doubt the scythe has anything to do with her, if she was without it when you saw her awake,' my aunt tried to explain. 'You're frightened of what's in this house, that little girl, and you're associating her with dead. The Grim Reaper's scythe, that's what you're thinking of.'

'This is a load of rubbish!' I exploded, storming into my kitchen, a little more relaxed now with the addition of another tangible person in the house. Daylight also comforted me, although before moving to White Lilies I had never minded the darkness. 'This is my imagination working because I found out that people died here, that's all.'

'Then why did you ring me up in the middle of the night?' my aunt asked patiently. 'You certainly weren't dreaming then.'

'I must have been! There's no other explanation for it!'

'What did she look like?' asked my aunt, tutting as she tidied the pile of herbs I had dumped in the kitchen.

'She had a thin dress, pale blue, I think. Look, this is ridiculous, there was nothing there!'

'Just tell me what she looked like. Then I'll tell you if there was anyone there or not,' my aunt said, pouring herself a cup of tea.

Frustrated, I continued. 'She had long black hair, er, blue eyes, she was quite pale, like she'd seen a . . .' I stopped short, and my aunt finished the sentence for me.

'Ghost? That's what you were going to say, wasn't it?'

I nodded, ashamed.

'There's nothing wrong with believing in ghosts,' she reasoned.

'But I don't believe in ghosts!' I shouted, feeling like a child who had to prove a point. I fumbled on regardless of my aunt's own beliefs. 'They don't exist, they can't exist! I won't accept that... that... whatever I saw was a spirit, a ghost, or anything else you'd like to christen it!'

'Then I will prove it to you,' she settled calmly, 'And I will stay here tonight, with you, and we'll wait up until that little girl of yours comes along and you can prove to me that she isn't real, alright?'

Irritated, but secretly glad I would have a companion as the daylight faded, I agreed. 'Fine. But if this isn't resolved by tomorrow morning, I move back to the city.'

'Deal.'

'Good.' I wandered into the living room and looked out of the bay window, in time to see my aunt walk out of the house and down the gravel driveway. I ran out after her, calling, 'Where are you going?

'I'm going back to my house,' she replied, as I caught up with her. 'I'm going to make some flapjacks and some cocoa and bring them back here and then I'll spot ghosts with you. I don't stay up all night without something decent to wet my whistle, and I'm certainly not putting up with your lousy tea.'

I smiled, for the first time in days, and held an elbow out for my aunt to lean on. She linked arms gratefully, and I walked her home.

'All set up?' she asked, plumping up a cushion. I had let her have the armchair, while I took up residence in a beautiful old rocking chair that had been left here along with the ancient desk. I nodded in response to my aunt's question, and settled the mugs of cocoa and boxes of food between our two chairs. 'Everything's in order.'

'Good,' she nodded, sitting herself down in the armchair.

I noticed the fact that it was only just five o'clock, and raised a questioning eyebrow. 'We're not going to just wait here for six hours, are we?'

'Of course not,' my aunt scoffed. 'Do you think I would plonk myself down for long enough to get a bedsore? I'm just making sure it's comfortable. I don't trust your furniture, not even that old thing.' She pointed at the rocking chair.

'What's wrong with it?' I asked defensively, quite in love with the ancient thing. So much care had obviously gone into making it, it seemed sacrilegious to let it go unappreciated.

'Oh, there's nothing wrong with it,' she answered cryptically. 'But I'm guessing it belonged to whoever lived here last.'

Nothing clicked. 'So?'

'So,' my aunt said, patronising, 'No-one's lived here since the Emersons.'

Click. 'Oh.' I looked at the chair, its beautiful filigree patterns intricately carved in the back and over the arms. 'You think Daniel made it?'

'I've no doubt about it, kiddo,' my aunt replied.

We made dinner and ate together, and after I showed my aunt around the house, pointing out every small change I had instituted, every place I had painted, or every discovery I'd made when cleaning up and rearranging my furniture. She was suitably impressed.

'You did all this yourself?'

I nodded.

'Even the gardening?'

I nodded again, smiling.

'Well I'll be... I'm proud of you, kiddo, this old place needed someone to make a few changes.' She grew solemn. 'Maybe that's what they don't like.'

'Who?' I asked, distracted by the rain clouds I could now see gathering.

'The ghosts,' she replied. 'Maybe they don't like us changing things.'

'Oh, don't start that again,' I sighed, a little disappointed that all these days of good weather were suddenly to be spoilt as the first few spatters of springs rain turned the dusty ground to mud.

'No, I'm serious,' my aunt said, looking out of the window with me. 'Most hauntings occur in old houses when the owners change something that the ghosts don't like.'

I was about to laugh, but my aunt sounded so serious it made me stop to think. It would make sense, my mind argued. If no one had lived here since the Emersons, then there would have been no one to make any changes. Then I came along, and made myself at home and disturbed the ghosts that had lived here so long without interference.

I kicked myself. I don't believe in ghosts.

'Come on,' my aunt said, interrupting my reverie, 'It's getting dark.'

I looked out. She was right, the looming storm clouds had turned the quiet evening dull and lifeless. 'But it's not even 6 o'clock yet,' I argued.

'Never mind that,' she called back, halfway up the stairs. 'They can come out at any time, as long as it's dark.'

I rolled my eyes and followed her, but made sure my front door was locked and bolted anyway.

We spent the evening on the landing, talking. After an hour, conversation drew to a close. My aunt believed that noise would frighten the ghosts away and refused to say much at all. Every few minutes I would get up and pace about the landing, torch in hand, and every time my aunt would scold me like a little child and order me to sit again. Eventually, about 9pm, I grew so bored and restless that I fell asleep.

My aunt must have been grateful for the respite from my pacing, because she didn't wake me until 11.30pm. A distracted shake brought me back to the real world, and I rubbed the sleep from my eyes before looking up and realising where I was . . . as well as what it was that was stood just feet from me.

'Do you see them?' my aunt cried excitedly, shaking me even though I was awake. But, like mine, her eyes were glued to the pale, opaque figures that littered my landing.

'No,' I whispered, 'No, I don't see anything.'

'Don't be stupid,' my aunt said excitedly, too engulfed to note the lie.

I couldn't believe my own eyes. Now I couldn't be dreaming—my aunt was here; I could feel her shaking my arm. Now I had no reason not to believe.

They stood before us, dotted about, unmoving, two boys, a young girl, a woman and a man, and the little raven-haired beauty I had seen so many times before. 'When . . .' I whispered, not daring to speak any louder should my voice betray the apprehension I felt inside.

'Just a moment ago,' my aunt replied, 'I just looked up and they were there. They haven't moved.'

Each figure stood motionless, dead still, mannequins in a haunted display. The little girl at the fore-front, my raven-haired, mournful soul, was watching me, her eyes endlessly blue and wiser than their years. The thin line was still there, as vivid as the first time she had appeared.

'Demie,' I whispered, suddenly understanding.

'What?'

'The raven-girl—I'm willing to bet that's Demie Emerson. Her father slit her throat.'

My aunt nodded in sudden understanding. She pointed to the two boys, who stood side-by-side and as like as two pennies. 'They'll be the twins then, Ian Andrew and William, and that,' she pointed to the smaller girl, in a petite pinafore the same grey-blue as her eyes, 'will be Alice, the youngest daughter.'

I silently agreed, the pieces of this long-dead family slotting into place. It was as though we were watching a slide show of family portraits, not being confronted by what I can only deem the 'ghosts' of the Emerson family.

'What shall we do?' I asked, hoping my aunt would know better than I.

Wordlessly, my aunt rose and walked slowly towards the apparitions. I was too shocked to move, but watched the expressions on each pale face remain constant as only the eyes moved to watch my aunt. When she came to Demie, my aunt stopped. The girl's eyes were locked with mine, and I could do nothing but gaze straight back, regardless of the others or even of my aunt.

Then an unearthly scream shattered the fragile air, and all erupted into chaos. Mary Emerson, black hair tailing behind as she ran, dove for the spectre of her former husband, Daniel, as he in turn set upon the two young twins. Their agonised yells tore open the very air around, and ghostly blood was spilled as if by act of an invisible knife.

'Oh my God,' my aunt cried, backing hurriedly away from the terrifying scene, as though it was actually happening around her. A fan of dark blood spattered up the wall to her right, narrowly missing her.

Unthinking, I broke the link between myself and the ghost of Demie Emerson and ran across to my aunt, dragging her from the melee. One twin yelped in despair and his hand grasped the air by my leg, before time swallowed his memory and he faded, like smoke on the wind, in a pool of blood and tears, his father, Daniel, driving the knife in for the last time. Both twins faded together, and disappeared.

I covered my ears as the screaming continued, and Alice's young cries were cut short by murderous hands closing around her neck. Mary Emerson was trapped in a nightmare that seemed so real to me it was as if I was living her life. Her children became my children, and died before my eyes.

I almost stepped down the first stair, pushing my aunt before me, when I hesitated. Demie's eyes were again on mine, drawing me in to the 155-year-old murder. I froze, then raced back, jumping into the melee.

'No!' my aunt screamed, watching with horror as I hit the floor, grasping at the ghostly figure of Daniel Emerson as he crushed the last of his youngest daughter's life from her fragile body.

'Stop!' I sobbed, 'Please stop...' but I could no more stop the killing than I could turn back time and stop it as it happened, 155 years ago. Then, to my helpless horror, Daniel Emerson turned on Demie, my raven-haired little ghost. I wept brokenly, feeling as powerless as a baby in the face of the purpose in Daniel Emerson's eyes. I clutched my way across the floor, in Daniel's wake, desperate to stop him from hurting Demie again.

Blue eyes sadly looked on from the beautiful face as Daniel Emerson slit the throat of his eldest daughter. Her life-blood spilled away, and Demie almost floated to the floor, her raven-hair splaying across her limp body, before she faded away, forever. Again.

I was too weak to watch any more. I heard the lonely, terrified screams of Mary Emerson, as they were heard 155 years earlier, and buried my face in my arms. Daniel Emerson beat his wife to death, only a few feet away.

After a moment, the screams faded, and chopped to empty silence. Mary Emerson lay dead, faded, amidst the memories of her dead children. Then, slowly at first, sobbing filled the air. Soft and pitiful, these weren't the cries of a shocked old woman—these were the desperate, anguished cries of a broken man. Daniel Emerson.

I looked up, my entire body shaking with more violence than I could have thought possible. The faded apparition of the Emerson father was on his knees, stained with the blood of his family, howling and choking with heart-wrenching sobs that wracked his pale form. Gone from his hollow eyes was the murderous light, replaced by pure grief. Despite what I had just witnessed, I felt absolute pity for this man.

A hand on my shoulder made me gasp in shock, but only my aunt's creased and harrowed face greeted mine, and the distress in her grey eyes gave me the strength to stumble upright. Regardless of the ghost condemned to an eternity of mourning, I led my aunt away from the bloodstained landing and out onto the gravel driveway.

Dawn was breaking on the horizon, the pale rays of the sun filtering through the leaves of the forest behind us. Tiny offerings of warmth dotted my skin, flecking through the leaves of the ancient apple trees. Gone were the heavy grey clouds of last night, and the early light quickly banished the vivid images from our tired, tortured minds.

PIERRE LOUYS (1870-1925)
An Essay Of Introduction by Rhys Hughes

Pierre Louys was an expert on the culture of Ancient Greece. He was also a sexual pervert. There is no other way of stating it. He was infatuated with lesbian sadism. His novels and poems are full of the degradation of innocent young girls by decadent elder women. Sometimes, as in his most famous work, *Aphrodite* (1896), the sadism becomes fatal. The crucifixion scene in that novel is such a devout fusion of cruelty and ecstasy that it functions almost as religious satire. While writhing in agony upon the cross, the blameless victim is given a lecture on the unimportance of sensations by a philosopher. This blatant assault on the hypocrisy of Stoicism serves also to illuminate Louys' own hypocrisy. He is offering a scene which he has enjoyed writing, and which he expects his readers to relish, but from which he wants to remove any traces of personal responsibility. Within the space of a single paragraph, something which appeals to the lowest instincts becomes a cerebral message. Louys is a monstrous titillator who covers himself with the aegis of irony. It was a common error in the working methods of many writers who reposed and respired in the perfumed climate of *fin de siècle* Paris and who looked to Classical sources to justify their tastes in substance, but who insured themselves and their readers against subsequent feelings of guilt by adopting and evolving a sophisticated tone.

It is easy amusement to dwell on Louys' faults. They are glaringly obvious in *Aphrodite*, but strangely enough they do not grow worse with the books that followed. Nor were they stronger in the poems that preceded it. The reader who samples his entire oeuvre is forced to conclude that Louys was neither mad nor truly a misogynist, in the manner of his contemporary, Octave Mirbeau. The humiliation of women in Louys is generally less gratuitous, almost as if *Aphrodite* really was an attempt to shock the literary world and gain some notoriety, despite the fact that he was a man who loved seclusion. Perhaps there is substance in the claim that he was only interested in mimicking Classical literature for its own sake, for although the French elements of his novels and poems now creak and steam among his sentences like the snappings of fresh baguettes, his contemporaries were fooled by at least one of his experiments. His *Songs of Bilitis* (1894), which purport to be lesbian love-songs from the time of Sappho, were accepted as such by more than one scholar. These prose-poems best illustrate Louys' attitude to his favourite subject. The suspicion is that far from taking revenge upon women by degrading them in his fictions, he is really expressing an enormous impossible *envy*. Louys wants to be a lesbian too, and he is not bothered whether he is the innocent young girl or the decadent elder woman, so long as he can get in on the act. He may never do that, of course, and so has to content himself with mere voyeurism and theatre. He is the Peeping Timon lurking under the altar of the Temple of Astarte while the huge crimson phallus is shared among the weeping initiates. If the instrument was hollow, and he small enough, he would probably prefer to crouch inside, eye pressed to the slit. No, that is too crude for his sense of occasion. These are *religious* ceremonies and the orgasms are praise as well as pleasure. Louys must remain forever an outsider, and his readers are doubly detached from those affections "which have, whatever men may think, more of true passion than invoked viciousness." It is no great surprise to discover that Louys, almost alone among the male writers who treated the theme a century ago, has been adopted as an exemplar by modern lesbians. Certainly he would be more than a little pleased by this circumstance.

As his style became less deliberately cruel, it also grew wittier. *The Adventures of King Pausole* (1901) ought to be as famous as any picaresque novel of its age, not excluding Dunsany's *The Chronicles of Rodriguez* or even Cabell's *Figures of Earth*. It is a fantastical comedy which equals them both. Again there is reliance on sapphism, but now in a romantic context. This tale of callow intrigue, elopement and the flexing of manners in the country of Tryphême, a secret land hidden between France and Spain, is nearly a lazy statement of Louys' utopia, despite a final paragraph that denies this. Unlike most ideal societies, it is barely ordered. There are only two rules: (a) do no wrong to thy neighbour, and (b) observing this, do as thou pleasest. It is a philosophy of anarchism without the troublesome barricades. For a political activist, Louys was far too languid. If one can imagine Ronald Firbank throwing a stick of dynamite, taking care not to crease his jacket by stretching his arm too far, then one might almost extend the same hallucinatory courtesy to Louys. But like Firbank (whose *Sorrow in Sunlight* has real anger fermenting under its wordplay) it is surely unfair to accuse Louys of a lack of involvement with the politics of his own time. His friendship with André Gide provides circumstantial evidence of that. And yet he does often seem happy on the streets only when they are the alleys of some Classical metropolis, the Sardis, Athens or Mytilene which existed in his head, built up by overexposure to ancient writers such as Sappho and Longus. In the present, the boudoir does tend to detain him. It is safer among scents and silks, for they are not passed by centuries, unlike unjust laws by governments.

Louys wrote very few short stories. His single collection of short fiction was called *Sanguines* and appeared in 1903. Many of his tales are minor variations upon the themes of *Aphrodite* and *Bilitis*, but there are a handful that are not. 'A New Sensation' is a peculiar piece about an Ancient Greek tomb which is transported by archaeologists to Paris, where its occupant, a beautiful young girl called Callisto, is summoned back from the dead by a curious scholar versed in the appropriate rites. She is permitted to wander the streets of Paris every night and indulges herself seeking something new in her surroundings. But it turns out that *fin de siècle* Paris compares unfavourably with ancient Antioch, and that every experience the 'modern' world has to offer had its counterpart in her own time. At long last the narrator confounds her disappointment by giving her a cigarette. The excellent opening, almost worthy of one of Poe's absurdist comedies, is thus ruined by an inconsequential solution. The tale becomes little more than propaganda for the tobacco companies, and the final twist of the plot and the product is boudoir bathos at its least forgivable. At the other extreme, Louys was capable of dangerously succinct and menacing tales, in which the Classical elements generate a real feeling of antique power and mystery. One of the best is 'An Ascent of the Venusberg', the horrible simplicity of its situation enhanced by its removal from the centre of the plot. A pure air of menace also lurks around the distancing device (a tale within a tale) employed in 'A Landing From the Roadstead of Nemours'. It is the *smell* in the language of Louys that disturbs, for he has a sensitive nose for colours as well as aromas, and such colours can include blood and things darker than shadows. But he is never quite a horror writer, except in the domestic tragedy 'The Venetian Blind'. These three are perhaps his finest stories and it is a small act of justice to forgotten dreams that their republication is at last imminent.

AN ASCENT OF THE VENUSBERG
Pierre Louys

In the month of August 1891, after hearing at Bayreuth *Tannhäuser, Tristan,* and, for the ninth time, *Parsifal,* I lived for a fortnight or so in the green valley of Marienthal, near the ancient city of Eisenach.

The room which I occupied had a window opening westwards on to the heights of the Wartburg, and had a view, to the east, of Mount Hoersel, called by priests and poets, in the old days, the Venusberg. The actual Star of Wolfram was visible in the clear sky of that Wagnerian countryside.

I was at that time of such a sinful disposition that after I had once leaned from the western window, looking towards the towers of Luther, I never had any idea of respecting the experience, even in dreams. It was the Venusberg that attracted me.

Amid all the neighbouring mountains which, in their clothing of black fir-trees or damp meadows, spread a pattern like a garment upon the earth, the Venusberg alone was bare, and looked exactly like the swelling breast of a woman. Sometimes the floating red gleams of twilight gave it the purple tinges of human flesh. It quivered; positively seemed to be alive at certain hours of the evening; and at such times one would have said that Thuringia, like a goddess reclining in a tunic of green and black, was letting the blood rise, in her passion, to the summit of her bare breast.

I spent whole long evenings watching, day after day, this transfiguration of the hill of Venus. I watched it from afar. I did not approach it. It was my fancy not to believe in its existence in nature, for it is an exquisite pleasure to simplify reality to the abstract appearance of its symbol, and to remain at a distance from which the eye is not compelled to see things as they really exist. I was afraid that on the day I set foot on the actual soil of the mountain, the illusion would vanish once for all and never return.

However, one morning I started . . .

At first I followed the Gotha road with its intersections of bridges and green rivulets, later a field path. I had not raised my eyes from the level of the meadows when I arrived, three hours afterwards, at their boundary. Then I looked up.

Seen from near at hand Mount Hoersel was reddish in colour, and appeared stripped of all vegetation, without trees, grass, or water; it seemed to be consumed by an internal fire, as if the curse of the legend were still arresting at its base all such new green growths as gave life to the other mountains. The path I took was all pebbles and dead lichen, sometimes scarcely visible in a wilderness of rocks, sometimes clearly marked between tall weatherworn crags. It rose to the very summit, where a small grey house had been built, with thick walls to resist the wild violence of the winds.

I went into the building and learned that lunch was to be had there. Lunch on the Venusberg! It was the final blow to my expectations. I received it, to my shame, willingly enough, for, in spite of my disappointment, I was hungry.

The two daughters of the innkeeper, who was absent, served me, at a little table, with a *Wiener Schnitzel*, which was, perhaps, more Saxon than Viennese, and a bottle of rather sour Niersteiner. I was in the midst of the most commonplace reality. The clean, bright room, the white curtains at the windows, the freshly scrubbed tiles of the flooring, a well-lighted bedroom visible through an open door, all ended by convincing me that I was not being entertained by witches, as for a moment, alas, I had hoped. The two girls were practical people who did not propose to take any part in the damnation of the district.

It is true that at the end of the meal the elder of them discreetly withdrew, whereupon the second girl immediately produced an inviting smile which was a proof of her obliging disposition; but in German inns the maids hardly set any limits to the favours they consider due to a young tourist on his travels, and as a general rule it does not follow that they have made a compact, in the shadows, with an accursed goddess.

We talked. She was good enough to understand my German, though I spoke it something like a Cameroon negro. I asked her for a certain quantity of topographical information regarding local matters of which I knew nothing. She answered me with great readiness.

'Do not forget,' said she, 'to visit the grotto.'

'What grotto?'

'The Venushoehle.'

'There is a grotto of Venus, then?'

'Certainly! That is what they call it; I don't know why the Venushoehle. You must not leave the mountain without visiting the Venushoehle.'

Uneasily, and actually with a sort of jealousy in my mind, I desired to learn whether many foreigners were in the habit of coming to see the grotto, whose name alone had given me so distinct a thrill

The girl answered sadly: 'No one at all! You know, the mountain is not high enough to tempt expert climbers, and at the same time it is too high for people who only want a stroll. We never see any foreigners. Just occasionally, a hunter from Eisenach comes here for his lunch or to sleep; but you are the first Frenchman I have seen since I was born . . . '

'Which is the way to the grotto?'

'Take the left-hand path. You will be there in five minutes. You may find a man seated on a stone at the entrance. Do not pay any attention to what he may say to you; he is out of his mind.'

* * *

Actually, then, there was a grotto of Venus in the side of the Hoerselberg! In that case the Tannhäuser country had preserved the whole apparatus of its terrible legend!

. . . The grotto of the Goddess did, in fact, exist. And so did the man.

It was small, in the form of a vertical ellipse crowned with slender brown brambles, and seemed the necessary symbol of the mountain, like a further vindication of the old Germanic tale, still more striking than the flesh like appearance of the Venusberg on the horizon . . . The interior, as I stared into it, was dark, narrow, and low-roofed. Pools of water, bays of gloom, covered the indistinctly seen ground of the place. It would certainly be difficult to go right into it without getting muddy, but some strange incomprehensible spell drew me on into its damp nocturnal air . . .

'Where are you going?' said the man suddenly.

'To the end of the grotto . . . '

'To the end of the grotto but there is no end, Monsieur. It is the Orifice of the Earth.'

'Quite so,' I answered patiently. 'I shall not go far. I shall soon be back.'

His long hollow cheeks turned purple. He struck the stick he held in his clenched fist against the earth.

'Ah, you'll soon be back! Ha, ha! You think you can go in there and come out when you like! Perhaps you mistake this grotto for a climber's goal or a geological curiosity? Are you from Cooks or from one of the Natural History museums? Do you want to write your name on the rock or gather stones for your collection? . . . You think you are going to find subterranean lakes here, or blind fishes, or architectural stalactites and vaults of rock all covered with crystals! You're going to study the spelleology of the Venushoehle! Ha, ha! That's capital! But you're as mad as the rest, then! You don't understand! You don't know . . . that Venus dwells there herself in the flesh with her millions of nymphs about her, more alive than you are, because immortal!'

'Monsieur,' I answered, 'I believe what you tell me; but you little know me if you imagine that the presence of Venus can keep me from entering this place.'

'Hell-fire!' he shouted.

'I am quite willing to deserve it as the price of the favours she bestows.'

The madman made a brief gesture, which evidently meant: You do not understand me at all. Then he seized his head in his hands and went on speaking 'Hoerselberg! Hoerselberg, rather! They shall come to thee without foreboding of eternal horror, thou that awaitest the innocent, thou that dost punish the chaste, thou that shalt consume in eternity the wretched niggards of the flesh, thou Furnace! They shall have lived their solitary lives in revolt against the great, the divine law, and they shall know not thy dreadful kindling until the day when, by the might of the Sword, the Bearer of Souls shall plunge them into the abyss. They have eyes and they see not, they have ears and they hear not, they have mouths and they . . . God! They are mad, mad, mad!'

Suddenly, turning towards me, he shrieked: 'How can you dream that the Venusberg can bring men to damnation, when *the Venusberg is Hell itself!*'

I stirred slightly.

'Alas!' he groaned. 'Alas, O God!' He drew his hands from his eyes down on to his beard.

'Alas! Must I be the only living thing that knows the Truth, the Truth, the Truth . . . Must it have been in vain that all the Patriarchs set up Venus, in relation to God, as His own fearful antithesis, and must none have ever known that she was Satan? It shall have been in vain, then, that the antique tradition depicted Satyrs with those horns, that black tail, those goat-legs, those cloven feet: none shall ever have guessed that they were Demons. And as for the eternal flames, no one on earth shall ever have understood that they are thousands of millions of naked women dancing there . . . '

He struck the ground.

. . . 'There! Under our feet!'

He shivered to the very nape of his neck.

'Since man was first able to think, since man first wrote and taught, he gave out, he repeated, he cried aloud, that there is no worse torment than love. How could he not foresee that in the world of eternal torment that torment alone would be his' And what other could he imagine more awful?'

He assumed an attitude, then, of prophecy, and shook his hand before his staring eyes:

'Ay,' said he, "tis there . . . there . . . From the day on which we shall be nothing more than rotting corpses and souls mad with terror 'tis there we shall go in our myriads, we, all of us, all of us sinners, to burn with the terrible fire of Lust. Each day, each hour, we shall long, to the point of agony, for women more beautiful than women are, and at the moment of possession we shall see them vanish, as on earth, into the empty vapours of a dream. But what is here a spasm, an anxious fear, a cry, a sob, enough, indeed, to bring a curse upon some human life through the birth of the memory to be, shall be, there below, the perpetual shudder, the unbroken anguish, the torture, of years, of centuries of centuries . . . Ah, God! Such is the fate that I must meet.'

He fixed his eyes upon a stone on the ground. Shaking his head, he continued, in a frightfully changed tone:

'I have lived evilly, Monsieur; this was the way of it. I was born of Protestant parents on Mount Wartburg, the very place where Luther, more than three centuries ago, set up his accursed doctrine. My youth was pious, my life austere and honourable. Nevertheless, from my fourteenth year I could not look at a woman without being assailed by desires of terrible intensity. I mortified them. I had appalling struggles from which I emerged, at daybreak, with my forehead streaming with sweat and my jaws trembling. I believed I could remain pure by living without love, insane fool that I was, blind to my own passions! To remain pure I would have killed myself with my own hand rather than commit sin. Those who have not experienced such nocturnal conflicts between religious duty and the frantic caprice of the body have never experienced suffering! And I struggled thus for a shadow, and I know now I struggled against God! Later on I married, Monsieur, but married only in the eyes of the world. My wife and myself had sworn to unite our souls alone, in order to preserve them, as we thought, in a state of grace. That was how little by little I damned myself by my mistake in telling a lie, each day, to the law of life; and henceforth it is too late for me to follow the strait path of my lost youth. I am virgin. Ah! Woe to all virgins! For the love they have rejected, all their short lives will justly torture them in the infinity of the wrath to come!

* * *

He seized my arm.

'Hark ye!... The sun is setting.... This is the time.... Every evening I come here, and the Goddess sings a sweet song.... She calls me from afar... she draws me to her.... I come as on the day of my death, as on the day of my final downfall into the Venushoehle... Ah, do not utter a word. *She is going to speak to us.*'

I do not know whether the calm tone of these last words or the expression of the man's face or the grip of his hand persuaded me that he was telling the truth—but a quick shudder passed over me, and I listened attentively.

It was an unfamiliar feeling. I was waiting, not on chance, but with an absolutely exact anticipation, the event foretold by the lunatic.

I cannot compare my state of mind to anything better than the sensation of a traveller who, having seen the lightning and knowing the distance between himself and the storm, expects to hear the thunder of heaven at a preordained second.

The time which separated me from the miracle diminished first by a quarter, then by a half, then by three-quarters; and at the precise instant when I perceived that it was at an end a breath of perfumes bore to our ears the languishing echo of a... Voice...

THE ELEMENTAL CHILD
Beth Lewis

She gazed listlessly up at the star strewn sky; a dark blanket of night stretched across the fabric of space, a shield against the prying eyes of alien kind. The wind brushed through the dry leaves hanging lifeless from the bowers of the old oak that grew next to the cliff. The Old World screamed release from the cracked bark; she could hear it echoing in her mind as she neared the edge. The icy wind of late November blew across her skin, making the hairs on her arms reach to the heavens for salvation from the white waters that lay beneath her. She was utterly alone, standing at the edge of a cliff; to anyone but herself she looked suicidal but to her she was nearly home. A girl dressed in plain white standing at the edge of a cliff, the wind whipping her hair, black as a raven's wing, into the darkness.

They wanted freedom. Freedom to reign from the heavens and bring order to a world of chaos, she would help it, she would unify it. If she went home, the Old World would be free. She wanted to go home, she knew she didn't belong in the human world.

As she stared down at the ocean spread before her, reaching beyond the horizon and beyond her dreams she thought. It was the first time she'd thought all day. She'd walked alone through the corridors, talking to no one, looking at less.

The ocean crashed against the rocks, the sound of her mother calling, forcing its spray into her face, her mothers touch. The water wanted her. Just as much as she wanted it. It wanted to swallow her in its icy embrace, take her life in its dark waters to make itself whole again, a family. She smiled into the darkness. The moonlight bounced off her pale skin, illuminating a tiny part of her before ravenous black clouds engulfed the glowing orb. The water was calling her; she could hear her mother's voice. An elemental melody, like water trickling over rocks, a perfect voice, a perfect face. As the spray hit her face again, she imagined it was her mother's hand, stretching up from the cold depths to claim her daughter back from the human kind. She saw her mother's fingers reaching for her body, reaching for her child. She reveled in the dream before a siren woke her, tearing her away from the perfect end.

She had to act quickly if that dream was to become a reality; she took another step towards the cliff edge. The wind blasted against her freezing body, whipping the air from her lungs and making her heart pound in her numb chest.

She glanced behind, the sirens had come closer, and now she could see the flashing. The red and blue lights of the police cars. The woman, parading as her mother, had called after she'd fled the house without tears. The woman didn't care for her; it was all a ruse, an act for the neighborhood. Behind the red brick walls and hideous flowery wallpaper was an evil woman with an ugly heart. The woman had hated her, despised her very being, beaten her, destroyed her confidence and self-esteem but felt no remorse at her terrible acts, only pride.

Her return meant everything to the elements; they would be free, as would she.

The sea spray was getting closer and more powerful; it was time to come home.

Another step—another and it would be over.

She heard the fuzzy police voices through a broken megaphone, but she wasn't listening. It was time. She was not afraid. The last time she'd stood on this cliff she couldn't bring herself to walk any further, the sea was calm that night so she would probably have lived, she didn't want that. She didn't want the judgement of the people around her; she didn't want their sympathy or their opinions. She wanted no part of their world.

The oak standing strong by the cliff encouraged her; she could hear its old, croaky voice telling her exactly what she needed to hear.

We want you back, you belong with us child, you are ours, and we are your roots.

It spoke without audible words, directly into her mind, its voice warm and familiar.

My child, my beautiful child, the waters have done well for you, made you the paradigm of light, we need you my child, make us whole once again . . .

The loving, mellifluous voice of the water sung out to her, she was standing at the brink of creation, her mother's voice flitting into her mind. The ancient tongue of the ocean familiar to her. The girl heard music in the sunrise; she woke up before dawn every morning to hear the melody.

Nature was hers, she was its. Nature's child, it's now ripened fruit, ready to be harvested. The ground pulsated beneath her; its throbs soothing the soles of her tired, bare feet. It was urging her to return home. She was a being of the sea, a life-giving being. The water loved her as she loved it, it was her home, her life, her everything. The earth was alive with hatred for all humans but her, she wasn't of the human kind and they knew it. She was different, special. The whole planet wanted their lost child to be found again and this time she would not fail them. The icy waters beckoned her home; back to a home that sustains life, douses flames, and can take lives back into the darkness without a moment of hesitation.

The elements were her friends; she had never been burned or hurt in any of the earthquakes that constantly plagued her country. They were her friends yet they were each other's enemies, fighting over her. The earth wanted to bury her, fire, to consume her, and water to drown her. Air was the only neutral element, wanting no part of the fray. Her sacrifice meant their unity, their equality. Now the elements would have their daughter home again. It was time for the final judgement on her soul, a judgement by the icy throes of life itself. One more step, just one more and everything would stop forever, they wouldn't even notice her demise. She was the after all elemental child. She would be absorbed into the ether; there would be no trace of her existence on any human record. She would disappear as a flame in the wind.

She could see the police lights in the corner of her eye. The woman, her false mother, stood outside one of the cars. Invisible words escaping her strict lips, hands waving in futile gestures of forgiveness. It was too late. One more, just one more.

She took that final step and as she plummeted to the waters she listened for the woman's screams but none came. She hit the sea and simply waited; lying on the surface, ready for her body to become water and her memories just a ripple on the surface of nowhere.

BIOGRAPHIES

Phill Beynon lives in Sheffield, England with his partner and two small children. He writes fantasy and supernatural fiction as well as articles and reviews for a gaming magazine. He is currently working on his first novel. As fame and fortune have yet to come his way, Phill has a day job. He works in a child and family Therapy clinic in Nottinghamshire. When he's not writing he enjoys fantasy role-playing games and gardening!

Steve Redwood. Started writing short stories around three years ago, about thirty now published or accepted. Publications in England include Roadworks, Sci-fright, Sackcloth & Ashes, Enigmatic Tales, Unhinged, Dead things, Planet Prozak, Hidden Corners. In America publications are Talebones, Eureka Literary Magazine, Happy, Matriarch's Way, Realities Escape, etc. Though a plug here for the mag which published my first ever story, a Michigan Punk-Gothic zine called 'Dead Fun'. A novel, **Fisher of Devils**, is being published by prime, and a couple of stories should be appearing in another anthology.

Scott Emerson Bull has been weaving creepy tales for seven years now, scribbling them down in an old stone cottage nestled in rural Carroll County, Maryland. His first published story, "Champion of Lost Causes," (*Terminal Fright*, Winter '95) received an honorable mention in *The Year's Best Fantasy and Horror*. Since then he has appeared in issues of *Outer Darkness*, *The Grimoire*, *Gathering Darkness*, *Nocturnal Mutterings*, and *White Knuckles*.

Pam Chillemi-Yeager is a writer and editor from USA with several credits to her name.

William P. Simmons is a fiction author, poet, critic and editor. He pens the "Literary Lesions" review column for Gauntlet magazine and works as a roof reader for Gauntlet Press. He also writes Digging Up Bones a classic horror review for Hellnotes, the "Savoring Darkness" fiction and film review for Horrorfind, the Folk Fears folklore column for Twilight Showcase, and the Folk Ways column for the HWA newsletter. His reviews, feature articles, commentary, interviews, and fiction have appeared in Dark Echo, Gothic.Net, Green Man Review, Haunted, Project Pulp, Masters Of Terror, At The World's End, etc. His interviews with Maynard and Sims appear in their collections [**Selling Dark Miracles**] and [**The Secret Geography Of Dreams**]. He can be contacted at wsimmons@catskill.net

Rhys Hughes. His books include **Worming The Harpy**, **Romance With Capsicum**, **Eyelidiad**, **Rawhead & Bloody Bones** and **The Smell Of Telescopes**. Others are due out soon! He insists that he is the cleverest and most underrated author currently alive, but his rivals and readers like to pretend this is not true. It is, honest. He is also the nicest and most unjustly maligned person in the northern hemisphere. (We are delighted he took the time and trouble to research and unearth these stories from two lost writers and to find out the stories behind the writers themselves.)

Gerd Maximovic is a German science fiction writer with numerous credits to his name. His stories have appeared in Playboy, Omni and have been read on radio and translated into six languages. The translator here is Isabel Cole, a US citizen.

Richard Sheppard is twenty-three years old and currently lives and works in Portsmouth. This is his first published story and the second one he has ever written. He is currently working on 'The idiot's guide to writing short autobiographical notes to short story anthologies'. It's not going well.

Brendan Connell lives in California where he translates texts from the Tibetan and Sanskrit. He has just finished his first novel, as well as a collection of short stories. His translations have been published in Literature of Asia, Africa and Latin America, Prentice Hall 1999. He has both fiction and poetry forthcoming, or already published, in a number of literary journals and zines, including RE:AL, The Journal of Liberal Arts, Tabu, Edgar, Frisson, Devil Blossoms, The Haunted, Darkzine.net, Deeply Shallow, Crossconnect, Fishdrum and Lethologica.

Simon Wood. I am English, living in US with my American wife. Rounding off my wholesome family is Royston, a Longhaired Dachshund, and Streetcar, a kitty, both rescued from the barbaric Californian streets. I have only been writing for two years, but I've had nearly forty stories published in the US, UK and Australia. Some of those publishers include: Millennium Science Fiction & Fantasy, Blue Murder, Fables and Muse-It. Readers can visit me at: http://members.home.net/sjwood3/Simonmain.htm

D F Lewis or Des as he is known has had over 1300 stories published in a long career. He now publishes a magazine at http://www.nemonymous.com He is a living legend and a thoroughly nice chap.

Donald Murphy was born in Denver and currently lives in Madrid, where he works as a teacher and translator. His stories have appeared in Enigmatic Tales Electronic, Darkling Plain, Quantum Muse, and in volume one of Darkness Rising.

Andrew Roberts considers himself a horror writer and is unconcerned at the negative connotations attached to this label (although he is glad book covers seem to have moved on since the 80s). By the time you read this, his published short stories will probably still be in single figures. He promises to try harder.

Alastair G Gunn is a professional astrophysicist by trade. As well as writing on scientific subjects, particularly astronomy, for national and international press, he is a frequent contributor to radio and TV media in UK. His debut in ghostly fiction occurred with appearance of Ballymoon in 2000, a collection of three stories published by Enigmatic Press. Since then Alastair has been working on other supernatural stories but has recently been concentrating on his first novel.

Richard Gavin is the author of nearly fifty published short stories and poems, all in the horror/dark fantasy vein. He lives in Ontario, Canada.

Martyn Prince. I'm 32, married, divorced, married again, and I've even lived on a kibbutz to get away from it all. I've been writing for longer than I can remember, perhaps in earnest for the last six or seven years. I started by writing the first draught of a full-length novel, which I later tore up in disgust, but it gave me the impetus to start taking things more seriously. After that I began writing short stories and entering competitions. It wasn't until I'd been short-listed a few times that I decided to actually submit anything to a magazine, and the results of these endeavours appear below. I now work full-time in London as a copywriter and web designer. Though my spare time is limited, commuting everyday from my home in Kent, I still find time for writing and research. I have two novels underway, and an entire library of short stories in various stages of disrepair. Spending so little time with my wife in favour of a noisy keyboard and a stack of crumpled notes proves somewhat hazardous, but a best seller or a Hugo might at least restore some domestic contentment.

Lucy Fryer. I am the author of 'In Memories' and my name is Lucy Elizabeth Fryer. At 16 years old, this is the first story I have had published, although I now have three printed poems to my name—the first is entitled 'The Thousand' and can be found at www.horsereview.com and the second and third are published in two anthologies printed by United Press Ltd. I have dreamed about being an author since I was old enough to dream, and when I'm older and have a few books under my belt, I wouldn't mind trying my hand at turning one or two of them into films. For more information about my writing, please email: hallieparis@yahoo.com

Beth Lewis is a 15-year-old girl from England who has had poems published in the UK. This story is one of several we are publishing and have published in DR which we are confident will be the first of many successes for a new and extremely promising literary talent.

Hugh Lamb is one of the most respected editors and anthologists in the genre. His numerous books such as **A Tide Of Terror, Victorian Tales Of Terror,** and **The Taste Of Fear,** introduced rare and forgotten stories to the present day reader. He provided stories for Enigmatic Tales, and edits books for Ash Tree Press as well as working as a free-lance proof-reader. He is a giant in the field of supernatural fiction.

Len Maynard & Mick Sims www.maynard-sims.com are writers as well as editors, and have been publishers (Enigmatic Press). By the end of 2002 they will have been responsible for 40 books in the genre. These include collections such as **Shadows At Midnight, Echoes Of Darkness, Selling Dark Miracles, The Secret Geography Of Nightmare** and the imminent **Incantations** from prime. Novellas **The Hidden Language Of Demons** and **Moths** are both available. As well as editing Darkness Rising, and previously F20, 2002 will see from them Best Of Enigmatic Tales and Cold Touch.

Iain Maynard is a talented UK artist who has also seen his stories published in magazines. His artwork has graced a number of magazines and anthologies, and can be seen on the covers of the hardback collection **Echoes Of Darkness**, as well as all the Darkness Rising covers.

Printed in the United States
4149